TABULA RASA

TABULA
RASA

KRISTEN LIPPERT-MARTIN

EGMONT
USA

EGMONT

We bring stories to life

First published by Egmont USA, 2014
443 Park Avenue South, Suite 806
New York, NY 10016

Copyright © Kristen Lippert-Martin, 2014
All rights reserved
1 3 5 7 9 8 6 4 2

WWW.EGMONTUSA.COM
WWW.KRISTENLIPPERTMARTIN.COM

Library of Congress Cataloging-in-Publication Data
Lippert-Martin, Kristen.
Tabula rasa / Kristen Lippert-Martin.
pages cm
Summary: A girl who has been held in an experimental medical facility to remove the memories that gave her post-traumatic stress disorder begins to recover her memory after fleeing mercenaries sent to eliminate her.
ISBN 978-1-60684-518-9 (hardcover) -- ISBN 978-1-60684-519-6 (eBook) [1. Science fiction. 2. Memory--Fiction. 3. Adventure and adventurers--Fiction.] I. Title.
PZ7.L6646Tab 2014
[Fic]--DC23
2013030315

FOR PHILIP. OF COURSE.

TABULA RASA

CHAPTER 1

She points to the chair. "Sit."

I don't want to sit. The chair is cold metal, and I'm wearing a backless hospital gown. So I stand there staring at it until Nurse Jenner clears her throat.

"Come on now, Sarah. We can't keep the doctor waiting."

The first time I saw this chair, I thought it was an electric chair. I thought they were going to kill me.

But they're not. I know they're not. I remind myself of that again.

The chair keeps me upright so they can access any part of my skull—front, back, sides. Long-term memories are scattered throughout the upper brain, and getting at just the right ones so they can be neutralized is nearly impossible. But that's what we're here for today. Stage six of the nearly impossible.

"I thought I was scheduled for next week," I say.

"Schedules change. Just be glad. It means you're that much closer to a fresh start."

She's right.

And so I sit.

Nurse Jenner starts securing my restraints: first the one around my neck, then the ones for my wrists and ankles, and finally the belt that goes around my chest. She fastens all of them a little too tightly and then gives me two pats on the shoulder.

"Try to relax now. This isn't your first trip to the rodeo, remember."

I know what's coming next, and I hate it. She's going to lock me into the halo. It's this metal birdcage thing that holds my head completely still while the doctor works on me. I have four metal inserts embedded in my scalp and forehead, and the points of the halo snap into the inserts. I feel the *click-click-click* against my skull as she finishes locking down all the prongs.

"What's the matter with you today? You're shaking all over."

"I'm a little cold."

"You know you're not supposed to move *at all*."

"Yes, ma'am."

She heaves a sigh and hurries away. A moment later she returns and drapes a scratchy blanket across my bare knees. After checking my blood pressure, she gives the thumbs-up to the doctor in the booth above the operating room. I hear the door latch as she departs.

Now we can get started.

A spotlight comes on above my bald head. Once all the injections are done, my hair will be allowed to grow back, but right now I'm on a special chemo regimen to keep me completely hairless. Otherwise they'd have to shave my head every time they did a memory modification. Bald makes it easier for them, and it doesn't really matter to me, since I can't see what I look like anyway. There are no mirrors or shiny surfaces to be found in this place.

Well, not many.

In the outdoor exercise area, there's a small pond with goldfish and water lilies. It's a nice spot to relax. Or it was, right up until a girl fell in and drowned. An orderly found her floating facedown in the black water, her hospital gown spread out at her sides like wings. Afterward, Nurse Jenner said to me, "I bet she fell in while she was trying to see her reflection." I got the message: *This is what happens when you don't follow the rules.*

The doctors tell us it's got to be this way. Seeing things from our past—even our own faces—can cause a setback in our treatment. They go to great lengths to make sure we remain unknown to ourselves. Not that any of their precautions can keep me from wondering. I've tried to put together a mental sketch of myself by running my hands over my face. I must have done it a thousand times, but I still have no idea if I got anything right. The girl I see in my mind's eye remains a blurry, half-formed image.

The only thing I'm pretty sure of is that I normally have dark hair. My skin is sort of olive toned, and usually olive skin goes with dark hair, not blonde. I figure I'd be a warm, toasty brown if I could just get a little sunshine, but we don't get a lot of sun here. Wherever we are. In every direction there are jagged, white-capped mountains like rows of shark teeth. What's beyond those mountains, I don't know. Maybe if you walk out there, you get to a point where the world simply falls away.

Just like my memories.

Any minute now, a male voice will address me. It'll be Dr. Buckley. I've met him just once, in the hallway outside the director's office on the first floor. He looks like a middle-aged Santa Claus: brown beard streaked with gray, bright red cheeks, and a twinkle in his blue eyes. He's up in the surgical booth right now, behind smoke-colored glass, operating the injection needles with a robotic arm to ensure absolute precision.

"Are you ready, Sarah?"

And there's Dr. Buckley now. *Ho, ho, ho.*

His question is just a formality. What am I going to say, *no*? Besides, now comes the only good part. I talk with Larry. He's Dr. Buckley's research partner.

Larry is the one who reads the CAT scans and the MRIs and then decides where to drill during these head-mining operations. He figures out the *this* to take and the *that* to leave alone. He's also an expert on hypnosis.

Larry talks to me throughout the operation. I have to be awake and alert during surgery so they'll know immediately if they're damaging something important. While

Dr. Buckley is busy puncturing my brain with needles, Larry will have me count backward from one hundred by sevens, or he'll read me lines of poetry and ask me to repeat them back. Sometimes he tells me really bad knock-knock jokes, and I just have to say, "Who's there?" at the right moment. Larry assures me that laughing at the punch line is not required or expected, which is good, because the jokes are never funny.

"Good morning."

Larry's voice startles me. He sounds so close, but I know he's not. He's up in the surgical booth. I've never seen him, and I only hear him through a speaker on procedure days.

"Big day today," he says.

"Is it?"

"I'm sure you'll be ready for whatever comes your way, though."

It's strange, I know. We seem to talk about nothing, and yet I feel like everything Larry says to me is somehow important. Maybe it's just that his voice is the only thing that keeps me from drifting away for good. Sometimes— maybe a lot of times—I want one of those needles to go in a little too deep, in just the wrong place. Would it really be so bad? I'm sure there are worse ways to die. Loads of them.

I could never say this out loud. Nothing gets the staff riled up like saying you don't care. These memory modifications are a chance for a new life. *And* they cost a fortune. The huge expense gets mentioned a lot, especially if the nurses think we're being uncooperative. They seem to think all the research money they've invested in us to help get our lives back on track will make us feel obligated and appreciative. Maybe it should, but it doesn't.

"What's on your mind, Sarah?"

Sarah.

Can that really be my name? I've said it over and over again, trying to force this square peg into its round hole. It never fits.

Just as I'm about to answer Larry, I hear the high-pitched whine of the drill starting up. Dr. Buckley is in a hurry.

"Hold still now. You'll feel a sharp prick and then pressure in *juuuuust* a moment. . . ."

I'd rather not picture the drill that's about to bore its way through my skull, even if Santa Claus is the one operating on me. I need to distract myself. I know my post-op recovery is going to be deadly dull. The only things we get to watch on TV are old cartoons, and I'm tired of watching *Tom and Jerry* in the rec lounge.

"Larry, can you sign off on a reading request for me?"

Only Dr. Buckley and Dr. Ladner can give permission for us to read. And like the cartoons, the books they approve are usually really old. I guess they figure old books don't matter anymore.

"Sure," he says. "How about *Hamlet*?"

Hamlet?

Dr. Buckley must also think it's a strange suggestion, because he abruptly turns the drill off.

"I tried out for a part in *Hamlet* when I was in college. Did I ever tell you that, Sarah?"

Larry has never shared anything personal before. He knows that.

"I wanted to play Polonius."

"Oh yeah?" I ask. "Why not Hamlet?"

"Because Polonius has the best line in the whole play."

"Which is?"

"'This above all: to thine own self be true.' Good advice. Though not always easy to follow."

"Or in my case, it's impossible."

Larry knows what I mean. I can't be true to myself if I don't know who I am.

"Don't be so sure, Sarah. I'm less worried about you than I am about me."

Should I ask him why he said that? Reassure him that he'll be all right?

I say nothing.

A moment later, I get that sharp prick that Dr. Buckley warned me about. I suck in my breath and feel an intense cold where he's stuck the needle in. Once the area is numb, Dr. Buckley will begin drilling. That's the worst. I hate the smell of the bone dust.

"Just remember, Sarah, sometimes the answers to all our questions are staring us right in the face."

I'm not sure what Larry's talking about, but I stop wondering about it almost instantly. They give me something to keep me calm during these procedures, and it must be kicking in.

"Dr. Ladner," Dr. Buckley says. "Are you *quite* ready to continue?"

The drill starts up again, but I don't care. I don't care about anything. I feel like my body is a wagon and my mind is a horse, and somebody just unhitched the two.

Despite what I tell them—that I'm ready to start my life over as a *tabula rasa*, a blank slate, whatever you want to call it—right now all I want to do is slip away into the cool, velvet nothingness that's calling to me.

Oblivion.

That's what I want. That's what I need.

With each slow blink, time passes quickly, and nothing happens. No more needles, no more drilling. I'm just sitting here, waiting. Whatever happy juice they squirted into me is wearing off, and worse, I'm getting feeling back in my scalp. I'd ask what's going on, but that would be a waste of time. They never, ever give you reasons for their delays.

I'm able to move my eyes just far enough to see the observation window. It's up high, on the other side of the room, opposite the doctors' booth.

Someone is up there watching me.

It's *her*.

HER.

I feel something rise in my throat, fierce and foul. My teeth clench together, and an intense hatred fills me up so hot, so fast.

It takes all my strength to force my fisted hands to open and relax. I need to stop this. It's ridiculous for me to feel this way. She's some consultant they've brought in from New York. I don't know her. I've never seen her before this week.

Ms. Hodges. That's her name.

Hodges.

"Whoa. Everything all right, Sarah? Your heart is racing," Larry says.

"I'm fine."

"You sure?"

"Yeah. Totally fine."

There's no reason for me to have such a strong reaction to this woman. She's a stranger, and though it's possible she reminds me of someone I used to know, there's no way to be sure. I need to ignore these feelings. That's all. Ignore them. Because I don't know what's real and what isn't.

As the woman looks toward the surgeon's booth, I sneak a quick glance at her. She's wearing an ivory dress with lots of draped fabric. It's elegant. Toga-like. Several gold bracelets circle her wrist. She spins them around, but as our eyes meet, she stops and lets her hands drop to her sides.

It's hard to tell how old she is. Fortysomething, maybe?

My eyes dart toward her hair. It's the most perfect shade of red, and if I didn't feel so murderous right now, I'd admit that she's beautiful.

You know, for her age.

I squeeze my eyes shut, hoping that when I open them again, she'll be gone. But she isn't. I want to make these feelings go away, but hatred is a sticky, clingy thing, and I can't seem to get rid of it.

I remind myself what I've been told nearly every day since I arrived. Paranoia is a side effect of these *tabula rasa* treatments. So is a strong feeling of déjà vu, loss of depth perception, balance problems, color blindness, and, according to Larry, an inexplicable affinity for people wearing wooden clogs.

That breaks the spell a little. A smile tugs at the corner of my mouth. I wait for Larry to ask me what I'm thinking. He's probably the only person who could tell me exactly how many times I've smiled since I got here.

Suddenly all the lights go out.

The room is black and instantly colder. The darkness only lasts a moment, but it feels much longer.

When the lights come back on, so does Larry's microphone. "You okay down there?"

"I don't know."

A drop of blood drips onto my lap. I must have jumped when the lights went out. I didn't think it was even possible, but somehow I tore one of the metal inserts loose from my skull.

The lights flicker and the heart rate monitor leaps back to life long enough to beep once.

"Sarah," Dr. Buckley says through the balky speaker system. "I guess . . . having . . . technical . . . someone . . . will . . . try to . . . calm—"

The power goes out again, and this time the outage drags on.

Just as I'm starting to panic, I hear a door open and then footsteps. My whole body stiffens at the sound of someone hurtling toward me. Whoever it is knocks a piece of equipment onto the floor as he approaches.

I hear him breathing hard. He's right there, right next to me, but he says nothing.

Aftershave.

That's what I smell. I have no association to go with it, which makes me think it can't be one of the orderlies. I know each of them by their body spray or shampoo or mouthwash.

I hold my breath, waiting, completely aware of how helpless I am. The man grabs my upper arm and then fumbles toward my wrist, finally locating my hand. He presses something into my palm and wraps my fingers around it. It feels like a plastic bag.

A moment later, he retreats, and then I hear the door click shut.

I'm alone in the dark again, but I feel a rush of something that I haven't felt in a long time: hope, curiosity, and a little bit of anger.

I feel alive.

CHAPTER 2

Twenty minutes later I'm out of the halo, and the lights are back on full blast. I haven't dared to look down at what's in my hand. I keep my fist at my side, practically sitting on it.

I'm being transferred back to my room in a wheelchair. One of the orderlies, Steve, is pushing me down the hall. Steve is this huge, tall black guy with feet like canoes. I spend a lot of time looking down at the floor, and I figure his feet for a size fourteen, easily. He wears a scarf all the time and usually a cap, too. I wonder if he has trouble keeping his head warm—too far for the blood to travel. He's probably the only person in this place I feel comfortable around. I have no idea why.

"Key lime pie with dinner tonight, Sarah! You like that. I know you do."

I have no real feelings one way or the other about key

lime pie, but it seems rude to contradict him when he's trying to be nice.

He whistles as we roll along and asks me for the second time, "So, how're you doing today?"

We're always supposed to say *good* when someone asks how we are. It shows we've got a positive attitude.

"Mmm, okay," I say.

"You'll be done soon. Then you can get on with your life. Fresh start, and all that."

Even though the power has returned, things are not back to normal yet. I can still feel something in the air, some echo of fear. As we pass the first-floor nurses' station, I see that it's empty.

"Where is everybody?"

"Of course you'd notice. I knew you would. You notice everything."

"That's why I'm your favorite."

"That's right." He rubs my head, and I wince when he accidentally presses down on the bandage covering the loose halo insert. "Whoops. Sorry about that. You okay?"

"I'll live."

He leans over me and whispers, "I'm not supposed to tell you this, because the doctors don't like us to say anything that might worry the patients, but we're expecting a big blizzard tonight."

"Oh."

"Yeah. They're sending people home. Last flight out's in

thirty minutes. Down to a skeleton crew tonight. But don't you worry. You'll still be in good hands."

Last flight out. Something about that idea makes me jumpy.

"Did the storm cause the power outage earlier?" I ask.

"Which power outage?"

"There's been more than one?"

"Yeah. Three or four, mostly in areas of the compound we don't use much. If you ask me, it's all this fancy equipment they got here. Wind turbines, solar panels, geothermal whatnot. I'm telling you, the least little problem and it's on the fritz."

"Where are we, Steve?"

"You know I can't tell you that."

"We're so far from civilization they can't use electrical cables to bring us power?"

"I'll tell you this much: We're off the grid. Way, way off the grid!"

"I hear helicopters a lot," I say. "That's how you guys get to and from work, isn't it?"

He ignores me and starts whistling again.

"I get it. It's a secret. How about I just guess what state we're in? It's somewhere with a lot of snow. And mountains. Maine? Montana? Some other state that starts with an *M*?"

"Hawaii. We're in Hawaii."

"Ha-ha."

He walks on with his big, canoe-length steps. I keep my fist tight around the little plastic bag.

"Have you seen Jori lately?" I ask.

He gives a cough and waits a moment before answering. "She's fine."

"Is she?"

"You just worry about you, Miss Nosy."

Jori is another patient here, and I haven't seen her in weeks. I'm worried that something happened to her. People have a way of vanishing from this place. One day they're here; the next day they're not. I don't know if it's because their treatment is completed or because something else happened to them. Something potentially "upsetting" to the rest of us. All they'll say is that a patient is "gone." That could mean anything from transferred to released to dead. You don't mess around with people's brains without losing a few, but they don't want to come right out and tell us when people die.

Except Nurse Jenner. She doesn't mind sharing bad news.

I have trouble believing Jori's been cured and released. She's a terribly limp thing, short and skinny, with skin the color of undercooked fish. She's always hunched over, with her hands clutched in front of her chest like she's trying not to crush the wings of a butterfly she's managed to catch. She's fragile, nervous, and more than a little weird, even by the standards of this place. And though no one on staff will admit it, I'm pretty sure girls like that don't go on to live happily ever after, no matter how many bad memories are cut out of their brains.

Steve steers me toward the elevators and presses the

button. We wait, but no car comes. He keeps pressing and pressing the call button. Still nothing.

"Maybe it's out because of the storm?" I say.

"Yeah. I bet that's it." He yanks the wheelchair back. "We'll go around the other way."

Going around the other way means cutting through the main lobby to get to the north bank of elevators, which takes a few minutes of backtracking. As we pass the lobby's floor-to-ceiling windows, I see that the mountains in the distance have been erased by heavy gray sky.

Just then the wind kicks up. At the harsh, skittering sound of icy snow against glass, Steve starts taking longer and longer strides across the marble floor. I don't know that I've ever seen him move this fast before.

We pass the entrance to the first-floor ward, which is unused. From deep inside the pitch-black hallway, there's a rumble and crack that sounds just like a thunderclap. It's followed seconds later by the creak of hinges.

Steve stops.

I tip my head back and look up at his face as he stares into the darkness. A strong draft blows toward us, and then the unmistakable scent of "outside" hits me.

"Smells like snow," I say.

Steve sucks his teeth. "Yeah. One of the doors must've blown open. I'll have maintenance look into it."

I don't know how a door could have possibly blown open. This whole place is locked up tight. Plus, they built this hospital complex into the side of a hill. First the main building, where we are now, and then the smaller building next to it—South Wing. As Steve wheels me past the walkway that connects the two buildings, my eyes are drawn to it. Something strange goes on in there. No one ever talks about South Wing.

Steve yanks the wheelchair abruptly, and steps up the pace even more. I turn around in the chair, staring at the walkway. I've always wondered why the letters *E* and *C* are etched into the glass. The staff only call this place "the Center." Or sometimes, when they refer to the two adjoining buildings along with the grounds themselves, they'll say, "the Compound." But the *E.C.* has to stand for something.

"Steve?"

"Eyes in front, Miss Sarah," he says, gently turning my head back around. "And don't be asking any more questions. You just think about getting better."

Getting better. That's what I'm here for. And *getting better* means forgetting the past. Because the past is bad. Very bad. Worse than very bad. So much worse than very bad that I might not get over it otherwise.

Drastic measures. These are them.

When traditional therapy, drug therapy, and behavioral therapy all fail, you land here, and they drill through your skull and pull out the bad memories like they're pulling weeds.

Everyone at the Center is being treated for severe posttraumatic stress disorder. At first, I thought that meant something traumatic had happened to me. But then one day I realized that assumption might be wrong. Probably around the time I noticed that my ward seemed to be the only one with round-the-clock security guards and a bank of monitors that displayed every inch of the floor. And there's this feeling I get from the staff, like they're all wary of me but pretending not to be. I asked my therapist if maybe I was the cause of whatever traumatic event I was supposed to forget. She just sniffed, pushed her glasses up onto her nose, and said, "Of course not."

Of course not.

Then there was the time—after my third injection series—when a new orderly was wheeling me back to my room. He smirked at me and asked, "So which kind are you?"

"Which kind of what?" I didn't know what he meant.

"Victim or perpetrator," he said.

"What do you think I am?"

He looked me up and down and laughed. "You ain't no angel, that's for sure."

I'm bored. All the time, horribly, horribly bored. I'm also filled with this sense of unease that I can't ever shake. It's like, even though my mind can't remember why, my body is straining to get back to whatever it was doing before I came here.

At some point I started counting the doors, the light fixtures, the floor tiles. Anything and everything, until I could visualize this entire place in my head. I know the layout of every floor and every ward—well, everywhere I'm allowed to go. And I do all this to stop myself from dwelling on "unproductive" thinking.

As Steve wheels me down the hallway, I look at the floor. I know there are eighteen black tiles between the elevator and the rec lounge, and as I count the final tile, I lift my eyes and see that that's exactly where we are.

The rec lounge is one of the few places I'm allowed to go without supervision. I'd much rather go to the gym and burn off some energy, but they won't let me do that anymore. Not since I pushed myself as hard as I could for as long as I could, just to see what I was capable of. I did seventy-four push-ups in a row and went up the climbing wall like a monkey. After that they rationed my gym time. They told me I was at risk for a treatment setback.

As we move past the glass partition between the hallway and the lounge, I sit up tall in the wheelchair to see if there's anyone inside.

There is. Jori.

I wave to her, and she waves back with twice the enthusiasm. I have to say, even if she does sort of give me the creeps, I'm glad to know she's not dead.

"Can't we stop a minute?" I ask.

"Nope."

"Why?"

"It's not good for either of you."

I guess they must have found out what Jori and I were

talking about last time I saw her. We were watching Bugs Bunny, and she whispered to me, "Quick. Tell me what I look like before the nurse comes back."

So I did, even though we're not supposed to.

"You've got blue eyes, a high forehead, a small nose with kind of a ball on the end of it."

"Really?" She pinched the end of her nose, trying to feel it. "Am I pretty?"

I lied. "Sure, I'd say you're pretty."

"Good. How old do you think I am?"

"Fifteen?" I was being generous. She really looks like she's thirteen, twelve even.

"Maybe. I think I'm older than that, though. I think . . . I just have a feeling. I think I may have had a baby."

"Really?"

"Yes. I had a memory of touching my tummy. And it was round and kind of hard."

When I asked her what I looked like, she smiled and said, "Strong."

That's when the nurse appeared and shooed her away from me. I didn't get a chance to ask her what color my eyes are, but I guess they're probably brown. Most people in the world have brown eyes. Like seventy-five percent. I'm not sure how I know that.

When Jori sees that Steve's not stopping, she rushes toward the glass, putting her fingertips on the window like a lizard crawling up the sides of a terrarium. I turn toward her and raise my hands like, *What can I do?* Jori's face falls as Steve whisks me around the next corner.

We're halfway up the hall when a nurse trots after us.

"She's very agitated right now," she says, looking back over her shoulder. "Could I borrow Sarah for a few minutes? She's the only one who can calm the girl down."

Steve rubs his chin. "Doc said not to."

"Come on. I've been dealing with her outbursts all day. I need a break."

He takes his hands off the wheelchair. "I'm gonna get a cup of coffee. You get caught, it's on you."

A moment later I'm doubling back toward the lounge, and as I get closer, Jori starts clapping. The nurse opens the door and nods toward me. "Five minutes, Jori. That's it."

"Thank you, Nurse Lemontree!"

As soon as she's gone I say, "Your nurse's last name is Lemontree?"

"Oh, no. It's something with a lot of *s*'s and *z*'s, and I think there's an *icki* at the end. I thought Lemontree sounded much nicer."

I get up from the wheelchair and walk toward the couch. As soon as I sit down, Jori slides in next to me, pushing herself up under my arm and pulling her knees to her chest. She always does this. I must remind her of someone who once made her feel safe.

"I've been wanting to see you, but they wouldn't let me," she says in a whisper.

"Yeah. I know."

The nurse wasn't kidding. Jori is agitated. And twitchy. She keeps looking toward the observation window to make sure the nurse's back is turned to us.

"I need to tell you something."

"What's that?"

"They were talking about you," she says quickly, lacing her fingers together in front of her chest.

"Of course they were. They talk about all of us."

"This is different. It's that woman from New York. The one with the red hair."

"Ms. Hodges?"

"Is that her name?"

"Yeah."

I close my eyes and see her in my mind. A fiery hatred engulfs me, but once again I force myself to ignore it.

"She doesn't like you. I think she . . . I think she's up to something, Sarah. Something really bad."

I can't help but shift myself away from Jori. Yes, I had similar feelings about that Hodges lady not even an hour ago, but hearing Jori say it makes me feel like Jori and me, we're the same, and I don't like that idea one bit. Even in a place like this, you want to believe that you're not the worst off.

I cock my head to the side and try to smile. "Jori. Come on. You know what the doctors tell us. Sometimes we have these feelings like people want to hurt us, but it's not true. All that stuff is just in our heads."

"I know, I know, but I'm telling you, this is different. You need to stay away from her. Get out of here, even."

"Where would I go? Down to the corner to wait for the next bus in my hospital gown and slipper socks?"

"I don't know, but I'm really worried about you!"

I know this is nothing but crazy Jori talk, but it still upsets me. Paranoia is usually a pretty selfish thing. I, for one, have never been paranoid about anyone else's safety. Only my own.

"I'm sure I'll be fine. Really."

"You won't. I heard her talking on her cell phone with Dr. Buckley, getting impatient. She was spinning her bracelets. Then she started pacing in her fancy shoes."

"When was this?"

"I don't know. I'm not so good with time."

Neither am I. A day is as a week is as a month. I used to scratch little hash marks on the wall next to my bed. I counted them every day to remind myself how long I'd been here. But then they switched my room and I lost track.

"Are you sure it was Dr. Buckley she was talking to?"

"I'm sure."

"But why would she be on the phone with him when she could just talk to him in person? And besides, I don't think cell phones work here."

"Satellite phones work here. Maybe that's what she had."

I'm surprised by this. I wouldn't expect Jori to know what a satellite phone is. I'm not even sure I do.

"Sarah, if you'd heard her, you'd believe me. She said to Buckley"—and here Jori uses a different voice, with a Southern accent—"'This is not what we agreed to. You've got one more chance to get rid of our *little problem* before I take care of things myself. And if I have to do that, you'll be drumming up research funds running a lemonade stand, because I'll make sure no one gives you another penny. *Ever. Again.*'"

The details of the story make me nervous, but I try not to show it. "Okay, Jori. I promise I'll be careful."

Jori squeezes me around my waist. "Good. I don't want anything bad to happen to you."

"I don't want anything bad to happen to me, either. Or you."

I rub her arm and put my head against hers. We sit for a moment, baldness to baldness, silent.

"Sarah?"

"Yes?"

"Do you want to leave here?"

Do I? I know I *should* want to leave. I should want to embrace this brand-new future, my clean slate free of trauma, anger, and pain. But it's not that simple.

"I don't want to be here," I say, "but I don't want to be out there, either."

"Yeah. Me too. I wish there was a better here or a better there to pick from."

Jori's nurse returns. Seeing us—and, more to the point, seeing Jori calm—pleases her so much that she smiles at me. I'm not often on the receiving end of smiles. I mean, I'm sure Larry smiles at me, but I've never seen his face, so that doesn't count.

I get back into the wheelchair, and the nurse thanks

me quietly, almost reluctantly. Before I go, Jori rushes me again.

"I almost forgot." She reaches into her bathrobe pocket and then opens up her palm, revealing a handful of jelly beans. "Nurse Lemontree gives me these if I don't make any trouble."

She picks up a red jelly bean and holds it up. I know what she wants. She wants to see me do my trick. I wink at her.

"Ready?" she asks.

"I'm ready."

"Anywhere?"

"Anywhere."

She tosses the jelly bean into the far corner of the room. She thinks she's thrown it out of my reach, but I put one foot on the coffee table, then another on the arm of the sofa, and I hop into the air, twist, and catch the jelly bean in my mouth, landing softly on the cushions, sideways.

"Amazing!"

It's a silly, worthless talent, but I never miss. I think I might have been a seal in a former life.

Jori hugs me. I put my arms around her tiny frame. It's like hugging a marionette.

I'm eager to get away. Five minutes of Jori is all I think I can take right now. I wave good-bye to her just as Steve reappears, huddling for warmth over his coffee mug like it's a campfire. The poor guy is freezing.

I guess I am, too. That must be why I'm shivering.

Once I'm finally back in my room, Steve helps me into bed and then dims the lights. He hovers for a moment, and I wonder if he's waiting for a tip.

"Try to get some rest. They'll get you fixed up next time. As soon as this storm blows over." He puts his hand on my head, gently this time. "Someone will bring your dinner tray in a little while."

"Thanks."

He winks and points at me. "I'll see if I can pull some strings and get you two pieces of that key lime pie."

"That would be great. Thanks, Steve."

"Take care now."

As soon as he walks out of the room, I sit up and turn my body away from the security camera's steady gaze, hoping it looks like I'm just adjusting my blankets. I examine the plastic bag in my hand at last. It holds three clear gel capsules, along with a piece of paper. On one side of the paper are instructions:

TAKE ONE PILL AT A TIME, AT 24-HOUR INTERVALS.
24 HOURS EXACTLY.
REMAIN STILL AFTER TAKING.

I turn the paper over and see there's something more. The handwriting is hard to make out, but it says,

FOR WE KNOW WHAT WE ARE, BUT NOT WHAT WE MAY BECOME.

Okay.

I should probably wonder what the pills are for, who gave them to me, why. I know the medical staff would disapprove of me putting an unknown medicine into my system. It might cause a setback.

I reread both sides of the note. Someone wants me to take these pills. Someone wants to help me.

I pop a pill into my mouth without another thought.

CHAPTER 3

What did I expect?

Something. Something more than disappointment.

I lie in bed for a long time. Whatever the pill is supposed to do, it isn't working. After an hour or so, I get up.

No sooner am I upright than it hits me.

A memory. So fast and furious, I understand why I'm supposed to remain still. I fall to the floor as the room seems to expand and contract around me, like I'm in the middle of a camera lens trying to focus.

Worse, this isn't a memory. It's more like a reenactment, and I'm not prepared for the intensity of it.

I'm hanging in the air, my legs swinging freely. I'm high up. So, so high!

Whatever I'm holding on to is swaying. Some piece of machinery. It groans as the metal contorts in the wind. The hood of my jacket is lifting up around my ears with every gust. I feel my hair lashing my cheeks. I should have pulled it back into a ponytail before I started climbing.

I can just make out the faint sounds of the city below. Taxi cabs. Trucks. Everyone so eager to get somewhere. That's what's so thrilling and horrible about the city—all those layers of urgency working against each other.

New York City.

I look at the lights spread out across the city. This is my starry sky. So what if I look down at it instead of up? It's just as beautiful to me.

I'm hanging from a construction crane poised beside a half-completed skyscraper. I must be a hundred feet in the air. My arm is hooked over one of the metal struts. I can stay here for a while so long as I don't look straight down. If I do, I feel the pull of it—the seduction of falling. All I have to do is let go.

But I can't give in. I need to finish what I'm doing. I need to tie this banner onto the arm of the crane. It's a message. I want the whole city to see it.

My face is wet with tears, tears from the wind in my eyes and the pain in my chest, but I do what I need to do. I finish, and I know I shouldn't, but I look down and feel it right away. That something that teases me and tells me it knows everything in my heart. It knows the strain of these last few months. Come to me, *it whispers. It's so hard not to listen. So many things would be solved if I just let go. What's the difference, really? Forgetting is the antidote for every problem.*

Let go, *it says.*

But I hold on.

• • •

I'm back in my hospital room, hyperventilating. I put my head between my knees and try to slow my breathing and heart rate, but it's like trying to calm a charging bull with soothing words. Inside my head is the strangest sensation, like there's something dripping, melting. It isn't painful, but it isn't pleasant, either. I wonder if something has gone wrong. All that drilling they do—maybe I'm bleeding. Maybe my cerebral fluid is draining away. Maybe taking that pill was a really bad idea.

Too late now.

I stand up, but I'm too dizzy to walk. I force myself to do it anyway. As I lurch toward the door, I stumble and fall hard onto my hip. I wonder why no nurse has come in. The camera in the corner is on. Surely they've seen me fall, but no one comes to help.

That's when I notice something odd under my bed. Clothing. And shoes. No, not shoes—boots. Big, heavy work boots. All I ever wear are hospital gowns and socks with little no-slip rubber pads on the bottom. I've hardly even seen regular street clothes in months. Everyone here is either in a hospital gown or a white medical coat and scrubs.

I shake my head and then tap it hard, like I'm trying to get some wonky remote control working again. I crawl across the floor and then press myself down onto my belly so I can reach the clothes under the bed.

How did these get here? *Why* did these get here? It's a pair of pants and a dark green hooded sweatshirt. The pants have grass stains on the knees. I immediately stand up, pull my hospital gown over my head, and begin to dress. The pants turn out to be huge, but there's a belt, which I tighten to the last notch. There's no shirt, so I put the hoodie on over my bare chest. I push my foot into one of the boots. Loose but usable.

I wad my hospital gown into a ball and throw it onto my bed. I check all the pockets of the pants and find something else: one of those magnetic cards the staff uses to open doors. It's white with a rainbow holographic *E.C.* on it, whatever that stands for.

Suddenly, a series of sharp pops makes the floor quiver. I don't know what could have caused that sound, but my instincts shout at me, *Get out of here now!*

My instincts don't seem to understand that I'm in a locked hospital ward and getting out is impossible. But I go to the door and pull it anyway.

It opens.

I can't believe it. I stick my head out into the hallway and look back and forth. I see no one and hear nothing, so I walk out of my room, and after a moment, I realize there's no reason to hide. It's not just the hallway that's empty; it's the whole ward. *How is this possible? Where are the nurses? They haven't abandoned us all and gone home because of this storm, have they?*

That's when I hear the pulsing beat of a helicopter. The windows rattle as it gets closer. It hovers right above the building for a solid minute before moving away.

I walk up to the nurses' station and look around. Mounted on the wall above the desk are a dozen video monitors, but only three are turned on. One of them shows the coma kid in the room diagonally across the hall from mine. I knew about him because I once heard Nurse Jenner make a joke about how he was her favorite patient. Never gave her a bit of trouble.

Another monitor shows a guy in bed with an IV. I've never seen him before.

The last monitor is focused on an empty bed. Mine.

Are there really only three of us here?

I pick up a remote control for the video monitors and start pressing buttons. Somehow I make the pictures on one of the monitors shift like a slide show. The screen displays various sights around the compound. I see the outer exercise yard. Snow is starting to accumulate on the benches and paths.

Next, there's a panoramic shot, blurred by the storm, and I can just make out the main hospital building from a distance. There are a few other places I don't recognize. It's like watching the universe expand.

And look at that! A sleek black helicopter is landing outside. The rotors come to a quick stop and fold up like some kind of mechanical insect.

The windows shake once again as the helicopter that was hovering over the roof descends. It moves slowly, following the contour of the building like it's prowling for something, looking into all the windows.

The next image that comes up on the monitor is startling and eerie: a small group of people rushing somewhere, frantically falling over each other as they run. That's when I notice the familiar pattern of marble tiles on the floor—a mosaic of the rising sun.

That's the main lobby.

I go to the window and look through the blinds. The helicopter is now twenty yards away, a couple floors up. It begins to move off, and I think it's leaving, but then the nose turns toward the building. Seconds later, there are three quick blasts of fire, followed by a whistling sound.

I'm able to think the word *rockets* just as they hit. *BOOM. BOOM. BOOM.*

Ceiling tiles and light fixtures rain down on me. Clouds of dust explode from every direction. The cracking and breaking seem to go on endlessly. I hear another series of three explosions—three more rockets—this time on the wing opposite mine. That's Jori's side of the fourth floor.

I scramble under the desk. The windows have popped and sprayed glass pellets everywhere. The ward doors swing open slowly, like the building's been turned sideways. I stand and then walk slowly to the stairwell, but seconds later, I'm on my hands and knees again as another explosion buckles the floor. The watercooler tank tips over, and I hear it glugging as it rolls away.

What was once my hospital room is now a ragged hole, and through this opening I watch the helicopter as it turns and rises. Once it moves away from the building, I rush toward the coma kid's room. *Why? This is stupid. How can I save someone in a coma?*

It's hard to climb over the fallen debris, but I make it to his door and see a huge beam lying on top of the kid's bed, across his chest.

I spin and run, searching from room to room as the snow blows into the hallway, melting instantly. Finally, at the end of the hallway, I find the guy I just saw on the monitor. He looks to be in his late teens. A bunch of tubes are connecting him to an IV and a catheter. His thickly muscled arms, chest, and neck are covered with tattoos, some of which have been "scrubbed" off with a laser. That's another thing they do here.

I count half a dozen incision scars on his head, and there's one that's freshly stitched. He also has what might be a bullet wound scar just below his collarbone. I lift his arm and try to tug him off the mattress. He's rock-solid dead weight, and I know there's no way I can carry him.

I put my hand over the kid's heart, feel his chest rise and fall. Something about him is familiar to me. Like I don't know him specifically, but I know people like him. I pull his IV out, make the sign of the cross on his forehead, lips, and chest. It's all I can do for him, and I'm well aware of how pathetically little it is.

I run out the door, slip on the wet floor, and land on my tailbone. That's when I hear them. There are people in the building. People who shouldn't be here. I know this because they're making a lot of noise, stomping up the stairs rather than running for cover. I look down at myself—the boots, the clothing, the passcard. Someone's trying to help me. Why? Maybe because someone else is planning to hurt me. Maybe Jori was right after all.

Jori.

I run past the nurses' station toward her wing, my boots crunching against the gritty layer of concrete that's popped off the walls. Each wing has a set of security doors, and when I reach the ones leading to Jori's side of the floor, I have to let the handle go because it's so hot. Dropping to my knees, I try to look underneath the door. I smell smoke . . . and something else.

Tear gas.

Up until this moment I had no clue what tear gas smelled like, but I don't really need that much training. It feels like someone just jammed a blowtorch into both my eyes and down my throat.

I pull the neck of the hoodie up over my mouth and nose. I'll have to get to Jori a different way.

I listen at the stairwell door. The people who were just coming up the steps have opened the door to the floor below. I wait a second until they're gone and then go down two floors, thinking I might be able to loop back around and use the stairs on the opposite end of the floor to go back up, but when I pull the door open at the second floor, I instantly regret it. Two men in black-and-gray military camos turn and fire at me. I let go of the handle and drop onto the floor as bullets rip into the metal fire door.

Sliding down the handrail, I practically fall the rest of the way to the first floor, bursting out of the stairwell into smoke and mayhem in the main lobby. An injured nurse, dragging one leg, is moving toward the front door, trying to stay behind the huge potted palm trees next to the ceiling-high windows. I dive behind the security guard's desk and find I'm not the only one taking cover there. There are two others.

Make that one other. One of the physical therapists is there. Dead. That leaves a nurse I've never seen before. She's completely rigid and her eyes are unblinking. If she weren't breathing so rapidly, I'd think she was dead, too.

I feel the prickly sensation of adrenaline in the tips of my fingers. My mouth fills with metallic-tasting saliva. Someone speaks. It could be a man or a woman. Whoever it is sounds like one of those computer-translator thingies. Like a voice you'd hear on a GPS. Robotic. Jerky. Not human.

"We are here for Sarah Ramos. She is sixteen years old. Tell us where she is and we will leave."

Behind one of the potted palms I see Steve crouched down. I make eye contact with him. He mouths, "I'm sorry."

I shake my head violently because I know what he's about to do.

He stands and points. "She's there. Behind the desk."

I stare at him in terrified disbelief. Two hours ago he was promising me extra pie, and now he's betraying me? He hangs his head, pulls his scarf practically over his face, perhaps out of shame. I can see he's genuinely sorry.

When they shoot him, I can't say I feel the same way.

CHAPTER 4

A hurricane of hot metal sweeps toward me. The windows behind the guard's desk collapse in on themselves. Through sheer luck, I've crouched down behind a filing cabinet and I'm not hit, but the gunfire is so loud I can hardly hear anything for a full ten seconds after it stops.

The woman lying next to me is staring up at the ceiling with lightless eyes. I hear the sound of boots making their way through a field of glass and debris.

Another hail of bullets flies over my head. How many bullets do these people need to kill one girl?

I hear a woman's voice. "Have your people put their guns down." Her voice seems to curl around every word. It's soft, Southern, sweet.

The computer voice responds, "Hold your fire until my signal."

"My signal, darling. *My* signal. Let's not forget who's in charge."

They take their time coming to check on me. I guess they figure that no sound and no movement might be proof in itself. I reach across to the dead woman next to me and put my hand on her chest. After wiping her blood onto the side of my face and neck, I sit as still as I can, open palms resting in my lap.

"Is she dead?" the Southern woman asks hopefully.

It's Hodges. I know it is. I've never heard her speak before, but I hear her bracelets jingling on her wrist.

The guy with the gun leans over the top of the guard's desk. He looks down at me, and I know he can only see the top of my bald head.

"I think."

Hodges sighs dramatically. "We didn't come all this way and spend all this money to *think* we killed her."

The soldier hops over the counter of the guard's desk and lands with one foot on the body next to me. He's off-balance as he reaches down and tips my chin up with the still-smoking muzzle of his rifle. I feel my skin blister but force myself to stay limp.

"Yeah," he says. "Dead."

"You're absolutely sure?" Hodges asks.

He pulls his glove off with his teeth and reaches down to put his fingers on the side of my neck. When his hand is right next to my face, I bite him as hard as I can and bring one of my boots up into his crotch.

As he doubles over, I grab the hand that grips his rifle and squeeze his finger, firing toward the ceiling directly above where his fellow soldiers and Hodges are standing.

She screams as the overhead lights explode. I also hit one of the sprinkler heads, or maybe the line that feeds them, because water suddenly pours down. I'm soaked within seconds.

I slide on my stomach across the wet, glass-strewn floor and dive through the window behind the desk. That's when I realize that I've miscalculated. I knew we were on the first floor; I just didn't realize that the first floor wasn't necessarily the ground level.

I fall fifteen feet and land smack on my chest and face. My jaw snaps shut and my teeth close onto my tongue. I spit blood and touch my front teeth, shocked that they're still there. I don't move right away. Not until I look up and see a man with a gun leaning out from the window, getting ready to fire down at me. Then I move real fast.

I roll toward the building and tuck myself flat against the wall. The jutting overhang of the upper floor gives me six inches of cover at most. As bullets dive into the ground near my feet, I scramble clumsily along the wall, then lose my balance, smacking my head against the rough granite wall in almost the exact spot where the insert came loose from my skull. The pain is blinding, but I keep going.

I'm so cold I can hardly get my body to work. I think my wet clothes are starting to freeze. The cold obliterates every thought in my head, and my need to get away from it overpowers every other instinct, even my urge to flee. I try every door I pass, but none of them budge.

Looking over my shoulder, I wonder when one of those soldiers is going to track me down. I shove my hands into the front pockets of the hoodie, but the wet fabric gives no warmth. I feel something, though. Something small, plastic, rectangular.

The passcard!

Maybe I can find a place to hide, some little mouse hole or a cabinet under a sink somewhere. The police will come eventually. You can't attack a hospital and expect to get away with it.

Not unless you attack in the middle of a blizzard. And the hospital is in the middle of nowhere. And help couldn't arrive even if it wanted to.

There's a sudden, painful heaviness in my rib cage, and it tells me that I've hit the dark truth. I'm on my own, stranded here, and no one is coming to help me.

I close my frozen fingers around the passcard and continue running along the side of the building until I come to a huge garage bay door. There's a magnetic card reader on the wall, so I zip the card through it and immediately wish I hadn't. The door rises, incredibly slowly and incredibly loudly. I might as well have sent up a flare to let the soldiers know where I am.

Once the door rattles to a halt, I don't want to risk lowering it again. Someone will hear it for sure. I'll have to leave the door wide open. *Forget about staying warm.*

I press my hands to my head. I still feel that slow dripping sensation now, and with it, something much worse—a terrible, budding sadness unfolding inside my mind. It feels like something bad has already happened, and something worse is about to follow. I'm more afraid of this sudden ache than I am of the men with guns who are after me. Because this thing—whatever it is—is coming from deep inside me. I can't run from it.

I'm momentarily paralyzed. I keep gripping my head and staring down at the floor, at the wisps of snow swirling around the lawn mowers. I need a plan. I need . . . I need . . .

"You need wings, little one. But no one has wings."

My mother speaks these words to me as if she's standing just over my shoulder. I jerk to my right to look, even though I know she can't be here. Because she's dead. They told me that much.

But I remember her. A little bit, anyway.

I remember that she said these words to me, and how she said them—the last traces of her accent hugging each word. But I cannot remember her face.

The next thing I know, I'm pulled into the past.

I'm sitting on a stool, staring at a fat woman with rings on every finger. It's not my mother. It's Mrs. Esteban. She's stirring a pot in a too-small restaurant kitchen, her long skirt shifting with each stroke. The scent of cooking rice and spice and hot lard fills the room. I could lick the air, it smells so good.

I am seven, maybe eight. Some kids were chasing me, so I ducked down an alley and then into the back of this pupusería, smack into the large back end of Mrs. Esteban. She is a cook here, and she also lives in the third-floor apartment directly below my mother and me. She let me hide from the kids who were chasing me, but now she's impatient for me to go. She has work to do, and I'm distracting her.

"Why won't they just leave me alone?" I say, slapping away my stupid, stupid tears. I hate that anyone can make me feel like this, that I have no defense against it.

"Because you are different from them."

"How?"

"You go to a different school than they do. You talk differently than they do," she says. Then she sighs. "And you are different in other ways."

"What ways?"

"Has no one told you this?"

"Told me what?"

She shakes her head and looks up at the ceiling. "You have green eyes."

"So?"

"So? So? Ay!"

She wipes her hands on a kitchen towel and slings it over her shoulder. "Your mother used to work for a very wealthy man who has green eyes. You're old enough to figure it out."

I don't understand what she means right away. Then I jump up from the stool and yank on her apron. "Who was it?"

"Oh, chica. Your mother should be the one to tell you this."

"Who!"

"I can't think of his name. He builds all the big buildings in *the city." She is snapping her fingers, trying to jog her memory, but nothing comes.*

I kick her in the ankle and run outside as she shouts names at me. I am in a blind rage as I run back out into the alley—right into the group of kids who were taunting and chasing me. Suddenly I am on the pavement, my face pushed into a grease-slicked puddle. I hear a group of girls giggle. The sound of girls laughing can be the ugliest sound in the world. I feel someone walk over my back, and I raise my head to see several pairs of shiny black loafers and ruffled socks skipping away.

The memory ends abruptly, like someone's shaken me to get my attention back. I'm facing the garage wall. I see a hedge trimmer, a pair of clippers, a small scythe.

A weapon. That's what I need. That's what I want.

Hiding doesn't suit me at all.

CHAPTER 5

I look around for something. Anything. I don't even know what.

In the garage there are three huge lawn mowers. They're the kind the landscapers here stand on to mow the acres of grass that surround this place. Next to them is a small tractor, with belt treads instead of tires. I look at it longingly, but I know I can't take it. Where would I go, especially in this weather? And it would draw a lot of attention. If I'm going to escape, I'll need to do it quietly. I have a feeling no one is going to let me leave if they can possibly help it.

A row of lockers lines one wall. Maybe there's something in one of them that can help me. I find a hammer in a nearby toolbox and give one of the keypad locks a couple hard whacks. The first locker springs open; it's full of nothing. The next one is more helpful. There's a set of blue coveralls and a big overcoat; it's green canvas on the outside and flannel on the inside. I strip off my wet clothes and put the coveralls on. I've got to roll the sleeves and pant legs up about six inches. I put the overcoat on, and it's so warm and soft I momentarily hug myself in grateful relief. In the next locker I find a lunch box with a sandwich and an apple inside. I stuff them into my pockets. Then I remember the passcard and the pills. I need to get them out of my wet clothes.

I put my hand in the pocket of the hoodie and come away with the plastic bag. One of the two remaining gel capsules has popped, and the baggy is leaking whatever was inside. It probably happened when I slid out the window and landed on my chest. I put the baggy in the coat pocket.

I smash another few lockers before I come up with a stretchy black cap. I put that on and instantly feel a thousand times warmer. I find a pair of leather work gloves lying on a nearby bench and put those on, too.

This garage is full of landscaping tools, but what am I going to do? Carry a rake with me to defend myself? I need something smaller.

I go back to the tool closet where I got the hammer and have another look around. At first I think I see a gun, but then I realize it's a nailer. It's about two feet long—the kind you use to fire nails into concrete with a shotgun shell. I have no idea how I know what it is and how it works, but I do. I put it in the inside pocket of the huge overcoat, holding the handle of it with my armpit. I take a handful each of shells and nails and put them in the pocket, too.

Improvising seems familiar. Like it's my style.

I notice an interior door in the corner of the garage. There's probably a hallway on the other side. It might lead toward a basement, but I can't chance it. Since this place is built into the side of a hill, I can't be sure what level the garage connects to, and I don't want to end up anywhere near the lobby. Run? Don't run? I do nothing. I can't do nothing. I hear footsteps on the other side of the door. Heavy and urgent. These guys are fast.

I can hear them shouting to each other in their weird, digitized voices. I run to the other side of the garage, where the big lawn mowers are parked, and squat down behind one of them.

I hear the chirp of a magnetized card reader and see the light near the door turn from red to green. The door opens an inch.

I wait. They wait. They're testing me.

"Sarah Ramos. Walk to the center of the room and lie face down on the floor with your arms and legs fully extended."

I say nothing. Still the door doesn't open. What are they waiting for?

I jump up from behind the mower and pull the engine cord. It springs to life, coughing black smoke. I squeeze one handle, but nothing happens. Then I try both at the same time and the lawn mower jumps forward, but as soon as I let go of both handles, it stalls.

Behind me on a workbench is a roll of duct tape. I tear

a piece off with my teeth and wrap it around each handle of the mower.

Just as the door springs open, I pop the brake and the mower takes off toward the door. I don't care how many guns you have—when a huge lawn mower is coming at you, you get out of the way. They reflexively shoot and then retreat back to the hallway as it smashes into the door. The screeching of metal echoes through the garage.

I hit the button to lower the garage door, waiting until it's almost all the way down before slipping out underneath.

I'm alive. But I need to keep moving if I want to stay that way.

Keeping close to the building, I hope the outcroppings and contours will provide me some cover. After a hundred feet or so, I come to the edge of my known world: a huge metal trellis mounted to the side of the building. It runs almost all the way to the roof and has thousands of pieces of copper foil attached to the lattice. When the wind blows, the foil strips spin around, making patterns in the shifting breezes. Pretty, yes, but it's also capturing the wind's energy to help supply power to the building. Somebody once told me it's called "functional sculpture."

As I try to decide what my next move should be, I see a figure ahead of me in the snow. It isn't one of the guys with guns. It isn't someone on staff. Another patient? It can't be. For one thing, he isn't bald. I can see dark hair sticking out from underneath his ski hat. Also, he's wearing a big white puffy ski jacket and goggles, and carrying what looks like a computer bag. As he skulks along, I skulk behind him. Something in the way he moves tells me he's young. I follow as he picks his way around the edge of the building. In his left hand, he's carrying a walkie-talkie, and when he disappears around the next corner, I run faster to gain ground.

I chance a look around the corner and stop in my tracks. There's a work site. It's huge. The hole they've dug for this construction project runs as deep as the main hospital building is tall. Excavated dirt is piled in every direction. There are dump trucks, cement mixers, backhoes, and, looming above it all, a tower crane. I see the trunk of it, but the top has disappeared into the veil of snow. Obviously, they wouldn't be working in this weather, but there's something about the site that's not quite right. Maybe it's the tall weeds around the tires of the cement mixer, the sheets of plastic that have torn loose and blown into the fence, the way the piles of dirt look hardened. No one's been here for a while.

The kid is making his way toward the small outbuilding that's connected to the main facility by a glass walkway. He's crouched low, definitely trying to stay hidden. It makes me feel better about him. Plus, he doesn't have a gun. Right now, my favorite people on earth are those without guns.

When the kid gets to the building, he squats down near the door at the side and pulls out a passcard. It's just like mine: white. He seems unsure about whether he wants to use it. He waits, then finally scans the card and opens the door.

As soon as he goes in, I make my move. I sprint for the opening like I'm trying to steal home, catching the door with my boot just before it closes all the way. I wait a minute before looking inside, just in case the guy is still there. He isn't.

I've clearly come in a back door or a side door. It's kind of odd, the way this place is separate from the main building, but I'm sure there must be a reason. There always is.

The stairs go one direction: down. I move as quietly as I can. This might be a good place to lie low for a while. I come to a set of doors, each with a magnetized card reader next to it. Judging by the unmelted snow on the floor, the kid went to the right, which means I'll go left.

I use my passcard and pull the door open. The air's so cold I wonder if I've walked back outside. As I enter the room, the lights come on. I take two steps back, and the security camera in the upper corner of the room adjusts itself to capture my movement.

No! No! No!

Turning back, I hear a strange sound, like something deflating. Someone has just turned off the lights, along with every machine in the place—all that white noise you don't notice until it's gone. A moment later, a series of greenish emergency lights come on.

I hear the beep of the card reader. Someone is coming. I press myself against the wall. It must be the kid I saw outside. Maybe he saw my snow tracks in the hall. I need to think fast.

The door swings open all the way, letting in just enough light so I can aim.

Apparently I know how to throw a pretty good punch.

CHAPTER 6

The kid flies backward. His head hits the wall hard, but the thud is muffled by his ski hat. He slides down into a sitting position as his computer bag spills onto the floor next to him.

He looks up at me, amazed and slightly offended, and then touches his bleeding nose. "What did you do that for?"

My head tips to the side; my lips part. I look at my fist because I'm pretty sure it's never punched such a good-looking face before. I can't dwell on this fact for very long, though, because for all I know, this boy could be helping those killers hunt me down.

I put my boot on his ankle and press down with all my weight.

"Hey! That hurts!"

"It's supposed to," I say. "Did you turn the lights out?"

"Who *are* you?"

I growl at him. "All you need to know right now is that I'm the girl with the gun."

"*That* is not a gun."

"A projectile is a projectile."

"You got me there."

I step back and he leans forward to rub his ankle. Then he starts to get up and actually holds out his hand for me to pull him to his feet.

"I didn't say you could get up."

"Just let me do what I was gonna do, all right?"

"Which is what?"

"Can't tell you that, but if I don't do it quick, a bunch of angry dudes with real guns are going to come rushing in here."

I look around the room. The green glow of the emergency lights has leached into the air like weak tea, but it reveals nothing familiar. At least not to my eyes.

"What is this place?" I ask.

"It's where they house the mainframe for this joint."

He points toward the other side of the room. Now I can see the outline of a series of small, rectangular towers. They're elevated off the floor behind a metal cage.

"Why would they have the computer so far from the main building?"

"This system needs to be kept super cool all the time, which is why this room is like a meat locker. And it needs to be kept safe. So it's in a bunker with four-foot-thick walls. Does that satisfy your curiosity?"

"Not really."

"Please. I'm running out of time. What do you want? You want me to beg?" He gets on his knees. "Here. I'm begging. Happy now?"

"Ecstatic."

He reaches for his pocket suddenly, and I point the nailer at his face.

"It's a headlamp, okay? As in, a lamp I wear on my head."

"Let me see it," I say, trying to sound menacing.

He takes the headlamp out, puts it on his head, and turns on the light. Then he throws his hands out to the sides. *Ta-da.*

I lower the nailer and kick his computer bag behind me. "I'll hold on to this for insurance."

"No, I need that for what I'm going to do."

I wait a moment. He makes a motion with his hand, like *gimme*, and I push the bag toward him with my foot. He grabs it and crosses the room in three strides. He takes a pair of glasses with thick brown frames from his coat pocket and puts them on. The glasses easily cut his attractiveness by half. Possibly three quarters.

"Why would you . . . what are you putting those on for?"

"Because you knocked my contacts out when you punched me in the face, and now I can't see."

I gape at his glasses, wondering if this is what people wear these days in the outside world. I feel my forehead crinkling in dismay at the pure, incandescent ugliness of them.

"Look, I got them in Pyongyang, okay? This was the only set of frames they had, and we were kind of in a hurry. Now stop distracting me."

At the door of the security cage, he punches in a code. Nothing happens. He tries again.

"Well, this is embarrassing. Thought I had that code cracked."

Scanning the room, he zeroes in on one particular server. He pulls a tool from his bag and uses it to cut away part of the cage so he can reach through. Then he pulls out his laptop, connects a cable, and starts typing madly. A moment later, he looks relieved and quickly tucks something into his pocket.

"What did you do?" I ask.

"Took some stuff. Then I killed it."

"Why?"

"Because that's what my boss told me to do."

"Your boss?" Now I'm good and mad. I point the nailer at his throat. "I thought you said you were trying to get away from those guys—"

I want to add *who are trying to kill me* but don't. Even I realize how crazy it would probably sound.

"My boss isn't with those guys," the boy says. "Well, actually, he is, but not in the way you think. It's complicated."

The boy takes his glasses off and puts them back in his inner coat pocket. Then he crouches down, packs away his laptop, and zips the bag shut. He looks up at me like he's not sure why I'm still here. His eyes are so brown they look black, or maybe it's just that his pupils are fully dilated in this dim light.

He starts for the door.

"Wait. What are you going to do now?" I ask.

"Leave."

"Leave?"

"Yeah. I'm getting my butt back to the yurt."

"What did you just say?"

"Yurt."

"What is that word?"

"Yurt. You know? It's like a tent. Or a hut."

"Take me with you."

"No."

"Please!" I want to spit that word out of my mouth; it tastes so much like desperation.

"No."

I try a different tack. "Look, I take rejection fairly well. My nailer? Not so much."

He looks toward the door again and then glances at his watch. "You don't seem to understand. . . ."

"No, I *don't* understand. I don't understand what's going on at all. There are guys here with guns who just killed everyone I know!"

He winces. "I'm sorry."

"You're *sorry*? Did you just say you're *sorry*?"

"I meant I'm sorry for you. Not that I'm apologizing for what's going on in there, because I had nothing to do with it. I've got my own problems, and I need to get out of here."

"You're complaining to *me*." I pull off my cap.

He stares at my bald head a moment and then looks me in the eye like I'm . . . like he knows I'm a lost cause, but can't quite bring himself to break the news to me.

"So you're one of them."

"One of who?"

"One of the lab rats here."

"Obviously."

He starts to speak, stops, then starts again. "I'm probably the last person who could help you. Believe me when I tell you that those guys inside are going to be very cranky when they realize what I just did. I wouldn't be doing you any favors if I let you come with me."

He's putting his gloves on now. I guess he assumes I'm going to just let him walk out the door.

"Tell me *something*," I say, trying to keep the anger out of my voice.

"Can't."

"Anything! I need something useful, now, or I will nail your feet to the floor!"

So much for containing my anger.

"I doubt you even know how that thing works."

I point the nailer at his computer bag. This gets his attention.

"Take it easy, okay? Just take it easy."

"Tell me one thing. That's all."

"Okay. One thing."

"How are you involved, but not involved?"

"My boss is the preeminent hacker in the entire world. He does jobs for people. People with a lot of money. He got paid to come here and remove some information."

"And shoot everyone in sight?"

"We didn't know they were going to do that. I swear. Why do you think I'm getting out of here?"

"I don't believe you. Why would somebody need help hacking a hospital computer?"

"*Hospital?* Is that where you think you are?"

I almost blurt out *yes*, but I know now that this answer is laughable.

"This ain't no hospital, sunshine," he says. "Or maybe I should say, it's a lot more than a hospital. This place is seriously state-of-the-art."

"Why?"

"You know what? No offense, but there's not much point in explaining this to someone who's brain-damaged."

"I am *not* brain-damaged."

"You are, and you've got the drill holes to prove it."

I shoot his computer with my nailer.

He starts howling, jumping, swearing, asking me if I realize what I've just done. I stare at him, unmoved. Nobody calls me brain-damaged. Even if, technically, I suppose I am.

Suddenly a voice comes over his radio. A woman's voice. "Who's there? Is there someone on the other end? Answer me."

The kid looks alarmed and holds the walkie-talkie away

from his body like whoever it is can see him through the speaker.

"I take it that's not your boss," I say.

He shakes his head and puts the radio back in his pocket.

Of course it's Hodges. Her voice is a razor blade covered in nectar. I know this, but I don't want to tell him. I won't be saying anything more to this kid until he's willing to trade more information with me.

"Why does she have your boss's radio?"

"I don't know, but I have to go. Now."

Like that hadn't occurred to me.

"How about you just tell me where I am," I say. "Tell me where the nearest highway is and point me in the right direction. That's all I need."

He snorts once. "That's all you need? One, you're assuming I even know that. Which I don't. If I didn't have this thing"—he pulls out a small, handheld GPS and shakes it in front of my face—"I couldn't find my own zipper. Two, even if you did know where you were going and had the right clothing and a snowmobile—which obviously you don't—you're not going to get anywhere in this freak of a storm."

"How did you get here?"

"How I got here is not relevant. Look, time is short. I really can't help you. I'm not even sure I can help myself. I'm sorry."

"Where is this yurt thing you were talking about? Can I just follow you there? Just for a little while? You don't have to help me after that. I need to get away from here . . . from them."

"Why?"

"What do you mean, *why*?"

"Look, those military guys inside are after someone. Some personal vendetta or something. I can't believe 8-Bit got involved with this. I don't care if it was a personal favor. I'm telling you, if you just lie low, they'll clear out eventually. They're not interested in you."

"No? Then why are they trying to kill me?"

"They're trying to kill you? *You?*" He looks me up and down, and for a moment, his eyes settle on my bare head.

"Yes."

He presses his lips together and says nothing for a few seconds. Then he points at my head. "You've got some dried blood. There. Above your left eye. And on your neck."

I lick my thumb and wipe the blood off my forehead. I'm not sure who this blood belongs to. I think of the woman who's probably still lying in the lobby right now. She's gone from being a person to being a thing. So have Steve and the coma kid. The horror of it, the unrealness of it, hits me like a wave of nausea. For all I know, Larry is also dead.

And Jori.

My face burns white-hot when I think about the way I ran out on her. The way I completely forgot about her.

I wipe my nose and eyes with the back of my hand. I

don't even realize I've let go of the nailer until I hear it hit the floor.

"I don't know what to do or where to go."

I'm half convinced that I've only said this to myself, but then I realize he heard me, because when I raise my head, I catch him looking at me. I can't tell if his expression shows pity or something far deeper. Something more like empathy.

His shoulders drop in resignation.

"Okay, fine. You can come with me for now. Maybe wait the storm out. But after that you're on your own. And we might not even make it. We might end up frozen in the woods."

I pick up the nailer and stick it in the inside pocket of my coat. "I'd rather freeze to death than get shot."

"That's the spirit," he says as he checks his watch again. After a minute, he closes his eyes and says quietly, "Where are you, man?"

"Are you waiting for someone?"

"I was. But now I've got to leave without him."

"Who?"

The kid kicks the mutilated body of his laptop across the floor and says, "Somebody who's going to be very annoyed when he finds out what you did to his twenty-thousand-dollar computer."

CHAPTER 7

We go back outside and stay close to the walls of the mainframe building. The snow is coming down so thick and fast that it builds up on the tops of our boots each time we stop to check if it's safe to move forward.

I've never been this far from the main building. Now that I'm closer to the fence line, I can see that this place is a fortress, just like the kid said. There's a twelve-foot-high fence with razor wire on the top. If there are roads leading here, I can't see them. This compound is an island in a sea of mountains.

I see a snowmobile with a sledge tied to the back. The kid points to it. "That's mine."

"We can't take it—they'll hear us." I don't have to translate that what I really mean is, *They'll shoot us.*

"I need to get some stuff from out of there. Come on."

He starts to run and I follow. We reach the snowmobile

and kneel behind it. The kid reaches under the tarp covering the sledge and pulls out a pair of rain ponchos, except they're white. A moment later he takes his GPS out of his pocket and hands it to me.

"You know how to use that?"

"I might. Give me a second."

This is an effect of the *tabula rasa* treatment. Sometimes we don't know what we can do until we do it. Something inside us takes over and suddenly we can paint or draw or read another language. Or in my case, climb the gym walls like they're nothing. Like I knew that being up high was where I belonged.

The GPS sits in my hand; I wait to see if I know what to do with it, but I guess I'm too slow. He takes it back from me and says, "It's okay if you don't. I'm surprised you'd remember how to use a light switch with all those holes in your head. I counted five of them, by the way."

"Five of what?"

"Holes in your head. Not including the metal studs in your skull for the halo."

How does he know about that?

I guess he heard me thinking this—or maybe he noticed that I jumped when he said it.

"I know a little about what goes on here. To be honest, there are days I'm half-tempted to check myself in."

"I don't think they take people like you."

"People like me? Who are 'people like me'?"

"You just don't seem to be as . . . you don't seem the type, is all."

"You don't know what type I am," he says darkly. He pulls a white poncho over his head and hands one to me.

"What's your name?" I ask.

He hesitates for a short, telling moment. "Pierce."

"Pierce what?"

"Pierce Belmont."

"Pierce Belmont?"

"That's right."

"That's obviously a fake name."

"No, it's . . . *not*."

"Whatever. Don't tell me."

We stay low as we head for the fence. *Pierce* takes out the bolt cutters he'd used inside. I put my hand on his arm before he can use them.

"What?"

A thought rushes at me suddenly, warningly, out of nowhere. "It might be electrified."

"You're right. I could have just fried myself."

He reaches into his pack and pulls out what looks like a small pair of scissors. The cutting end is shiny like black glass.

"Nonconductive," he says. "Thanks for the heads-up. You're already earning your keep."

Once we are both through, he takes a plastic zip tie out of his pocket and ties the fence flap back in place.

"From a distance they won't be able to tell where we went through. Might buy us a little time."

I'm suddenly annoyed. "Don't you want to know my name?"

He puts the tool back in his pack and says, "Do you even know what your real name is?"

"Sarah?"

He looks at me skeptically. "You sure about that?"

I open my mouth to respond but find I really don't have anything to say.

The woods are black and white. White from the snow coming down, black from night falling. We'd be walking in circles if not for the GPS.

By the time we get a few hundred yards into the woods, every step takes a huge amount of effort. The wind has blown the snow into drifts in places, and as we cross them, I sink up to the middle of my thighs. The cold has numbed my legs, and I'm only walking from memory, one foot in front of the other, over and over again.

Just as I'm about to tell Pierce that I'm done, I can't walk any farther, he looks at the GPS and says, "We've only got twenty more yards to go."

There could be a herd of elephants twenty yards ahead; I can't see more than a foot in front of my face. We walk another few steps and suddenly a small tent appears, as if Pierce waved a magic wand to summon it.

"So this is a yurt," I say.

It's a round structure, maybe fifteen feet wide. It looks like a miniature circus tent with a satellite dish on the top of the center pole.

"8-Bit got it from some guy he knew who quit the

Russian intelligence service. He was selling all his equipment off. The Russians will sell you anything. Secrets, guns, kidneys, their children. Anything." He grabs the flap of the tent and flips it over to show me the layer of fur on the other side. "That's reindeer hide."

He pushes the flaps back. "There's only room for one person at a time in the doorway. You'll see. Take your boots off and turn the lantern on when you go inside. It's hanging next to the inner door."

He holds the flap back enough for me to duck inside, into a small foyer kind of thing. I guess it was designed so you could take off your coat and boots without letting the cold air into the tent. Yurt. Whatever it's called.

I'm not sure if I should take my coat off, but then I feel warm air leaking from the inner chamber, so I figure it must be all right. My socks come off with my snow-packed boots. It's so cold the snow hasn't melted, even though it was pressed against my feet.

I push the inner flap back and go inside. I find the lantern and flick it on.

In the middle of the ceiling is an opening about two feet wide and, below that, what looks like a small cauldron with a perforated top. Something inside the cauldron is glowing orange—the last embers of some weird fire that's just about gone out.

There are two inflatable mattresses, a couple portable chairs, and a folding table with three large laptops the size of briefcases on it. Next to each mattress is a big, bulging backpack. I also see a portable camping stove near the table and some dirty plates with utensils stuck to them.

"Welcome to Hackville," Pierce says as he pushes the inner flap up and enters. "You won't be staying long enough to enjoy the amenities, which is just as well, because there are no amenities."

I stand in the center of the yurt, not sure what to do with myself. After a minute he smiles and points. "That right there is known as a chair. You sit on it. A lot of people find them quite handy."

"Thanks for the guidance."

I plunk myself down while he turns on all three computers. As he takes his hat and jacket off, he draws himself up to his full height. His head nearly touches the top of the yurt.

"This place makes my hospital room look huge by comparison. I hope your boss doesn't snore."

"As a matter of fact, he does."

"He's paying you extra for putting up with that, right?"

Pierce uses some bottled water to fill a small kettle and then lights a propane stove beneath it. "I'm not getting paid anything," he says, running his fingers through his hat-flattened hair. "Well, I get room and board, I suppose. 8-Bit is my father."

"Oh. Why didn't you just say that to begin with?"

"I'm not used to saying it yet. I only met the guy eight months ago." Pierce pauses a second and then says, "He doesn't want anyone to know."

"That he's your father or that you're his son?"

"What's the difference?"

"There's a difference, depending on who's ashamed of who."

He snorts. "I hadn't thought of that before, but I guess you're right."

He sits down in the computer chair. We're maybe three feet apart. I sneak a look at him while he's fiddling with one of the laptops. I've been in that hospital for who knows how long, and I can't remember the last time I saw a boy who wasn't bald with holes in his head.

Pierce catches me looking at him and smiles. My cheeks suddenly feel like they're a hundred degrees warmer than the rest of me. "Sorry. Didn't mean to stare."

"That's okay." He gives me a cocky grin. "I get that a lot."

He puts his ski hat back on and raises his eyebrows at me.

"Going somewhere?" I ask.

He points at my hat. "Didn't want you to feel all alone."

I touch the acrylic cap, which, now that it's wet from sweat and melted snow, is very itchy. I take it off, but once I do, I feel naked in front of him.

"So," I say. "What were you doing back there, to the computer system?"

He shrugs.

"What did you do to end up in that head lab?"

I shrug.

"What did they tell you?" he asks.

"Not much. Telling me why I was there would sort of defeat the purpose of erasing my memory."

"They had to have told you something."

"Just that my parents are both dead, and that I have PTSD. Like everyone else there. I guess we couldn't get over whatever it was, so we needed help forgetting."

"Help? You don't seem like you need help with anything."

"What does that mean?"

"Those treatments, they don't change your personality."

"How do you know?"

"I told you. I've done a little reading about what they do here. Point is, PTSD or not, you are who you are."

"Which means what?"

"Which means—how can I put this? You and your nailer don't seem like the kind who'd have trouble dealing with anybody's hurt feelings, including your own."

His words hit me hard. All I've feared, all I've suspected . . . could it be that obvious? Even to this stranger? Maybe that's what I really am.

Perpetrator.

I look up, expecting him to be disgusted by me, but instead I see a flicker of . . . not sympathy. Understanding, maybe? It's strange.

He stands up and moves toward me. I spring to my feet, slightly crouched, my hands already hardened into fists.

"Hey, relax, will you?"

"Sorry. I'm not very good at relaxing."

He pulls something out of his jacket pocket, and now I see what it is: a flash drive. "I need to do a few things." He takes me by the shoulders and moves me so he can skirt past. "This may take a while. Feel free to lie down and rest."

"I don't want to lie down," I say, even though all I want to do is lie down.

"Okay, tough girl. You can stare at the wall if you prefer. But you look exhausted."

He rolls his eyes a little, like he's known me forever and this is just the kind of thing I'm always doing, putting up a brave front. It makes me feel a little better about him. And about myself, too. The nurses were always so cautious and wary around me, but he's not. Even after I punched him in the face. And shot his computer with a nail gun. I'm very relieved to imagine that I might be whatever he thinks I am. Being plain old *all right* would be a huge step up for me.

Pierce sits down at one of the computers and takes out his heinous, thick-framed glasses. He hesitates a moment before putting them on.

"They're really, you know, not that . . . bad," I say.

"Don't patronize me."

"You're right. They're completely hideous."

He begins tapping away. I can tell that even if I ask him a question, he won't answer, because he won't even hear me. Whatever he's doing, though, it's clear that it's not making him very happy. Finally, my curiosity overpowers my exhaustion, and I get up and look over his shoulder.

He's staring at a screen filled with nothing but lines of numbers.

In the blackness of the screen, I see the dark reflection of my own face. I jerk my head back, averting my eyes. I'm not ready to look at myself yet.

"What's all that?" I ask.

He holds up his index finger momentarily and then keeps typing and grimacing. I wait another minute for a response, but he seems to have forgotten I'm standing there.

"I'm starving," I say.

I remember the sandwich I stuffed into my jacket pocket. I go back into the foyer to get it. The sandwich has congealed into a gooey ball. I walk back into the tent, sit down, and take a bite of the mess in my hand.

Pierce must smell the same thing I do as I bite down: slightly spoiled lunch meat. His lip curls in disgust. "What are you eating?"

"I don't know."

"You might be a lab rat, but you're not a real rat. No need to eat garbage. Go look over there. Lots of delicious freeze-dried food to choose from. The instructions are on the packets." He points toward the propane stove with the kettle on top. "Make me something, too. Not the beef enchiladas, though. They taste like Mexicans."

"Aren't enchiladas supposed to taste Mexican?"

"No, I mean they taste like actual Mexicans. Unwashed ones."

He looks at me, and his face goes red faster than a stop-light. "No offense."

"No offense about what?"

"Aren't you—I mean you could be . . . ?"

"I could be what?"

"Mexican maybe? Or something."

I stare at him.

"Although you've got green eyes, so maybe you're Mexican and something else mixed together."

If I had eyebrows, they'd be arching at that comment. "Maybe you should stop talking now."

"Yes, maybe I should, before you decide that I'm some huge racist jerk and not just an awkward idiot who was trying to be funny."

I turn away and look through the plastic packets of food. I have green eyes. That's what Mrs. Esteban told me, too. Until he said it, I wasn't sure my memory could be counted on. But this much is true: I have green eyes.

When the water in the kettle boils, I add it to the contents of the packet. A few minutes later we're both eating hot, gritty chili. I obviously didn't let the water hydrate the food properly, but I was too hungry to wait. My impatience has been rewarded with kidney beans hard as pebbles. Pierce doesn't seem to notice or care. He eats while looking at the computer screen. I guess this is how it's going to be—him doing whatever he's doing, and me just sitting here watching.

After a while he says, "Seriously, you might as well have

a rest. Maybe take a nap. This is going to take a lot longer than I thought."

He returns to the computer with a look on his face that I'd call "entranced." Maybe "obsessed."

I realize that I don't just *want* to sleep; I have to sleep. But I can't. The temperature in the yurt is dropping. After a few minutes of pacing around and rubbing my hands together to stay warm, I see Pierce start shivering, too. He keeps mistyping and swearing. Finally he gets up and puts a couple of brown bricks into the black pot. The bricks smolder, then catch. They smell like candle wax.

My head starts to throb. Maybe the sudden heat is getting to me. I sway and almost lose my balance.

"Whoa there. You all right?"

"I'm fine."

"You're fine? Well, then lie down until the *fineness* passes."

I'm about to say no, but can't think of why I should. Lying down is a perfectly good idea when you're about to fall down.

I sit down on the mattress, and Pierce lifts my feet up and positions them for me before covering me with a blanket. "Let me know if you need anything."

I am inexpressibly grateful and so, naturally, I say nothing.

Pierce sits back down and keeps working. The sound of his fingers on the keyboard, the sight of his profile in those awful glasses . . . I feel myself starting to drift off.

Just as the world's edges start to get fuzzy, I hear him talking to me, although his voice sounds different. It's deeper and slower and full of reverb; it's like he's reciting poetry from the far side of a metal tunnel. He's telling me something about how the storm is coming; that I can survive it. That I can survive anything, because I'm special, and he won't just stand by and let them kill me. . . .

Is this real?

I'm not sure. I don't care. All I know is that I feel safe for the first time that I can remember. Which isn't very long, I know, but I welcome the feeling just the same. For however long it's going to last.

CHAPTER 8

Voices. So many voices in my head. I hear someone talking. It's the red-haired woman, Hodges. She's talking to me. No, about me.

"What rotten timing, officer," she says. *"I was just on my way to see* La Bohème. *But I'm glad you finally caught her. Truly. Well done, NYPD."*

The red-haired woman is sitting across from me in a dress that seems to be made of a hundred yards of purple silk, seed pearls, and puffs of air.

Flouncy.

That's the word that comes to me when I look at her.

She's clutching a fur wrap around her narrow shoulders and holding a sequined purse in her hand. Her hair is pinned up with a sparkling hair clip.

We're in a police interrogation room. There's a table and four chairs. One wall is dark glass—an observation window. I glare at it, daring whoever is behind it to face me.

Sitting next to the red-haired woman is a middle-aged cop. His holster is visible underneath his suit jacket, and as he leans forward to pull his chair closer to the table, the handle of his gun knocks against the armrest and a sprinkle of dandruff lands on the table in front of him.

The red-haired woman pinches the bridge of her nose like she has a terrible headache. "I'm glad we can finally bring this to a close. This vandalism has gone on quite long enough, and as usual, the media have the story all wrong. She doesn't look like much of a hero to me. What do you think, officer?"

"Nah. Not much of one."

"So how did you catch her? I'm curious."

"We got an anonymous tip and just waited at the bottom of the crane. Treed her like a squirrel until she finally had to come down or fall."

"Thank you, lieutenant. If it's all right, do you think I could talk to her a moment? Privately, I mean. She might feel more comfortable if it's just me, and we might be able to get to the bottom of all this that much more quickly."

"Are you sure?"

"I'm sure."

"I'll be just outside the door if you need me."

As he gets up, he gives me a look that says, Don't try anything or I will stomp on your neck. *Then he leaves me with this woman who I've never seen before—even though she's acting like she knows me.*

The red-haired woman rests her elbows on the table and bats her eyelashes at me.

"New York City," *she says.*

She says nothing else for a long while. I look around the room like I can't be bothered talking to her and finally ask, "What about it?"

"New York is soooo *welcoming. I would never have believed it. Here I am, just a poor girl from Georgia. Yet I've come all this way to . . ."*

I roll my eyes.

"You should really listen to this, Sarah. It's important that you understand. You see, when people say they grew up poor and they're from Georgia, that's a very different kind of poor. A whole other level of poor. Even you and your tenement apartment and your mother who's worked as a domestic her whole life—even you can't begin to understand how poor Georgia poor really is."

"Is that right?"

"But I come here to New York, scratch and claw my way up through so many terrible, demeaning jobs. You have no idea how badly people will treat you when they know you have to take it. But I learned a few things over the years, and I've come to see what's really important."

I stare at her.

"You see, you have to set a goal and not let anything or anyone stand in the way of it. That's what I do, and that's the reason I'm here now, in this beautiful dress, on my way to the opera. A true New Yorker."

I raise my cuffed hands and let them plunk down onto the table. I'm wearing a tank top, jeans, and a beat-up pair of sneakers held together with duct tape around the toes. I have dirt under my fingernails and I smell like the streets, like bus exhaust and urine. I say nothing. I'm very sure that this woman in the flouncy purple dress has no idea what the real New York City is.

I'm New York City.

I sneer at her to let her know I think she's a pathetic poser.

"You could learn a thing or two from me, Sarah. You really could. About determination. And commitment." *She adjusts a small, diamond-encrusted C brooch on her dress.* "But of course you won't learn. Which is unfortunate for both of us."

I stretch my neck back and forth. My arms are still achy. I'd been hanging on to that crane for an hour when the police finally showed up. How could they have known where I'd be?

"Have you been listening to me, Sarah?"

"What? Yeah, sure. You were poor. Now you're not. Good for you. Is this little pep talk over now?"

She smacks the table with the palm of her hand and I jump. I glance at the dark glass, wondering if someone is going to come in, but no one does.

"Who are you? My new case manager?"

But as soon as I say it, I know it can't be true. This woman is not like anyone I've ever met. Not in school, not in the foster care system. Whoever she is, she's not here to spew the usual hopeful, encouraging pile of garbage they've tried to feed me regularly since my mother died.

"Who am I?" *she says.*

She extends her hand to shake mine, laughing lightly as if she'd completely forgotten I'm cuffed and shackled and can't possibly raise my hand to meet hers.

"My name is Evangeline Hodges, and sweetheart, right now you are ruining my whole damn life."

A loud burst of static jolts me fully awake. I roll onto my side, off the mattress, and then try to stand up.

Was I dreaming?

No. I was remembering—remembering the red-haired woman's voice. It's the very same voice I just heard come out of the radio before it landed on the other side of the yurt. Pierce startled when I got up, and the walkie-talkie he was cradling in his lap flew six feet.

"Hey! Careful! It took me an hour to figure this out."

"What?"

He picks the walkie-talkie up carefully by the antenna. The back of the radio has been removed, and some of the wires are sticking out. "8-Bit's radio. Those soldier dudes are using an encryption program. It changes frequencies a hundred times a second."

I'm hardly awake, and even if I were, I wouldn't understand what he's saying.

"I slowed down the interval that their frequency changes and . . . never mind. Point is, we can hear them for about a minute before the frequency hops again and we lose the signal. Assuming they're in range."

I sit down on the edge of the mattress, and we lean in close over the radio. It squelches and buzzes, and we hear nothing but static. Then, suddenly, a deep, digitized voice breaks through. The words are garbled, and the signal cuts out a couple times. A woman answers back. It's Hodges.

"Where is he?" she demands. "I want him found."

"We think he's on the sixth floor somewhere. We're searching room to room now, ma'am."

"Get him out of there. I don't care how. He's messed my plan up enough as it is."

"Most of the offices up here have coded locks. It could take some time."

"I don't want to hear excuses. Don't you people have things that go *boom*? Use them!"

I look up at Pierce. "Who are they looking for? Did you hear a name?"

"No. Now *shhhh*."

"She definitely said *he* though, right?"

"Yeah. That's what I heard." Pierce gives me an odd look, like he's trying to figure something out that makes no sense whatsoever. "Who *is* she?"

He says it like he's talking to himself, so I don't answer. We stay hunched over the radio for another minute, but the voices fade in and out and we hear nothing useful. Then the signal jumps again and all we hear is static.

"We lost them."

A sudden gust of wind shakes the yurt. I gasp.

Pierce puts his hand on my shoulder. "It's okay." He looks up at the ceiling, which is moving violently. "Well, okay-ish. Maybe."

I shoot to my feet. "What time is it?"

"Why?"

"Just tell me."

"You were only asleep for about ninety minutes."

I exhale in relief and sit back down. More than once, I've awakened to find that hours or even whole days have passed. But it's fine. There's no need for another pill just yet. That's all that matters.

I feel a backdraft through the hole in the roof. It scatters ash from the glowing brick in the black pot. I pace back and forth in the small space, going over the memory, trying to make sense of it, but I get nowhere.

"Sorry I fell asleep while you were talking to me," I say.

He looks at me, confused. "I wasn't talking to you. I've been sort of consumed with the radio and all this stuff on the flash drive 8-Bit left me."

"Oh."

I sit down in the chair opposite him and put my hands around my skull and squeeze gently. I do this every time I wake up.

"Are you in pain? I have something you can take."

"What? Oh, no, thanks. This is just a thing I do. I think I just need to check that my head's still there sometimes."

I raise my eyes and notice Pierce looking at me like he wants to ask me a question.

"I know what you're going to ask," I say.

"What?"

"Is it weird being bald?"

"Well, is it? I mean, for a girl."

"I guess it's no weirder than having no memory."

"You seriously don't remember anything? Like, not even what you had for breakfast?"

I'm not sure what, if anything, I should share about these confusing things coming back to me. It's almost like I'm being haunted, and I'm too afraid to tell anyone about the ghosts I see because they'll think I'm crazy. I don't want Pierce to think I'm crazy.

"Oatmeal and grapefruit juice."

"Good for you. I had a miniature candy bar and cold instant coffee."

We smile at each other, and I realize that you can half-trust someone for a while—maybe even a long while—but there will always come a moment when you must choose to let go and trust completely or withdraw. Somehow I've come to this point already, and I decide to let go. I'm surprised by how easy it is and how willing I am to do it.

"There's stuff I remember, but I'm not exactly sure when it happened or why. Most of the time I have this odd, drifting feeling, like the world isn't quite solid or I'm not. Other times I'll have these intense feelings that come out of nowhere. I have no idea what causes them. All I know is they're never good."

"I find that to be the case for me, too."

I rub my forehead. "I . . . I remember recent things, things that make no sense. Like playing with the Legos."

"Legos?"

"Yes. They were a therapy aid—you know, to help rebuild hand-eye coordination, if you were having trouble with that. Me and Nurse Jenner always fought about them."

"Why?"

"They said I was getting too fixated. I guess I kept trying to build something. This tower, or building, or whatever. I would get it mostly finished, but I could never get the top right. It was so frustrating. Every time I went to the rec lounge I'd try to build it. I did it over and over again. Then they made me stop."

"What do you think you were trying to build?"

"I don't know, but one day I went into the lounge and there it was. The tower I'd been trying to make. Someone had put it together for me. The top was like a . . . a sword, you know? Kind of tapered to a point at the top. And I had this feeling, like I'd seen that building before. That it was really important, but I had no idea why."

"Who finished it for you?"

"Don't know, but Nurse Jenner was furious when she saw it. She came in and started screaming at me, asking me if I was even trying to get better. Why was I always making trouble when they were just trying to help me? I didn't get a chance to tell her that I hadn't built the thing before she knocked it to the floor. Then she told me to clean up the mess. I had to crawl around picking up all the pieces while she watched to make sure I got every single one."

Pierce sighs and says, "Nurse Jenner sounds like just the sort of super lady who should be working in the mental health profession."

I wonder what's happened to Nurse Jenner. Maybe they shot her, too. I hope not. She isn't very nice, but no one deserves that sort of end. That's when I think of Jori. I can practically feel her bony shoulder against my side.

"What's up? You've got a weird look on your face," Pierce says.

"I was thinking of this girl, Jori. She's another patient. I don't know what happened to her. I tried to find her before, when the men were shooting at me. . . ."

"And?"

"I ran out on her. I left her behind. Nice, huh?"

"Men shooting at you does tend to distract one."

Pierce is trying to cheer me up, let me off the hook maybe, but I can't stop thinking that I let Jori down.

"I shouldn't have run. I should have protected her."

"How could you have done that?"

"You don't understand. She relies on me. She's very attached to me." I look at him, and when our eyes meet, I look away. "I know that's probably hard to believe."

"Why would that be hard to believe?"

"I mean, that anyone would feel, you know, that way about me."

"You think it's weird that someone would *like* you?"

"You said it yourself. That I don't seem like the type who has too many feelings, or whatever."

"I only meant that you seemed strong. Like you're no pushover. There's nothing wrong with that. In fact, there's everything right with it."

"But I'm not—"

Just then, the yurt shudders so violently, Pierce grabs one of the support poles and says something about securing a few of the ropes better, but it's like his words have been tossed into the wind. Another memory comes barging into my head.

I am ten years old, and my mother and I are standing in the nave of a large, beautiful church. I am hot with anger and humiliation, and at the same time I know I have no right to be. It's their church. Their rules. Their steeple.

My mother is being scolded by the church secretary. The secretary keeps fanning herself like she's on the verge of having a fit. You'd think she'd been the one sitting up in the bell tower, dangling her legs over the edge.

"You should mind your daughter more carefully! Heavens! She could have died!"

My mother does not look at the woman, just at me. She's checking me so thoroughly I wonder what she could be looking for. I'm fine. And besides, if I'd fallen from the steeple, I wouldn't have hairline cracks that needed close examination. Anything broken would be plenty obvious.

I really don't know what the fuss is about. I wanted to have a look around. From way up high. I'd always wondered what it was like at the tippy-top of the church.

My mother hugs me while the secretary scolds her, scolds me. Back and forth, like she can't make up her mind. It seems to go on for a long, long time, and I want to leave.

My mother is more gracious than I think she should be to the secretary. She thanks her, apologizes, accepts all the blame for not keeping a closer eye on me. I'm angry at the secretary for making my mother feel bad.

After promising to never ever go into the steeple or even the church again, we depart. When we are on the street again, I stop and look up longingly at the sharp tip of the bell tower. It's like a spear piercing the sky.

My mother shakes her head and says angrily, "Don't you ever do that again. I turn my back in the grocery store and you're gone! You can't just go wandering off like that, climbing into the rafters, just because you feel like it. That tower has been closed for repairs longer than you've been alive."

That would explain why the stairs were blocked off and why I'd had to climb over the barrier to get into the steeple.

"Why? Just tell me why you went up there."

I want to tell her. I want to explain that I like to be high up in the air because I like looking down at the apartment buildings on our street. And the stores. And the people. How I feel closer to people when I'm farther away. And they can't hurt me.

But I don't know how to say this. I don't know that I even understand what pulled me up those stairs, why I felt so free and comfortable with my feet dangling over the edge.

"I wasn't afraid," I tell her.

She pinches my nose and then whacks me lightly on the behind. "You should have been."

"I like to be up high," I finally blurt out.

"Well, maybe you'll be a construction worker someday. And you can skip along the beams of the skyscrapers."

"Really?"

"Yes. That's the only appropriate job for a girl who likes to hang around church steeples. That or becoming an angel, and somehow I don't think you're angel material."

My mother called me Angel from that day forward. It was a joke between us—a reminder of that day we both got in trouble at the church. But it was more than that. Sure, I wasn't the sort of girl anyone would mistake for an angel, but I also wasn't going to be pushed around easily. I wasn't going to let people walk all over me. Not even a little bit.

I think my mother was glad about that.

CHAPTER 9

Pierce is pressing me against his hip, his arm tight around my lower back to keep me standing up. He hands me a canteen, and I take a drink. The water is ice cold, and it hurts my teeth. I test my legs to see if they'll take my weight, and as I do, he slowly lets me go until I can stand on my own again.

"Sarah?" He whispers to me like he's not sure I'll respond. I feel the tickle of his breath on my cheek. It's like a gentle nudge to return to the here and now.

"You back?" he asks.

"Back?"

"From wherever you just went."

I must look frightened. I am frightened. I'm not sure if I should tell him what I just saw, but I blurt it out before I can stop myself. "Her face was blank."

"Whose face?"

"I remembered my mother, but I couldn't see her face. I

mean, I could see everything clearly. As clearly as I see you right now. But my mother's face was just this blank white space."

"You're all right," he says. "At least I think you're all right. Has this ever happened before?"

"Once. Right before I escaped. And then as I was waking up a little earlier." It's finally starting to register that without him standing here, I'd fall down. "Is this—"

I blink. I'm worried about something and afraid to say it out loud.

"What?"

By now I've fully come out of my daze, and I push back from Pierce a little.

"I was going to say *real*."

That I could be here, in a yurt, with this boy—I'm convinced I've made it all up. I must be lying in my hospital bed right now, dreaming the whole thing.

"Yeah. This is real. Here's a good way to figure out if something's real: Ask yourself, 'Does this suck?' and if the answer's yes, then it's probably real."

"That's actually not half bad."

"I have my moments."

I shake myself a little and then windmill my arms around. I take what few steps I can inside the yurt.

"What are you doing?"

"I don't know. The more I move around, the clearer my mind gets."

"Maybe it's like with dreams," he says. "They always

seem so real and vivid when you first wake up, but then five minutes after you get out of bed they're gone. I once read that there's something about moving around that does that. When you get up, go take a pee, whatever. It disturbs all those fragile neurotransmitters in your brain and— *whoosh!* It's all gone."

Maybe that's why the note said to lie still after taking the pills.

"What else did you see? Besides your mother. I mean, if you don't mind telling me."

"I don't. There wasn't much to it. Just a childhood memory. I remembered a nickname my mother had for me."

"Pumpkin?"

"No, not quite that bad."

"What then?"

"Angel."

He turns his head slightly and his eyes narrow. "Angel?"

"I know, right? Hard to imagine."

The wind blows so hard, the yurt buckles on one side. Pierce lunges for one of the tentpoles. "Help me."

Together we push it upright, but then freeze. There's another sound hiding behind the wind—like a small chainsaw revving up. Pierce leans toward me; his mouth is an inch from my ear.

"Did you hear that?"

I nod. I'm only just realizing that the woods—the outdoors, generally—are not my comfort zone. I may not remember everything about it, but something deep in me misses the glass-and-concrete world of New York City.

"If we're lucky, it's just the Mounties," he says.

"Mounties?"

"Canadian police. Used to ride horses; now they ride snowmobiles. Really fast ones. We're right up against the border here. I'd say yards from Canada at most. The storm should give us cover, but let's hope whoever it is doesn't have infrared technology. I'm sure we'd light up like a Christmas tree on fire."

"So we're sitting ducks?"

"We're definitely some kind of ducks. Probably slightly better than sitting. Let's say we're standing ducks. Maybe whoever it is will think we're just hunters or something."

"Hunters with a satellite dish on the top of their tent?"

"Yeah. You're right. We're in big, possibly dead, trouble if it's not the Mounties."

We stay motionless. Hoping the predator will move on. The motorized whine gets louder, then quieter several times. They're circling around.

"They're not shooting at us. That's a good sign," I say.

We hear the engines again, and finally, the sound is carried off by the wind. We stay still for a while longer, though. Just in case.

I suddenly remember being vigilant like this. I remember the thrill and fear of waiting in the dark until everyone had gone home from the work site, hoping my luck would hold out just one more day. I wasn't some careless daredevil when I climbed those tower cranes. Not for one second did I forget that every single handhold, every single step, was a chance to die. It was always on my mind.

Remembering these feelings is so frustrating. It's like remembering how I felt going to and then leaving a carnival, but not recalling anything about the carnival itself. The concrete things my feelings are attached to—I still can't get ahold of them.

"I think whoever's out there just drove off," Pierce says. He turns to me, eyes narrowed. "Hey, come here a sec."

"Why?"

"Just come here."

I take a step toward him.

"Closer."

I take another step, but I guess I'm still not close enough. He pulls me forward until I'm an inch from his chest. This is not the best moment to realize how bad I stink. Pierce seems so clean by comparison. Well, maybe it's not that he's all that clean, either, but he smells good.

I look up at him and see that he's staring down at my head. "Look here," he says. He holds up one hand, pulls his sleeve down, and then turns his hand around so I can see there's nothing in it.

"Are you going to do a magic trick?" I ask.

"Watch," he says, snapping the fingers of his left hand. I do. A moment later, I feel a sharp pain.

"Ow!" I slap my hand against my head, furious. "What was that?"

He holds his right hand out—the one I wasn't looking at. There's a small piece of metal in the center of his palm. It's one of the inserts for the halo.

"This was wiggling back and forth, so I pulled it out. You could probably use a stitch or two, but I doubt either of us wants this to be my first experience as a medic. I have some butterfly bandages that should help keep the wound closed well enough."

I pick up the metal insert, look at it briefly, and then throw it toward the door of the yurt.

"Sorry about the sleight of hand, but I figured it was better that way."

"Where'd you learn to do that?"

"I went through a magic phase when I was twelve. I read books, practiced; I even had a cape. I used to pull quarters out of my kid sister's ears."

"I bet she loved that."

"She did."

Two emotions march across his face in quick succession. Sadness, then revulsion.

"She's gone now," he says. "She died."

"I'm sorry."

"Happened a few months ago." He moves me back a little and says, "You've got another wound near your temple. The dressing is pretty well soaked through with blood. Here. Sit down."

He retrieves a first aid kit from his backpack and kneels in front of me. He's only inches away, and I feel frozen in place, like I'm back in the halo.

"I'm going to pull this bandage off. You want me to do it fast or slow?"

"Slow."

"Wrong answer."

He rips it off, and I jump up, practically landing in his arms.

"Fast is always better," he says as he dabs some antibiotic cream on the wound. "There's another insert that's almost out. You want me to pull it out, too?"

After a second I give half a nod. "Okay. Yeah. Let's get it over with."

This one doesn't come out cleanly. I bite down hard and stay motionless as he digs it out with his fingernail.

"Sorry about that," he says. "It's out now. See?" He shows me the bloody piece of metal in his hand.

"I guess we're even for the punch in the face."

"Yeah. Not that I'm keeping track. I mean, it's not payback. I didn't like hurting you just now."

I stare into his chest. I feel his chin bump against my forehead, and then I slide back away from him, onto the mattress. He clears his throat and our eyes lock.

He leans toward me and puts a Band-Aid on my head.

"Thank you," I say. "You're a good guy."

He smirks.

"You don't know many guys, do you?"

"I think you might be the only one at the moment."

He laughs, but I was being serious. I have no idea who's left up there at the hospital. It's kind of sickening to think about.

"Hey, look," I say. "I've got a trick, too."

I stand up, take a freeze-dried bean from the foil packet, and then toss it high into the air. It almost touches the top of the tent before dropping in a straight line directly into my mouth.

"That's your trick? *That?*"

"You try it. It's not as easy as it looks."

He stands up next to me. Several minutes of throwing another kidney bean go by.

"It has to go all the way to the top of the tent or else it doesn't count," I say.

On his fifteenth attempt, he manages to catch it.

"See? Piece of cake."

We sit down on one of the mattresses, side by side, and watch the heated air rising in a column in the center of the yurt. All the tension in my body seems to flow up and out through the roof along with it.

But almost as soon as I let myself start to relax, there's a rustling sound outside. A moment later, the whole yurt seems to shimmy.

Someone's found us. Someone's coming inside.

Seems we're sitting ducks after all.

CHAPTER 10

Pierce turns to me and puts his finger to his lips. Then he calls out, "Hey, 8-Bit? That you?"

The inner tent flap flies up and we see the metal tips of two snowshoes come through the opening, followed by the barrel of a pistol. Pierce puts his arm in front of me and then tries to push me behind him.

A man enters. He's got ice clinging to his bushy, blond beard. He lifts his goggles as he turns to look at us. We're both gaping back at him like he's an especially dangerous sort of armed bear. He points the gun toward the floor.

"Two days of storm. Big delay. Not have delay."

He's got a thick accent and, besides that, seems to be speaking through his nose.

"Excuse me?" Pierce says.

"Delay. Storm." He slices the air with the pistol in his hand. Then does it again in the opposite direction.

Pierce looks at me, then back up at the bear man. "Um . . . what?"

The man grunts and shrugs. "Deal off. Have other jobs."

Pierce scrambles to his feet as the man turns to go. "Wait!"

The man waves his hand at us and then leaves. We hear the sound of him trudging away from the yurt. A minute later, a snowmobile engine roars to life.

"I think that may have been the person 8-Bit and I were supposed to rendezvous with. The guy who was going to fly us out."

"Looks like he just bailed on you."

"Yeah, that's the impression I got from the . . ." He imitates the man's grunting and the way he made an X in the air with his gun. "You know, this is the problem with paying people to save your butt. Their hearts just aren't in it."

"This storm is really going to last two whole days?"

"So says the Russki."

"So what now?"

"We wait."

"For what?"

"For someone to find us and kill us. Or morning. You know, whichever comes first."

I don't know how Pierce managed to fall asleep so fast, but now that he's out, I think this may be the most alone I've ever felt. Before these few memories came back to me, I didn't have a strong sense of what was missing. But now that I realize how many pieces of me have been stolen, I can feel what's gone even if I don't know everything that's been taken. I had a mother, a city, a whole other life before I came here. It's like this massive ship has sunk, and though I dive and dive, all I can find are the smallest treasures from the wreck: a coin, a few broken pieces of china, a child's shoe. Things that imply there was once so much before the weight of time and cold darkness separated me from it.

Ignorance is not bliss. Not for me, anyway.

The pitch-black yurt isn't helping me sleep, either. I'm used to lights and machines beeping and people checking on me every two hours. With the lantern off and the computers shut down, there's nothing to focus on.

But the biggest reason I can't get to sleep is that the coveralls I'm wearing are scratching me raw. I can't stand it one more second, so I sit up and peel the top of the coveralls off. I try to remember where Pierce left his backpack. Maybe he has something in there I can borrow. I just need a T-shirt underneath as a buffer.

As I start to get up, I misjudge where the edge of the mattress is and slip to the yurt floor like a clumsy cat missing the windowsill. Pierce wakes with a jolt, rolls on top of me, and presses his forearm across my throat. He yawns.

"What're you doing?"

"You're choking me!"

"That's what I'm doing. What are you doing?" He lifts his arm so that he's no longer pressing all his weight onto my windpipe. "Why are you out of bed after lights out?"

"I was looking for something to wear."

"What?"

"I think these coveralls are made of burlap."

He rolls off me and gives a small huff of amusement.

"What's so funny?" I ask.

"Nothing. I'm just relieved that I was dreaming after all. I was listening to 8-Bit argue with that Russian dude, and 8-Bit offered to sell me to the guy for a thousand rubles and a sack of beets."

"That's crazy. You're easily worth three sacks of beets. Maybe even four."

"Thanks." He yawns loudly. "Just to refresh my memory, we're in a yurt near the Canadian border and people are trying to kill you?"

"Correct. Possibly you as well."

"Right. Forgot about that second part. I've got a shirt you can wear. If you help me find the flashlight. It's in the pack on the floor over—"

"Don't turn the light on!"

But he flicks the light on before I can pull the coveralls back up to cover my chest. I dive onto the mattress, face down.

"Whoops. Sorry. I didn't realize . . ."

I have my arms pulled in next to my chest. I keep waiting for him to hand me a shirt, but he doesn't. He's not doing anything, as far as I can tell. Finally I say, "Can I have the shirt, please?"

"Here you go."

I feel it land on my back. My face is against the pillow and I can't tell where he is. "Are you turned around?"

"No."

"Well, turn around."

"Your back," he whispers.

"What about it? What's the matter?"

He comes closer. For a second I think he's going to tell me that I have a bullet wound that I somehow hadn't noticed. "What's the matter? Is there blood or something?"

"No blood. Just wings."

CHAPTER 11

He kneels on the mattress next to me and traces something on my back with his finger. His touch is light, and I feel a shiver rise up from my spine, into my neck.

"I don't do ink on underage kids. Period. End of story."

He's got a beard down to his chest and a barbell stud through each eyebrow. He keeps his heavily tattooed arms crossed over his chest. He's not going to budge.

"I'll pay you," I say. "A lot. Twice what you normally get."

"Money's not the issue. Last thing I need is some kid's mom coming in here, threatening to have me arrested for ruining her poor, sweet angel's perfect skin."

"No one's going to do that," I say. "No one will ever do that."

I tell him about me. I tell him about my mom.

He does the tattoo half price.

• • •

I pull away so suddenly, Pierce is startled. His finger is still extended, like he'd been painting and I've snatched his canvas away. He's looking at my back, and his eyes do not meet mine. He withdraws his hand slowly and lets it drop.

I try to look over my shoulder. "What do you mean, I have wings?"

He turns away, allowing me to pull the T-shirt over my head quickly. When I spin back around, I see his profile. He's staring into space, his hand covering his mouth. After a minute, I wave my hand in front of his eyes.

"Pierce?"

He says nothing.

"What's the matter with you?"

He looks at me in wonder and starts shaking his head. "I don't believe it."

"What? What is it?"

"I think I know who you are." He gets up, flips his laptop open, and types something. Then he hoists me up and stands me in front of the computer. "Look."

In the center of the screen there is a black-and-white picture of a young woman, her back exposed by a low-cut tank top, her arms extended like she's about to dive. Her head is turned to the side, and you can just make out her ear, which has three piercings in the cartilage. You can also see part of her cheek, but her dark brown hair is blowing around her face. She's standing on the ledge of a roof. The background is a sea of buildings and rooftops with small wooden water towers. It's New York City. I'm sure of it. And I feel a surge of warm, gushing affection.

Home.

"That's New York City."

"Yes, but look at this." He points to the girl's back, to the wings tattoo. They spread across her shoulder blades. "That's what's on your back. Or most of it, anyway. It looks like someone got a start on removing it. The tip of one of your wings is missing."

"Who is that? What's this website?"

"That's Angel. And I guess you could call this a fan site. Or maybe a memorial, depending on which theory you believe."

I can't reconcile this powerful image on the computer screen with how I feel right now: not powerful at all.

"How do you know I didn't just see this picture and copy it?"

"Turn your head."

I do.

"May I?" he asks, but before I can answer, he's already touching my ear, comparing it to the picture.

More shivering.

"That's your ear. Ears are like fingerprints. Distinct."

I touch my upper ear as I stare at the screen.

"And look, you've got three holes in your ear. Just like her."

I pinch my ear. "I didn't know that."

"Didn't you ever notice the piercings in the mirror?"

"I haven't looked in a mirror since I arrived at the hospital. I mean, here. Whatever this place really is."

"Really?"

"Really."

"You don't know what you look like?"

"No, and I'm afraid to ask." I feel my eyes stinging, because I can hardly blink. "So . . . what *do* I look like?"

"You look like an escaped mental patient."

"Thanks."

"A cute one, but still."

He smiles at me, and I can't help but smile back. I lean toward the computer and look closely at the image on the screen, focusing less on the girl than the background, trying to see past her and into the city where she lives. I wish the screen were a window, so I could look out at the streets below.

"Let me see it again."

"What?"

"Your back."

I turn around and lift up my shirt a little, trying to make sure my back is all he can see.

"It's so intricate. Who could copy it exactly? I'm telling you," he says, looking back and forth from the computer screen to my back, "the tattoo on your back and that one in the picture—they're exactly the same."

He shakes his head, smiling in awe. "Wow. That's—I mean . . . you're, like, a legend."

A legend? I cringe a little, because I suddenly feel like an impostor. "What did I do?"

"Oh, nothing much. Just exposed a vast government scandal and then vanished into thin air, which is just the sort of thing that conspiracy theorists live for. Here, check it out." He types *Angel* and *New York City* and *government* into a search engine. "You kind of got famous for derailing this housing project they were going to build along the Hudson River. At least, that's what they said it was. The developer claimed it was condos. But you kept hanging these huge banners up nearby that had these numbers and stuff."

"What were they?"

"At first nobody knew. That was sort of the fun of it—figuring out the message. Turned out they were verse citations from *Hamlet*. I'm not a *Hamlet* kind of guy, but I think all the references were about lies and deception. Something like that."

I put my hand to my forehead. Larry! Had he been trying to tell me something? Trying to give me a clue about who I was? Why not just tell me?

"Nobody could figure out how you found out what was really going on, not to mention how you got those banners up once you did. Then the city started looking into the developer's building permits, and what do you know? It turned out the company was a shell corporation. From there it kind of snowballed, because the government stepped in and claimed whatever they were building was a matter of national security. A bunch of very important guys ended up in prison for lying to Congress about it. You bagged a sitting senator and two White House advisers. It was pretty cool. From a David versus Goliath standpoint, I mean."

He shows me another picture—a construction crane.

"See this? You hung banners on these. The police figured you shinnied up the things, freestyle. No ropes, nothing."

This would explain the images coming back to me.

"What happened to me? I mean her. Angel."

"There were all kinds of rumors about you. Some people thought you'd been snuffed out. Assassinated. People started painting angel wings all over the place in New York. *Where's Angel?* It became a thing. People had T-shirts printed up, and posters. You know how kids are these days, trying to borrow your mojo. Things died down a bit after a while."

"How long ago was that?"

"About eighteen months, I guess. How long you been in this joint?"

"A year maybe? I don't really know for sure." I look at Pierce and ask, "What were the other rumors about me?"

"Just some stuff," he says.

"What?"

"Keep in mind that these are *rumors*. Probably entirely made up."

"Tell me."

"Okay, there was a report that you tried to murder someone in the police station when you got arrested."

"Wow."

"After that, though, there was nothing else. Well, nothing else halfway credible. No one knew what happened to you, and not for lack of trying to find out. There must have been a dozen stories and at least that many theories about why you disappeared."

"I just . . . I can't believe it. I feel like you're telling me a story about someone else. Someone who can't possibly be me."

Pierce puts his hand out like he wants to shake, and I put my hand in his, even though I'm not entirely sure why. "Congratulations on not being dead," he says.

"For all that's worth."

"Hey, it's no small feat being alive. And it's even more amazing that you've survived this place."

"What do you mean?"

"This is a highly secret, highly secure, almost hack-proof place. It's not like it's juvie. They've been drilling into your head! Why did they put you in here? *How* did they put you in here?"

"I don't know."

"Do you remember anything about how you got here?"

"No. I always figured I must be some nobody if no one came looking for me."

He scratches his chin and squints. "Well, they're looking for you now."

"You believe me, then?"

"About the guys with guns coming here specifically to kill you?"

I nod.

"I guess I have to. Not that I understand it. It's hard to believe this whole operation is about killing a girl who hung up a bunch of protest banners. I mean, these guys inside? They are the elite of the elite. The kind of hired guns really powerful people employ to whack dictators and then get lost. They cost a whole lotta money. My boss's services do not come cheap, either."

"Your father's, you mean?"

"Right. My father. I may never get used to calling him that."

Pierce stands up and tries to pace back and forth in what little space is available. "What is it?" I ask.

"This is what's bugging me the most: I don't see why 8-Bit would get mixed up with this. I can't say I know him inside out or anything, but up until now we haven't done anything on this scale. And he's way too smart for someone to use him without him catching on to what's happening. Besides that, he's . . . he's not a bad guy. Obviously not the most responsible person ever, but I have a hard time believing he'd get involved with some plan to put a hit on someone."

"Even as a personal favor?"

"For someone who has no memory, you have a pretty good memory."

"Thanks."

"How we've gone from totally tame corporate espionage, stealing some company's idea for a new cell phone, to providing support to guys with more high-tech gadgets than the Navy SEALs—it's strange. I wish I knew what he was thinking, why we got involved."

Pierce takes the flash drive he was holding earlier out of his pocket. "And then there's this."

"What is it?"

"There's a file on this drive that's labeled 'In Case Something Happens to Me.' 8-Bit used his standard encryption on it, which means he knows I'll hack it eventually. Not that it'll be easy, but I'll get there."

"Have you tried to open it yet?"

"No."

"Why?"

"Because I'm still hoping that nothing's happened to him."

"I wish I had some hope." I walk to the door of the yurt and open the flaps. Cold air rushes in. "But there's no getting back what they took out of my head."

"Sure there is."

I whip my head around. "What do you mean?"

"They're not actually extracting anything. There's a small amount of brain tissue damaged during the needle insertion, but for the most part there is no real injury to the brain."

"Are you sure?"

"Like I said, I read through some of the reports. Kind of got the gist of how things work."

"They told me that they inject this stuff into my brain that kills off the neurons they've isolated. I had all these

CAT scans before they started working on me. I don't remember much of that process, though. I guess they erased that, too. All I know is what they told me."

"Who are *they*?"

"This guy named Larry. His real name is Dr. Ladner. Plus Dr. Buckley."

Pierce taps on the computer and brings up a grainy picture of a man with a beard. The picture must have been snapped while the guy was in motion, but I can still tell who it is easily enough. Middle-aged Santa Claus.

"That's Dr. Buckley."

"Buckley is the name he's using, is it?"

I give Pierce a confused look.

"He's the mastermind of the *Tabula Rasa* project. A very mysterious man. 8-Bit went to Harvard grad school with him. His real name is Joseph Purcell Wilson. And he's dead."

"Dead?"

"Yup. Supposedly he was killed four years ago. There was an obit and everything. A very carefully orchestrated story about his tragic death in a small aircraft crash. 8-Bit never believed it. 8-Bit's got a hang-up because the guy scored six points higher on his IQ test or something. Geniuses seem to be the most envious humans alive."

"Dr. Buckley was supposed to do my surgery this morning, but it got interrupted."

"Did it now?"

I explain about the power outage.

"What time was that?"

I point to my holey head. "Sorry. Time's not my best subject."

"It's just weird. Our not-so-friendly crew of mercenaries didn't cut the power to the main hospital building until right around the time the storm hit. So, say, early afternoon."

I suddenly have an idea that makes me feel momentarily better. "Dr. Buckley's probably still inside right now. Maybe it's him they're really after. I mean, maybe they were after me just to get to him. They want to kill all the patients he was working on as some kind of punishment or something. She said they were looking for a man."

"Who is she?"

"Hod—"

I freeze. I hadn't really thought of this before, but maybe there's a chance Hodges is after me—that she hates me—for a very good reason. Because of what Buckley did to us. Or specifically to me. Maybe there's a good reason the nurses were always so cautious around me.

"That woman we heard on the radio," I say.

"I'm sure they wish they could get to Buckley, but he's not here. He's hardly ever here."

"What do you mean? Where is he?"

"Best guess is Bethesda Naval Hospital in Maryland."

"That can't be."

"Let me ask you this: Was he actually in the room with you?"

"No, he was up in the surgeon's booth. He uses—"

"A robotic arm?"

"Yeah."

"Exactly. He does the surgeries remotely."

I start to speak, but stop myself. For some reason, I find this idea horribly offensive. All this time Dr. Buckley/Wilson/Whatever wasn't even in the same state while he was doing brain surgery on me?

"Why did you say the procedure isn't permanent?"

"It can become permanent. What they do is inject a sort of plasticizer compound into your head that seeks out certain kinds of nerve cells. Every time you think about an incident, the compound migrates to those nerve endings. Once all the nerve endings containing a certain memory are identified, they inject another compound that causes the plasticizer stuff to harden and kill the neuron for good. Before they do that, though, the process is reversible."

I touch my head in wonder. "I can still get my memories back? All of them?"

"If that's what you really want."

"Of course I do."

Don't I?

"There's a pill you can take that flushes the plasticizer out of your system through your cerebral spinal fluid."

"Pills," I say. I get up and put my hand in the pocket of the coat I stole from the locker. I pull out the baggy and show it to Pierce.

"Where'd you get this?"

"I don't know."

He sighs. "How can you not know? Did they just appear in your pocket?"

"Basically, yes." I tell him about what happened during the injection procedure, the clothes in my room, and the passcard.

He goes silent for a moment.

"What?"

"Pretty amazing timing, wouldn't you say? I mean, right before someone busts in to try to kill you, clothes and a passcard magically appear in your room?"

"I think it was Larry who gave them to me," I blurt out.

"Why?"

"I just do."

"I can understand why someone on staff might want to help you, you know, avoid getting whacked. But why would one of the doctors who've been trying to erase your memories want you to take those pills to bring them back?"

"I don't know."

Pierce laughs. "Okay, listen. You're not allowed to answer 'I don't know' to any more of my questions."

"Then you better stop asking me questions."

He sits down at the desk. "Well, whatever the story is, you're probably better off not knowing."

"Why?"

"Why put all that mud back in your head again? I wish I could chuck out half of what's in my brain and get a fresh start. Seriously, it's for the best that you never took them."

"I did take them," I say. "One of them, anyway."

"What?" He jostles the computer table with his leg and catches one of the computers before it hits the floor.

"I took one right before those soldiers busted in."

"That's a problem then," he says. "That's a big, huge problem."

CHAPTER 12

If my brain is in jeopardy, I know I should probably ask why, but it's still hard to get the question out of my mouth.

"Why is it bad that I took one of the pills?"

He rubs his eyes and says, "I don't understand all the medical stuff they talk about in their case studies. . . ."

"You have all their case studies? For everyone in the Center?"

"I do now. That and a whole lot more. Normally I don't come along on these kinds of projects, but 8-Bit set up this yurt and wanted me here, out of sight, so the soldiers don't know I'm here."

"To take their files?"

"To take everything. All their research data and patient files. Every last thing. And to leave with it if 8-Bit runs into any problems. I think that's what's in this encrypted file he left me. Instructions about what to do with all this data."

"Tell me what you know about the pills," I say.

"You have to take them at certain intervals. . . ."

"Yes! Twenty-four hours. That's what the instructions said."

"They get rid of the plasticizer, but it's an all-or-nothing kind of thing. If you don't get it all out, it floats around in there," he points to my head. "Then it adheres to whatever it feels like adhering to. Like, say, that part of your brain that tells you what the color red is, or what music sounds like, or how to breathe. Or that little thing called your conscience that makes sure you don't kill people just for the sheer pleasure of it."

"I'm one pill short."

I suddenly feel like too much energy is coursing through me. I can't contain it all. I realize that what I'm feeling is, weirdly, elation. I hug Pierce briefly, intensely, for telling me this. Yes, he's given me a lot of bad news, but he's also just given me something I need—hope.

"I just need to get one more, right?"

"Angel . . ."

"Where can I get more of them?"

He looks like he doesn't want to extinguish my hopes but knows he must. My heart tumbles onto this concrete reality: I have to go back in there.

I walk toward the computer desk and let myself fall into the chair, my head in my hands. I've got whiplash from jerking between the extremes of hope and dread in the span of seconds.

"Don't look so glum," Pierce says.

"Why shouldn't I?"

"Because there's no way I'm not going to let you go in there by yourself."

"Absolutely not! You can't!"

He shakes his head at me and says, "I think that as you get to know me better, you'll find that I'm rather difficult to control."

I look back at him, determined, adamant. I'm going to tell him no way, no how is he coming with me. I don't care what he says.

But then he smiles. And I give in.

He *is* difficult to control.

I suppose I like that about him.

We trudge along, taking turns in front to block the snow and wind. Dawn punches weakly at the clouds. Through the canopy of the pines I can see the occasional patch of fading stars. A couple times the storm eases up, only to get twice as bad the minute I think the worst is over.

It seems to take much longer to get from the yurt to the hospital than it did to go the other way. Pierce gave me a pair of liners to put under my leather work gloves, but my fingertips hurt from the cold—it's like someone has been hitting them with a hammer. I look at Pierce's ski pants and his puffy down parka. It's one of those real expensive ones, lightweight but warm. In the city, it's the kind of jacket people steal.

Now there's something else I can remember that I couldn't before.

When we get within fifty yards of the compound, I see it. The tower crane. It's swaying slightly, and we can hear the creaking of the cold metal even in the howling wind. I can just make out the heavy plates of the counterbalance. I wonder if they're enough to keep the crane stable in these high winds. Each time it moves, I feel my stomach lurch.

We arrive at the fence and find the point where we went through earlier. Pierce cuts the zip-ties. He slides through, careful not to touch the edges. I pass his backpack through and follow after.

We walk at an angle, pressing ourselves into the wind, and I look down into the excavation pit. A line of solar-powered lamps hang by their cords, swinging wildly back and forth. All the heavy equipment sits motionless, like bright yellow dinosaurs stuck in a tar pit.

Pierce looks up toward the hospital. He takes out the walkie-talkie and looks at it. "Maybe I could give it one more try. See if 8-Bit responds this time. See if he could help us."

"I wouldn't risk it," I say. "That woman's voice we heard earlier . . ."

"What? You know her?"

"I do. I don't."

"What's that supposed to mean?"

"You told me I couldn't say 'I don't know' anymore."

He throws his hands up in exasperation.

"Her name is Evangeline Hodges, and all I can tell you is that every time I think of her, I feel so much hate and anger I can't see straight. She's the link between this hospital, me, your boss, and those mercenary guys."

"If she was, I think I'd know about it."

"Don't take this the wrong way, but you seem to be out of the loop on some key aspects of 8-Bit's plan."

Pierce gives me a quick, pained smile. My eyes drift toward the main hospital building. I remember the warm, bland world I had there. I miss everyone telling me I should relax. It only lasts a moment, though, and I recognize it for what it is: a longing for safety. I would never want to go back to that life again.

We walk a few more yards, and I stop. I know I need to do something I don't want to do: I need to give him one last chance to leave.

"Pierce . . . I . . . this is far enough. Really. You've done more than enough." I point to the snowmobile. "Push that toward the woods and start it up when you're out of earshot."

"I was wondering when you were going to make this heroic little speech." He checks his watch. "Yep. Pretty much right on schedule."

I grab him by the wrist. "If I were truly being heroic, I'd actually mean what I'm saying right now. But I don't. I want you to stay with me, but I realize how selfish that is. That's why I'm telling you to go."

"You don't know this, Angel, but *you* are actually helping *me*. Not the other way around."

"I'm helping you by dragging you into a hospital filled with armed soldiers against the express wishes of your boss?"

"Father."

"Right."

"And yes, that's correct."

"Why are you doing this?"

"I have my reasons."

"No doubt very stupid, self-destructive ones."

He shrugs. "Aren't those the best kind?"

I look around, trying to get my bearings. Snow blows into my face, and for the next few seconds I see nothing at all. Then I turn toward Pierce. His scarf covers his nose and mouth. He lifts his goggles. All I see are his black-brown eyes.

"My name's not really Pierce, you know."

"Yeah, I know."

"I'd tell you what it really is, except 8-Bit made me swear never to tell anyone. He said it could get us both killed."

"Then you definitely shouldn't tell me."

"No, I want you to know. Every time you call me Pierce it reminds me that I'm lying to you."

He's just staring at me. I know he wants me to know that he trusts me, but he's afraid. There must be a good reason why.

"I forbid you to tell me," I say.

"You forbid me?"

"Yes." I put both forefingers to my temples. "I remember now. Yes . . . it's hazy, but I must admit that under even mild stress, I blurt out other people's deepest, darkest secrets."

"I think someone could threaten to cut off your head and you wouldn't tell them your shoe size."

I put my hands on my hips. "How about this? If you tell me your real name, I won't let you come along to help me."

"You won't *let* me come?"

"That's right, and then you'll have to find some other way to satisfy your self-destructive urges. And let's be honest, this is kind of a golden opportunity for self-destruction. I'd hate for you to miss it."

The warmth of his smile cuts through the freezing gusts of snow.

"Okay, I won't tell you."

"Swear?"

"I swear I will not tell you my real name."

"All right then. I'll *let* you come with me and risk getting killed."

"Thanks. I really appreciate the chance you're giving me here."

I put out my hand to shake, but then suddenly let it drop.

"Hey! I thought we had a deal!"

"It's not that. It's . . ."

I've caught something on the wind. A scent. Just for a

moment. It's a neutral kind of smell, but one I instantly recognize as the laundry detergent they used to wash our hospital gowns, robes, and bedding. I walk away from him, my head cocked slightly, trying to catch it again.

"What's the matter?" he asks.

I put my hand up. Close my eyes and sniff again. I turn and look toward the construction site, straining my eyes, willing them to penetrate the snow.

There it is. In this sea of white, I can see a different shade.

"Someone's there," I say, pointing.

I hunch down and run across an open area between some of the construction equipment and a trailer parked at the edge of the excavation pit. The person I see is not moving. She is small. I run faster, but I don't know why I'm bothering. I already know. I just know.

It's Jori. She's leaning with her back up against one of the big black rubber tires of a cement mixer. I don't think I would have seen her at all if I hadn't been trying. She was so pale to begin with, and the snow is already covering half her body. She's in her hospital gown; her legs and feet are bare and blue.

I use my teeth to get one of my gloves off, hoping I'm wrong. I touch her chest. If it's even possible, she's colder than the snow around her.

I remember the fire on her wing, the way I left her behind. I take one of her hands in mine, and I see that it's blistered. She burned and then she froze. For some reason,

I think of Hodges. A seething rage surges through me.

Pierce walks up behind me. "Oh man."

I kick the tire of the cement mixer, only succeeding in hurting myself. But I don't care.

"Someone you knew?"

"The girl I told you about. Jori."

My hot tears go cold almost instantly in the wind. I wipe my runny nose, and it hurts. The ice on my glove makes it feel like I'm rubbing sandpaper across my face. I feel like I deserve this pain.

"We should move her," I say.

I don't even know where to take her. I just know I don't want to leave her here, forgotten under the snow.

Pierce takes her by the armpits and I lift up her legs. As we shift her body, I see the snow swirl and realize that I'm seeing two sets of footprints. Hers and much larger ones. Not boot prints, either. Footprints. As in, bare feet.

CHAPTER 13

The footprints lead toward the construction pit, up to a double-wide trailer that sits on high ground next to the excavation area. The roof of the trailer is completely covered with solar panels, one or two of which are lifting up slightly as the wind gusts. The satellite dish that was once mounted at the top of the trailer has come loose and is rattling in the wind like a garbage can lid.

We carry Jori's body toward the trailer, and as we approach, the door blows open. It smacks against the side of the trailer again and again. If it had been open earlier, when we were heading toward the yurt, I'm sure we would have heard the door banging.

When we reach the trailer, I put one foot on the three-step staircase leading to the doorway, still holding Jori's upper body. Pierce stops, and for a moment we are pulling her in different directions.

"I don't mean to be, you know, gross or whatever," he says, "but it's probably better if we keep her outside. Decomposition, and all."

I know he's right, but I hate it.

Now that we're right up against the trailer, I notice something else. Near the door, I see a hospital gown snagged on a length of rebar that is sticking up through the snow. It can't be Jori's. She's still wearing hers.

We set her down in the snow. I turn her on her side and push her legs and arms together so she's somewhat in the fetal position. Pierce steps back and gives me a minute. Not that I have anything to say to Jori. Really, I didn't know her, and she didn't know me. If I measured it in hours, we probably shared a sum total of a few weeks together. But I know I gave her comfort and I wish I could give her comfort now. But I can't. The whole world seems like it's full of nothing but "I can't" and wishing I could have done more. The dead must be so disappointed in all of us.

Pierce is crouching near stacks of what look like the fancy, faceted concrete blocks they used to build this place. The flimsy trailer door is now whipping back and forth, smacking so hard against the side of the trailer, I'm sure it's going to snap off its hinges.

I automatically crouch down as I approach the door. I must have spent a lot of time sneaking around construction sites back when I was Angel, and now my reflexes have taken over. I pull my nailer out of the deep inside pocket of my coat. The trailer is dark. All the blinds are pulled tight, and I motion for Pierce to give me one of the flashlights he's packed. Instead he hands me his headlamp.

I put it on and step inside, Pierce close behind me. As I turn my head to look around, the white beam travels over the walls. We're in some sort of fancy, temporary construction office. There are leather chairs, a couch, even a Persian rug. I see the usual desk stuff: pens, paper, a desk lamp, a stapler. I look at the framed pictures on the walls. They're all line drawings of whatever the building is supposed to look like when it's completed.

At the opposite end of the trailer is a small kitchenette. I walk toward it and notice the clock on the microwave is flashing the wrong time, but it's still working.

I let the light sweep around the trailer again. Pierce is standing in the doorway. I turn to him, and I'm about to say that I think the trailer is empty when he points to something and pulls me back toward the door.

"There. Look."

I see the bottom of a bare foot. Someone is curled up on the floor, under the desk. Judging by the size of the foot, it's got to be a guy.

"Hey," I say.

I get no response.

"Are you okay?"

I move closer and around the corner of the desk. I shine the light on the person lying beneath it.

"Oh, geez," I say.

"Is it . . . is it another body?"

"Yes."

He pulls the trailer door shut and walks toward me. "Dead?"

"Nope. Buck naked, though."

He points a flashlight at the guy curled up under the desk. How the kid has even managed to squash himself in there, I don't know.

"Anyone you know?"

It's the tattoo-covered kid. "He was on my ward. But I only saw him once before now."

I'm about to say that this might be a problem. My ward was . . . well, my ward. The locked ward. But Pierce's voice is suddenly urgent.

"He's hypothermic."

"What?"

"He's burrowing. Help me get him out of there."

Pierce begins removing things from his pack. Then he takes off his jacket.

"What are you doing?"

"Body heat. Burrowing is a sign of advanced hypothermia. That's why he was stripping off his clothes."

"What?"

"It's what people do before freezing to death. They take their clothes off and find some place to curl up in the fetal position. Help me. Get on the other side of him."

Pierce takes his pullover off. I must look horrified, because he tells me, "You don't have to take your shirt off. Just get on the other side of him and we'll kind of sandwich him between us."

Pierce rummages through his pack and comes out with

a blanket that looks like a giant silver garbage bag. We pull the kid out from under the desk and roll him into the center of the blanket. Then I take one side of the blanket and Pierce takes the other and we wrap ourselves up with him.

"Ugh. It's like hugging an Alaskan mailbox," Pierce says.

We stay there for about half an hour, until the kid starts feeling warmer and begins shivering. Pierce says this is a good sign. "We need to get some clothes for him, and he's not going to fit into any of my stuff. See if there's anything around here."

I get up and poke around the trailer, looking for something that might pass as clothing. I find a pair of dirty overalls that crackle when I try to fold them over my arm and a yellow Windbreaker-type thing with an orange reflective triangle on the front. I also find a long, stretched-out sweater with a poinsettia design on the front. It has the name "Collins" written on the tag. I show it to Pierce.

"I guess even ugly holiday sweaters have their uses."

"You do the pants," I say, turning my head as Pierce pulls the overalls up over the guy's naked lower body. I help him put the sweater and windbreaker on the kid. I feel like I'm dressing an overgrown, tattoo-covered child to go sledding.

Pierce takes a pair of socks out of his backpack, looks at the kid, and sighs loudly.

"What's the matter?"

"This dude better appreciate this. These are my favorite socks."

CHAPTER 14

I spend most of the day exploring the drawers and cabinets of the trailer, minding the tattooed kid, and trying to distract myself from the bitter cold, which is pretty much impossible. Pierce has spent hours trying to find a way to get us inside without being detected, and so far that's proven to be equally impossible.

I look through the desk drawer for a key that might unlock some of the cabinets, but as time drags on, my patience runs out, so I start unlocking them with my boot.

"I'm trying to concentrate over here!" Pierce complains.

"And I'm foraging."

"Please forage more quietly, okay?"

I kick another door. Kick it again. The third try is the charm. Inside the cabinet I find something more valuable to me right now than my memory.

"A space heater!"

Pierce looks up and blows into his hands to keep them

warm. "We can plug it in for a little while, but not too long. It'll drain the batteries." He points to a cord running up the wall and into the ceiling. It says, *Powered by Green-Power!* "Powering a few computers is a lot different than heating an entire trailer. We'll be lucky to get thirty minutes of heat out of it, seeing as the batteries haven't been able to charge much in this storm."

"I don't care. I'll take it."

I carry the space heater over and bring it close to where the kid is lying on the floor. I turn it on full blast. After a few minutes, the kid's shivering lessens, and the trailer starts getting so warm, I take my jacket off and hang it over the back of the desk chair.

Pierce's watch starts beeping.

"What's that?"

"I set my alarm to remind you to take your meds."

"Oh. Thanks."

I walk to the watercooler and knock on the plastic bottle. It's frozen solid. In the corner I find a mini-fridge and open the door. Inside are a bunch of paper bags and, on the door, a small carton of orange juice that's already been opened. I throw the pill into my mouth and wash it down with what's left of the orange juice.

I start coughing and gagging.

Pierce jumps up and rushes over to me. He takes me by the shoulders and squeezes, trying to get me to look him in the face.

"What? What's the matter?"

"This orange juice is rancid!"

He sighs at me and rolls his eyes. "Don't do that again, okay?"

I smile at him, just a little. "Sorry." He's a surprisingly easy person to smile at. Maybe that's been my problem all along. I'll smile as much as anyone if I have a good enough reason.

"I thought you were dying."

"Not yet."

I think for a moment that he's actually really mad at me, but then his face relaxes and his eyes go wide.

"That's it! I should hack the medication timetables right now, so we can open the med locker. They might even have the locations of the pills listed in there!" He hugs me roughly, crushing my face into his chest. "Angel, that's brilliant!"

I push back from him, rubbing my nose, wondering if I should point out that it was his idea, not mine. "They keep the meds in a locker?"

"Definitely the painkillers and the sedatives. That's where most hospitals keep them, anyway, and we'll assume they've done the same thing here. Probably the pills you need will be even higher priority. All we need to do is find one of the lockers, unlock it, and then get back out again with the pill you need."

Pierce sits down, and within seconds he's swimming through the lines of code on the screen, oblivious to everything around him. I hover over the tattooed kid for a while. He looks like he's trying to wake up but can't. I spend another half hour looking at the pictures on the walls and going through the rest of the contents of the mini-fridge to see if anything is still edible. I find a couple of dried-out hard-boiled eggs, coffee creamer, and a brown paper bag with grease spots. I look inside.

"Where would you get Chinese food around here?" I ask aloud. I pull the takeout receipt off the side of the bag. "Johnnie Q's Szechuan."

Pierce looks up from his computer.

"You think Johnnie Q's delivers here?" I ask.

"Not unless their corporate jet has a little basket on the front of it. That restaurant's in L.A."

"The receipt says this stuff was ordered in August." I bring it to the desk and open the top of one of the containers. I sniff and groan at the rank odor.

Pierce coughs. "Kung Pao E. coli. My favorite." He pushes back in the wheeled chair and stands up. Something on the wall catches his eye. "Hey, look at this."

I close up the cartons and go to see what he's looking at. It's a framed magazine cover featuring a youngish Asian man standing in front of a strange building that looks like an upside-down bowler hat. The caption says, *William C. Chin in front of his newest creation, the Opera House, Dubai.*

He points to Chin's name on the edge of one of the blueprint drawings lying on the desk. "This guy's a rock star of architecture. They must be sinking a lot of money into this place if they're using Chin to design it." He continues to read the bottom of the blueprint and then says, "Ah! And now I see why."

"What?"

"Claymore Industries."

He looks at me and smiles weakly. "How about we just skip over the part where you tell me that you don't know who that is."

"No. I do. Sort of. I mean, that name does sound kind of familiar."

"Well, it should. Claymore Airlines, Claymore Studios, Claymore This, Claymore That. Erskine Claymore puts his name on everything."

I can see a building in my mind. A tall, thin skyscraper that looks like a perfectly formed icicle . . . or a sword. "Central Park South. Claymore Tower."

"Good girl! I'd throw you a biscuit if I had one."

I shoot him a dark look, but can't help feeling proud of myself for remembering.

"Claymore Industries also happens to be a big military contractor. Interesting, don't you think?"

"I guess."

"And perhaps you'd be interested to know that the building project, the one that you managed to derail by carrying on like a cross between Spider-Man and Robin Hood, was linked to none other than . . ."

"Erskine Claymore," I say.

"Direct hit on correct."

But the name means something more to me. I'm not

sure why, but suddenly I have a terrible feeling of . . . loss. Fury. Confusion. Curiosity. There's something about that name that reaches all the way down into me, like a memory stored in the marrow of my bones. If I were to yank it out, I'd end up pulling myself apart.

"He's a very powerful guy," Pierce says. "Not that having all the money in the world has done him much good in his personal life."

"Why?"

"All his kids have died. Well, except the youngest one, but he's got some problem. I forget what. He's really sick or a quadriplegic or something. And Claymore's wife had a breakdown a couple years ago, and hasn't been seen in public since. Thanksgiving in that family has got to be a real bummer. It's probably just Claymore and his butler watching football and eating turkey sandwiches together."

Across the room, we hear a moan. Or more of a growl, really. We look at each other and then slowly walk toward the tattooed kid. I reach down and touch him on the forehead. As soon as his eyes open, he tries to sit. He rolls onto his stomach and pushes himself up, kicking off the warming blanket like it was trying to smother him. He stumbles toward the desk, grabs it, and upends it with a crash.

Pierce and I both step back.

Seems we succeeded in bringing this kid back to life. Maybe that wasn't such a good idea.

CHAPTER 15

The kid immediately starts speaking Spanish. Pierce says out of the corner of his mouth, "Do you know what he's saying?"

"I think he's asking, 'Where is she?'"

Then it occurs to me that we found his footprints near Jori's body. It's possible that they'd tried to escape together.

The kid falls over, gets up, falls over again. He hits the floor like an anvil. He's not as tall as Pierce but twice as thick.

"Thirsty," he says.

I walk to the watercooler. The water is still mostly frozen, but the space heater has thawed it enough that I can get a few ounces of liquid out. I bring him a Styrofoam coffee cup of water. He drinks, crushes the cup in his fist, and flicks it away from him.

"Where's the girl?" he asks.

"Which girl?" Pierce says.

"I don't know."

The kid looks down at himself and says, "Sandhog."

Pierce looks at me. I have no idea what he means, either.

"My uncle's a sandhog."

"Ah, got it." Pierce whispers, "I think he means he's dressed like a construction worker. Sandhogs are subway tunnel workers."

"Oh."

"What's your name?" Pierce asks him.

"Oscar," he says. "Oscar . . ." He's trying to think of his last name. He shakes his head, and then starts smiling and putting his hands in the air like he's thinking, *How can I not know this?*

I start to introduce myself—"I'm . . ."—but then I realize I don't know what to say. I'm caught somewhere between Sarah and Angel. I'm not one, not the other. I guess I'm nothing.

Then I hear Pierce say, "Angel. This is Angel . . . and I'm Thomas."

Thomas?

I jerk my head to look at him, trying to ask with my eyes if that's his real name or one he's trying to pass off like counterfeit money. His eyes lock with mine, apologetic.

Yes, I think he's told the truth this time.

"You swore you wouldn't tell me."

"I didn't tell you. I told him."

I suck my teeth in irritation.

"It's only my first name. So I only half-broke our deal. There are a million Thomases in the world, right? I could be anybody."

Oscar looks back and forth between us like he's trying to figure why any of us is here.

"Who are you?" Oscar asks, his eyes narrowed.

I pull my cap off to show him my bare head. As soon as I do, he reaches out and touches it. "*Mija*, we got to stay together, eh?"

He starts laughing hysterically but then stops abruptly a few seconds later. His gaze shifts to Pierce, I mean Thomas—it's going to take a minute to get used to that. Oscar seems to realize that Thomas is not his kind, but I am. And not just because of the baldness thing. I guess I noticed the same thing about Thomas: He's unmistakably a rich kid.

Oscar puts his fist to his chin and pushes hard, cracking his neck and his knuckles at the same time. He points to the carton of Chinese food on the desk. "You want?"

"All yours, dude," Thomas says.

Oscar empties the container of greasy food into his mouth, tapping the bottom of it to get the last bits out. Thomas and I look at each other. Aside from being certain that he's going to be puking inside an hour, something about Oscar is making us both jumpy.

Oscar looks into the paper bag and then quickly finishes off a second carton of food. A few stray bits of rice and sauce stick to his chin. He walks up to Thomas and pulls Thomas's hat off. In this light I notice that Thomas colors his hair. It's a deep, flat black, a different color at the roots.

Oscar unzips Thomas's jacket a few inches and then runs his fingers along the edge of the material. He stares into Thomas's face, his lip curling slightly as he says, "Nice jacket, bro."

"He's okay," I say to Oscar. "He's helping me. He helped you, too. You were almost frozen to death when we found you."

Oscar ignores this and walks toward the other end of the trailer, looking around, tossing whatever doesn't interest him onto the floor, including a coffeepot, which shatters. He flicks piles of paper off tabletops, shakes out the contents of folders. Then he pushes a line of notebooks off a shelf and onto the floor.

"There's something really wrong with that guy," Thomas says.

"You think? And you color your hair, *Thomas*," I respond.

"A lot of people color their hair."

"True, but why do you do it?"

"8-Bit insists we disguise ourselves. Change our appearance from time to time. Just to be safe."

"From who?"

"A very long list of agencies, bureaus, and corporations. Plus several dozen irate Russian individuals with direct knowledge of our involvement in their organized crime."

Oscar is now rampaging around the opposite end of the trailer, pulling drawers out of the kitchenette and emptying them onto the floor. The warmth of the trailer seems to be strengthening him, and I'm not so sure that's a good thing. He stops suddenly, looks down at his feet, and says, "I need some shoes." He walks up to Thomas and looks down at his snow boots. "Wrong size, amigo. Lucky for you, eh?" Then he turns, opens the trailer door, and goes out into the storm.

I jump up and run to the door. Oscar lurches out of view, around the end of the trailer. "Should we go after him?"

Thomas shakes his head and then sighs. "The only reason I'd go after that freak is to get my socks back, but even that's not worth it."

He sits down at his computer.

"What are you doing?" I ask.

"Seeing if I can find out something about him."

I walk behind Thomas and look at the screen as he searches through case files.

"What floor did you say you were on?"

"Fourth."

"Looks like we can sort by room number. There were only three of you on the fourth floor. Six on the third floor. Two on the second floor. Oh, wait. The two on the second floor were discharged. Man, that's a big hospital for a handful of patients."

"Is there a file for me?"

I can barely stand it. I want to know, but I'm afraid of what I might find out.

"Let's see if we can find out more about Mr. Personality first," Thomas says. He opens a file and a picture appears. "Obviously not him."

"I saw that kid inside. He was crushed by a falling beam."

"Ouch."

"He was in a coma. I'm sure he didn't feel a thing."

Thomas opens the next file. Jori's picture comes up, and I'm startled by it. She has a full head of white-blonde hair and a dull, lifeless expression. Her picture is a cross between a bad yearbook photo and a mug shot.

We both read the file simultaneously.

Jori Elyse Harris. Age 16. Patient was referred by mental health providers in Kansas City. Excellent candidate. Otherwise healthy female. No history of violence prior to initiating incident that led to her incarceration. . . .

"Her initiating incident? I wonder what it was," Thomas says.

We both keep reading.

"Whoa," Thomas says. "She killed her parents."

"Yeah," I say, "after her father molested her and her kid sister and Jori ended up pregnant. The mother was an alcoholic. Put her out on the street when she was twelve. Close it up. I don't need to see any more."

We search the coma kid's record. *William Eggers, age 15.* He was the lone survivor of a house fire that killed the rest of his family. He was the one who started the fire.

We find files on three other kids, all of whom have been

discharged. One is listed as being a "partial success," and the two others are described as "unsuccessful."

Then we find him.

Oscar Ruiz Noriega. Street name: O-No.

"Cute," Thomas says. "I think it really suits him."

We read the file together. Oscar was a complete thug. Six counts of assault and battery. He broke a kid's skull with a two-by-four.

"Whoa. He killed his roommate in juvie with his bare hands. Tried as an adult and sentenced to thirty years," Thomas says. "His file says 'Experimental.' Seems like the kid's a starting player on the varsity psychopath team. You had some nice company there on the fourth floor."

I take a deep breath and feel a tremor passing through me, but this time it has nothing to do with the cold. I sit down on the sofa, take my cap off, and start twisting it in my hands.

"Stop," I say.

"Why?"

"Don't you see a trend here?"

"What do you mean?"

"You said there was a rumor I tried to kill someone. Maybe it's true. Maybe I'm here because I'm a murderer."

CHAPTER 16

Thomas kneels in front of me and takes the cap I'm strangling out of my hands.

"I'm going to tell you something, and you're going to have to trust that I know what I'm talking about. You are not guilty of anything."

"How can you possibly know that? Look at these files. Everyone they put on the fourth floor was a killer! I could be one, too!"

He puts his hand over my mouth. "Hush. This is the 'trust me' part. Now look at me."

I look up, but my eyes dart away almost instantly as fear and shame boil up inside me.

"I know what a guilty person looks like. And you are not it." I start to reply, but he covers my mouth again. "Am I a very smart guy?"

I nod.

"Yes, I am." He takes his hand away from my mouth.

"Did you already read my file? Do you know for sure?"

He clamps his hand over my mouth yet again. "There is no file for you."

I grab his hand and pull it back. "How—"

"I looked while you were asleep."

"Because you were worried about me."

He smiles. "Maybe a little."

"I don't blame you."

"All I know is that there was only one patient named Sarah in this whole place, and her file was removed by LLLadner58."

"Larry?"

"Could be. Whoever it was went so far as to delete it from long-term and backup storage."

"That doesn't prove anything."

"True. I could be wrong and you could turn out to be the worst mass murderer in the history of mass murderdom, but I don't think so. And if it was Larry who helped you, he obviously didn't think so, either, or you wouldn't be here right now. Feel better?"

I nod. He puts my cap back on my head. We both jump up as the trailer door pops open.

I walk over to the door and look out. The snow whirls inside and melts at my feet. No one is there. The wind changes direction, and then we both hear the sound of gears grinding in the distance.

"Thomas! The light!"

He hurries to close his laptop and turn off the desk lamp. I pull the door shut and lock it and then run to the opposite end of the trailer. I push the blinds out of the way and look out the window, but all I see is empty black night.

Thomas is looking out the window on the other end of the trailer. "Snowcats. Two of them."

"Heading toward the building or away?" I ask.

"Seem to be going away."

"Toward the fence?"

"Yeah."

"Maybe they won't see the snowmobile," I say.

"Of course they will, and when they do, they're going to know someone's creeping around out here. We need to go."

The wind is battering the trailer now. I can feel the cold air blowing through seams in the walls and up through the floor. Thomas is at one end of the darkness and I'm at the other. I walk toward his voice and then get down on my hands and knees to feel around for my jacket, wishing I hadn't taken the thing off in the first place.

In the darkness, I bump into Thomas, who's also searching the floor for something. I reach around for the nailer but can't find it. My hand touches something soft on the floor.

"Your hat," I say.

We stand up at the same time, both of us holding on to his hat.

I hear someone rattling the doorknob. Thomas exhales in annoyance, and says, "Who can that be at this hour?"

"Maybe Oscar finally realized that it's cold outside."

I walk toward the trailer door.

"Don't let him back in! Are you nuts?"

"But if they see him, they'll come over and investigate."

He groans. "I suppose."

I unlock the door and it instantly swings open. Someone grabs the front of my coveralls and pulls me out into the snow.

The back of my skull smacks against the frozen ground, and I see lights popping against a dark background and then afterimages of burned-out stars. I try to roll over, but there's a soldier sitting on me, pinning my arms against my sides with his legs. When I strain to get up again, he backhands me across the face with his glove, which is covered with jagged bits of ice. He's about to speak into the radio clipped to his collar when suddenly a blur of movement dislodges him.

I see a bright yellow flash and hear someone growl. Oscar. He pummels the soldier, his fists flying so fast, so hard, I'm sure the soldier's face must be shredding like wet paper. Oscar clasps his hands together and begins pounding the soldier's chest, like he's doing ultraviolent CPR. The soldier kicks both legs up in the air, but Oscar holds on to him with his legs and keeps squeezing. I hear a snap. I think it's one of the soldier's ribs. Oscar lets go, maybe thinking the soldier is now hobbled, but the guy rolls to the side and tries to reach for his weapon. Oscar grabs the rifle away from him and momentarily tries to figure out how to fire it. He puts his finger on the trigger, but nothing happens. The soldier manages to get a hand on the end of the gun and pulls on it. I can see the soldier has some kind of computer screen attached to his arm, just above his wrist.

Oscar kicks the soldier in the face, wrenches the rifle free, and tosses it as far as he can into the darkness, throwing it like a boomerang. I hear the sound of jingling metal coming from wherever it lands.

I look up at the trailer and see that Thomas has been watching this, too. I need to see where that gun landed. "Turn the lights on!"

Thomas is confused, but he does it. The lights from inside illuminate a small patch of ground, and I now see that the trailer is about fifteen feet from the edge of the construction pit. Between the trailer and the pit there's a series of chain-link fence sections. They're not sunk into the ground. The posts are anchored in buckets of hardened concrete, maybe to make the fence movable.

Now we can all see where the rifle landed. It's hanging by its strap from the top of one of the fence sections. The soldier is gasping for air, but he runs toward it. Oscar stays put, squatting in the snow, his black eyes blazing. When the soldier gets to the fence, he tries to lift the gun up, but he's having trouble getting the strap free.

Oscar looks over his shoulder and smiles at me with an expression that says, *Watch this.*

He sets himself up like a sprinter and takes off running

full tilt toward the fence. The soldier has just about untangled his gun when Oscar plows into his back and drives the guy headfirst into the fence, flattening both of them to the ground. The soldier must be unconscious, or at least dazed by the impact, because he hardly fights as Oscar grabs him by the front of his jacket and drags him toward the edge of the pit.

"Oscar, no!"

It's too late. Oscar positions the guy at the edge and rolls him into the darkness with his foot. I run to Oscar's side and stare into the black mouth in the earth. All I can hear is the moaning of the wind. There is no sound from below.

Oscar waves sweetly at the abyss. "Adios."

I take a few steps back. I notice that Oscar found some footwear—a pair of rubber boots. He's laughing hysterically as he slaps me on the back and points at the pit below.

Then we hear the sound of someone talking, calling out. Followed by a beep. The soldier's radio had been clipped to his collar, but it must have come loose in the struggle.

"Come back," a man's voice says. "Hey, where you at, Simmons? Answer me."

I search in the snow, trying to find the radio. When the guy at the other end calls out again, I find it, along with the soldier's pack. I shake the snow off the radio and press the call button. I hear a blip of static, followed by a beep.

"That you? Where you at? I've got nothing out here except frostbite."

"Go back in the trailer, Oscar. Turn all the lights out again. Now!"

He smiles at me and says, "*Si, si, mija.* Whatever you say." He takes his time walking toward the trailer, still laughing to himself. I press the radio button to speak as Oscar steps into the trailer. The lights go out. Suddenly, Thomas is at my side.

"I'm not staying inside the trailer alone with that guy."

Again the soldier on the radio speaks. "Simmons, man, what's up?"

I press the button and say, "He's dead."

Thomas hisses at me, "Angel! What are you doing?"

He tries to take the radio, but I swat his hand away and say, "Grab the backpack! It's your turn to trust me now."

Thomas snatches the pack off the ground.

"He's dead," I say into the radio again. "I . . . I don't know what happened. He fell. He fell into the construction pit."

"You better be lying to me or I'm coming for you!"

Thomas is freaking out pretty good now, but he steps back when I press the radio button again. "I'm sorry. It was an accident."

"Where are you?"

"Don't hurt me," I say. I'm trying to sound like Jori. It seems like the kind of thing she would say and the world would ignore. "I didn't know. I didn't mean to do it."

The guy's voice softens a little as he says, "Yeah. Okay. I'm sure it was an accident. Just tell me where you are."

I motion for Thomas to follow me, and we go back to where we put Jori. An inch of snow has covered her. I brush it off, startled at how much she resembles a child.

"Help me move her over near the fence," I say.

As we pick her up, her flimsy hospital gown rides up to her waist. I whisper to her again and again, "I'm so sorry for this."

"Are you still there?" I hear the soldier say over the radio after a minute.

I press the button. "Yes. I just want to go back inside. I'm so cold."

"I can help you with that. Tell me what's around you. I'll find you."

I prop Jori's body up against a section of the fence that rings the construction pit. We're now a good fifty yards from the trailer. I say into the radio, "I'm sitting by some big machine. It's orange with a big drill."

"I think I know where you are," he says. "I'll be there in a second. Do not move."

Thomas and I quickly scurry into the shadows. A few minutes pass. Then a shot rings out. It hits Jori in the chest, and her body momentarily jerks up into the air.

Thomas whispers to me, "And I thought I was smart. You're a genius. Holey head or no."

I don't feel like a genius. I feel sick as I watch the soldier walk up to Jori and give her a push with his boot. She falls over.

He speaks into his radio. "Simmons is dead."

Another voice on the radio. "Get his computer and pack and get back up here."

"Can't. They're both gone. The little nut-job pushed him into the construction pit."

The robot-voiced soldier on the other end says, "You're going to have to retrieve them before we leave."

"Understood."

The soldier takes a last look around and heads back toward the research building. Thomas whispers to me, "What computer is he talking about?"

"The guy had something strapped to his arm. Right here," I say as I point at my forearm. "What do you think it could be?"

Thomas's eyes narrow. "I'm not sure, but the fact that they want it back so badly makes me want it even more."

CHAPTER 17

One hour, one scavenged rope, and many slipknots later, Thomas is standing on the edge of the construction pit, looking scared to death but ready to descend. I explained to him that my experiences with freestyle climbing were exclusively on urban terrain. Giant black pits in the earth during a blizzard? I don't do those.

"Just go slowly," Thomas says. "And remember, if you drop me, I will kill you both."

Oscar gives his squinty-eyed smile and says, "I got you." Oscar seems to warm up to Thomas the crabbier he becomes, like he finds Thomas's annoyance amusing.

Thomas and I exchange looks of terror. Oscar is still suffering from a case of the psycho giggles, which is worrying, because each time he starts laughing, he lets go of the rope a little. But we both realize that I need Oscar's help. I don't think I can lower Thomas down on my own.

"Here we go," Thomas says as he positions himself and then leans back into the pit. I feel the rope go taut as he starts to rappel down.

Thomas had looked over the drawings in the trailer and determined that the pit was about fifty feet deep. What wasn't clear was how much progress they'd made in pouring the concrete for whatever this underground bunker was going to be.

I feel the rope tacking back and forth. I look over at Oscar, who has the rope braced against his back, his hands gripping it on either side of his hips. He's doing most of the work, and really, other than the fact that he might be a remorseless killer, he's just the kind of person you'd want as a spotter.

The rope goes momentarily slack and then taut, again and again. Just as I'm getting into the rhythm of lowering Thomas down, the rope goes limp. I wait for the pull of his weight again, but it doesn't come. The time seems to stretch out. He can't be more than halfway down.

"Thomas!" I shout, trying not to be too loud. I have no idea who else might be around, but it's hard to shout quietly.

"Thomas, can you hear me?"

I'm answered by nothing but silence for a long, frightening moment. Then I hear Thomas's voice. "I landed right on top of the guy. We're on some kind of scaffolding. Hold on."

Two minutes later, he calls for us to pull him up. Oscar

wastes no time hauling up the rope, pulling hand over hand like a machine. We soon see the light from Thomas's headlamp, and a second later his head emerges from the blackness. Oscar lets out a whoop.

Then he lets go of the rope.

He walks away with his head cocked in this weird way, menace and glee spreading across his face as he laughs to himself.

I still have the rope, but I'm not expecting to take the full brunt of Thomas's weight and I get pulled forward off my feet. Thomas is able to get a hand onto the section of the fence that had fallen over and hangs on. Then the whole fence section starts to sliding toward the edge of the pit.

I push myself forward with my elbows and grab hold of the fence even as I'm still holding the rope, but it's not enough to counter Thomas's weight against the pull of gravity. I crawl onto the fence, thinking my weight will anchor it in place, but as Thomas pulls himself up, the fence starts sliding down with both of us on it.

We're going over the edge. There's nothing I can do to stop it. The fence shoots forward, gaining speed, and I'm frozen to it, staring ahead into the void.

I think two things at the same time: *I'm going to die* and *Do something.*

I don't know how long this moment lasts, but even as I feel myself tipping forward, about to plunge into the pit, somehow I have time to wonder if I should hold on to the fence or let go of it. I grab the lattice with my fingers just as it jerks to a stop.

The fence sticks out like a diving board from the edge of the pit. It teeters slowly, and I hold my breath until it levels out again. The snow whips around my face, and a gust of wind unbalances me. I tip forward, my fingers frozen to the metal. I try to inch back slowly, but as I shift my weight, the fence dips again, sinking even farther this time.

Suddenly it snaps back.

"It's all right," Thomas says. "I've got you."

Somehow he must have scrambled up the fence as it was falling, like he was going up a down escalator.

"Angel. You need to come back. Come on. Just a little at a time."

The metal is bowing underneath my body, and my head and shoulders are hanging in midair. I can't make myself move, though. Not until I hear Thomas's voice again.

"I've got you. Come on back, Angel."

I crawl backward slowly, shaking more and more the closer I get to frozen ground. Finally, I feel the toes of my boots against the dirt. Two arms circle me, and Thomas pulls me the rest of the way.

The moment I'm clear, the fence plummets down into the darkness below, landing a few seconds later with a jingling crash. We both sit there, panting.

I look over at Oscar, who is doing some kind of shadowboxing thing. He jogs around raising his hands in victory like an imaginary crowd is cheering him on. He jogs off into the night. I get up but don't bother to chase him down.

"Not to make excuses," I say, "but I'm not sure how in touch with reality he is. I mean, he clearly doesn't realize how much all this sucks."

Thomas crawls a few feet, like he doesn't want to get up off the ground. I know the feeling. The front of his jacket is torn, and the downy fill is spilling out. In his hand is a black rectangle with two wrist straps attached to it. He holds the small computer up, victorious.

"At least I got this."

"But what is it?"

"Probably about a hundred million dollars in research and development. Let's go find out what it does."

We retreat to the trailer. Thomas's new toy has him occupied, so he tells me to go ahead and use his laptop. The trailer is once again freezing. Thomas doesn't want to waste power on running the space heater. I can see my breath as I hunch over and begin to read hungrily, wanting to know, afraid to know. I go through page after page of reports and memos on the *Tabula Rasa* project. The weirdest stuff is about the side effects. This whole treatment is nothing *but* side effects—and they're all over the map. Every patient seemed to display a different set of post-op behaviors—"extreme lethargy and suicidal impulses" to "hyperaggressive displays paired with loss of impulse control and empathy."

I know that this could be my fate if I don't get that last pill, but I don't want to know any more about this clinical stuff. I switch over to a file labeled "Grants and Funding," thinking it might be fairly harmless. Instead, I find a series of emails between Dr. Buckley and some guy at the National Institutes of Health. The first line of the first message I read says, "Effective immediately . . ."

"The government canceled the project!"

Thomas hardly responds. "Project canceled. Hold that thought. I've just figured out that this tablet is connected to their mainframe."

"I thought you said you killed the mainframe."

"I killed the hospital's mainframe. But this awesome little thing"—he shakes the tablet—"connects to these soldiers' portable mainframe. This is the highest of high-end stuff. Their portable mainframe can override every system in this place."

"How?"

"This thing blots out one signal and replaces it with a stronger one. It can even override hardwired connections. So these guys can basically come in and turn that sucker on, and what was once your mainframe now becomes *their* mainframe. But more importantly, what was once your security system now becomes their security system."

I get up and look over his shoulder. He points at a series of red dots on the screen. All of which are moving.

"Look what we have here."

"What are those?"

"This is a map of the compound, both inside and out. Each dot is a soldier."

He scrolls through some pages, and I can see that some of the dots are inside the building, and some are roaming around outside. He brings up each floor of the hospital in turn.

"Uggh," he says.

"What?"

"I count thirteen armed dots."

My heart sinks. "That's a lot of armed dots."

"Yeah, but this tells us something important. Wait. Look at this." Again he taps the screen, and this time I see the wreckage in the main lobby. Snow has blown in through the windows and collected in a drift near the front doors. They've stacked a pile of bodies near the potted palms.

"You have access to the security cameras?"

"Indeed. Now let's get back to finding those pills. I had no luck figuring out where the med locker is. It's not on the map, anyway. Where do you think they'd keep something super secret like that? I mean, do you remember someplace inside that was off-limits?"

"Pretty much everywhere was off-limits."

"But I mean, do you remember the staff ever talking about certain floors of the building being special for any reason?"

"The sixth floor," I say automatically. "That's where Larry's office was. I think that's where all the doctors' offices were. I once heard some of the nurses talking about how you had to have special clearance to get in and out of there."

"The sixth floor," he repeats. "Okay. We'll start there. But first we've got to get back inside."

"Wait. What does the fact that there are thirteen dots tell us?"

"What?"

"You said that the number of guys they've brought tells us something."

"Oh, right. Well, one assumes these guys know what they're doing, and since 8-Bit helped case the joint electronically for them, they must have decided that all they needed to raid this huge hospital was thirteen guys."

"Fourteen," I say.

"Oh, yeah. Right. They're down a man thanks to Oscar. Still, that's not much firepower for a compound this big."

"Maybe they knew that people would be clearing out for the storm."

"They didn't. They knew a storm was coming, but I don't think anybody expected it to be this bad."

"So that pretty much proves that there weren't many of us left in here."

"Yeah, something strange is going on. This hospital is pretty swank, considering it was about to become a ghost town."

He gets up and walks over to the little space heater. "No point in conserving energy now."

He turns it on full blast, and I let the warmth bathe me.

"What else was in the bag?" I ask.

"Lots of goodies. I don't know what they all do, but

I'm sure some of them blow things up." He rubs his hands together quickly, then says, "I'm going to do something now. Trust me?"

"I'll have to think about it."

He hits a button, and I see on the screen that the alarm system goes off in an area on the first floor. We watch on the soldier's computer as a bunch of red dots start moving toward that area.

Thomas turns the alarm off.

Then he turns it back on.

He waits about thirty seconds and does it all again. We wait another five minutes and suddenly the whole wing goes dark.

"What just happened?" I ask.

He raises his finger and points at the soldier's computer. Slowly, the red dots begin moving back toward the main lobby again.

"You made them think the system was glitching on and off," I say.

"Yep."

"So they shut all the power off in that section because the alarm was so annoying. Genius."

"'Annoying Genius.' That should be my slogan from now on." He points at the screen. "We should head toward this door. I think it'll be open now, so we don't have to use a passcard to get in. Plus, if we trip any alarms, they'll assume it's another problem with the security system."

We start to pack up our things, but I pause. "Oscar.

What should we do about him?"

"That nut-job is on his own as far as I'm concerned, especially after that hilarious attempt to drop me to my death."

"He didn't do it on purpose."

"You're defending him? He almost got you killed, too."

"I know, but I was reading some of the other staff reports about treatment effects. Oscar isn't sure what's real and what's just in his head."

"Yeah. Well, I hope he gets over that sometime soon or he's gonna fantasize us all into a bloody pulp."

The rumble of an engine makes us both turn toward the door. "Maybe those snowcats are back," Thomas says.

The sound gets louder and louder until it sounds like it's coming from right outside the trailer. Because it is. The whole trailer is trembling. Headlights come on directly outside the window, and we both freeze like deer waiting to be shot.

CHAPTER 18

Thomas grabs my hand and the tablet and dashes for the door, but we don't make it more than a few steps before the whole trailer starts rocking. We land on the floor and slide toward one wall and then back again. The furniture slides with us, including the heavy oak desk and the pictures dangling from their wall hooks. I hear glass cracking and metal twisting and a crunching sound that I think is coming from the roof. Thomas manages to get a hand on the laptop to keep it from sliding off the desk just as the desk smacks into the wall, and I barely escape being pinned by the leather sofa.

"Maybe my little security system trick didn't work so well after all," he says, dodging the desk chair as it flies by.

The trailer tips upright again and remains still for a moment. I crawl toward the window, expecting to see a snowcat, but what I see instead is only slightly less troubling.

Oscar is behind the controls of an excavator. He's using the digging arm to push the trailer, like he's trying to knock it off its foundation.

I watch as he swings the arm as far as it will go to the left. I have just enough time to scramble backward before he uses the claw to rip the end of the trailer off like he's opening a cereal box.

"Come on!" I grab Thomas's arm and pull him toward the trailer door. "It's Oscar!"

Just then, something crashes through the roof of the trailer, smashing the desk to splinters. The computer flies into the air, and when it hits the floor, the screen snaps off.

"What does he think he's doing?"

We roll into the opposite wall as the trailer tips so far to the left I'm sure it's going to fall onto its side. At least we'd be falling toward solid ground. I guess this is not what Oscar wants, though, because he lets the trailer slam flat upright again. I realize that he's trying to push the whole thing over and send it tumbling into that big hole in the ground.

Just as I reach the door, Thomas pulls away from my grasp. He stretches to retrieve the computer from where it's landed next to the mini-fridge. Through the opening in the roof, I see Oscar winding up again to punch straight down through the top of the trailer.

"Thomas, no!"

"I need the flash drive!"

He flattens his body completely, just able to reach the

drive with his fingertips. With the other hand he grabs the strap of the soldier's backpack and pulls it toward him. Oscar brings the arm of the excavator down. Inside my mind, I'm screaming at Thomas to get back, but there's not even time for my lips to form the words. He's trying to get up but can't get off his knees because the trailer has collapsed and fallen off its supports. He's sliding toward the end that Oscar ripped away. Thomas isn't going to make it out. The digger claw is going to cut him in two.

I reach through the door and grab him by his jacket just as the claw smashes what's left of the ceiling. He screams in pain, and at first I think he's been crushed, but then I see what's happened. The claw missed Thomas, but pinched a piece of metal from the roof against his lower leg. I have to wait for Oscar to lift the digger claw up again before I can try to get Thomas out.

Oscar struggles with the excavator's control levers. A moment later the arm swings upward, and I'm able to peel back the piece of debris and pull Thomas out through the door. We both land hard on the frozen ground and Thomas howls. His boot has been slashed all the way through. The cut runs from kneecap to ankle in almost a straight line along his shinbone.

Oscar looks directly at me; his eyes are innocent. He could be playing in a sandbox with a toy. He swings the excavator's arm up and brings it down again onto a porta-john, smashing it flat. He laughs as the putrid slush in the porta-potty gushes onto the ground and runs downhill toward the excavation pit.

I need a way to get Thomas out of here, because he won't be able to walk. I grab a plastic section of the porta-potty and retrieve the rope we used earlier. After threading it through the air vent at the top, I roll Thomas onto this makeshift sled and pull him out of range of the claw. Every bump makes him shriek in agony.

The storm is ferocious, and the wind slashes at my bare head. In the scramble to get out of the trailer, I've lost my hat, my gloves. We've lost Thomas's backpack, though he managed to hold on to the soldier's pack. He's clutching the flash drive in his hand so tightly I think he might be crushing it.

I've completely lost my bearings. I look up at the hospital. It's just a broad expanse of wall and rows of windows too high to reach. We might as well be trying to break into a prison.

"Thomas, where do we go?"

He points at a huge pile of dirt next to the construction site.

"Other side of that?"

He nods.

Of course. There's no way I'm going to get him up and over this mound of dirt, but I start to climb anyway. Each step I take, I use up all my strength, decide it's pointless, and then try one more time. I keep my eyes closed so I don't have to keep looking at how far I still have to go. After struggling up the hill for what seems like an hour, I feel a blast of wind hit me full in the face, shocked to find that I'm at the top.

I pull as hard as I can, but I can't get the sled up the final few feet. "You're going to have to climb the last bit, Thomas. I'm sorry. Can you do it?"

He lifts his body just enough to let the sled beneath him slide away. I lie flat and he uses my body like a ladder, pulling himself up until we're both sitting at the top. He bites down on his lip to keep from screaming.

I look down toward the door and realize getting down won't be so easy. The dirt pile is right up against the building, and the angle of the incline is steeper than on the side I just dragged Thomas up. I'm going to have to take him down inch by inch, and if I lose my grip on him, he could slide out of control, right into the wall.

We need to hurry. We're in open view, and snowcat headlights are now moving toward the trailer. Oscar seems oblivious. He begins working the excavator's arm up and down, up and down. The claw plunges repeatedly into the ground, right in the same spot, but the ground is so hard he's not making any progress. *What is he doing?*

Then I understand.

"I think he found Jori's body, and he's digging her a grave," I say.

Thomas raises his head and says, "I don't care what that lunatic is doing."

A second snowcat suddenly emerges from the swirling snow. It's further away, but I can tell by the way both snowcats are moving that they've caught sight of Oscar. He sees them, too, and steps out of the cab, onto the tire of the excavator.

I wave my arms and shout, "Hey! Here! Over here! Oscar!"

Thomas reaches up and tries to pull me down by the edge of my coat.

"Like it or not, he's our problem now."

I see Oscar turn toward me, unsure of where my voice is coming from. Then he looks back at the snowcats, which are getting closer. Still he does nothing. He ducks as a few sparks fly off the edge of the excavator. Apparently gunfire registers enough with him that he knows he's got to run and hide.

I see more sparks and then Oscar goes down. He grabs his shoulder and staggers to his feet. He's up the pile of dirt in a matter of seconds, shivering violently, his eyes wild and terrified.

"Help me," I say.

I tell him to get on Thomas's other side, and he follows my lead as we try to make a controlled slide down the dirt pile to the door. It doesn't work. We shoot to the bottom, and I end up acting as the bumper when we come to a stop against the side of the building. Thomas slams into my rib cage, but I stand up quickly and put my hand on the door handle. A prayer springs to my lips. I don't know if I believe a word of it, but when I yank the door open I know my prayer has been answered, and I'm grateful.

There is no light inside. Not even emergency lights. I have to leave the door propped open slightly to see anything at all. Oscar helps me drag Thomas, but I can see he's fading fast. Once we heave ourselves through the door,

Oscar makes a little gagging noise and passes out. His body is half in and half out of the door. I pull him across the threshold.

"Forget him, will you? And shut the door," Thomas says.

"It's pitch-black in here!"

"I've got a couple glow sticks in my inside pocket," he says, patting his jacket. I reach in, take them out, snap both, and hand one to him. As I do, he grabs my hand and presses it to his face, closing his eyes.

"Angel, you saved my stupid life."

I stroke his forehead. I can see he's fighting to remain coherent. The pain must be beyond excruciating. "You can thank me by telling me the layout for this area."

He pants in between every other word. "End of this hallway . . . set of double doors. There's a big open room. I don't know what it is."

"Okay. I'll be right back."

I use the glow stick like a sword, brandishing it at the blackness. The walls are bare concrete. I see a trowel and a bucket and a few other tools lying around. It makes sense now. All these places are unfinished because the government walked away from this hospital and left it to rot. Left us all to rot. But if that's the case, why was there still anyone here at all? Why were they still talking about finishing my treatment?

As I get to the end of the hallway, I see the double doors that Thomas mentioned. I go through and come to a T, turn right and continue along. There is a line of doors with small glass windows. It looks very familiar down here. These are hospital rooms. All the doors are open, but they have the same heavy lock mechanisms we had on the fourth floor. My back suddenly stiffens as I realize that this is a basement.

Who would they lock up down here?

I turn around and investigate in the other direction. At the very end of the hall, there's a swinging door. I'm about to enter when I hear a scraping sound behind me. I turn. A flashlight, a really bright one, shines in my face. I put my hand up to block the light. The beam drops to the floor, and I see a young, bald man, maybe in his midtwenties. He's wearing pants and a shirt that look very much like military fatigues, but he's barefoot. A fire ax dangles loosely at his side.

He looks at me, cocks his head to the side, and says, "Welcome."

CHAPTER 19

For some weird reason, I bow. I guess it's because I want to put my bald head front and center to make it clear: *I'm one of you. Whatever you are.*

Right now he's a guy with an ax in his hand. That's reason enough to show him some respect.

"Hello," I say. "We're . . . we're looking for . . ."

For what? I don't know what to say. Safety? I don't imagine there's much of that around here.

The man just looks at me. In his expression I read intelligence, exhaustion, and maybe pleasant surprise. He's not unhappy to see me.

I start to say, "I'm . . ." Then I wonder if I should tell him my name. I don't know who he is or anything about him, so I think fast and finish, ". . . sorry to intrude."

"It's no intrusion," the man says. "Misery loves company. And that's what we call ourselves. Misery Company."

Three other men suddenly step up behind him, emerging from the darkness like smoke. I can barely make them out. One of the men is carrying some kind of electric lantern. He turns it on and bright white light reveals the room behind me. It's a conference room.

"We thought they'd finally decided to kill us," the man with the lantern says, almost cheerfully.

"Who? The soldiers?"

He looks at me quizzically, and the man standing to his right says, "Our captors, of course."

I don't know what he means, but I say nothing. All four of them are dressed the same: green pants and T-shirts, barefoot.

"My friend . . . ," I start to say, turning back toward the dark hallway I just came down. "My friend is back there. He's injured. It's pretty bad."

The man holding the lantern points to the smaller man to his left. "Elmer here might be able to help you. We're allowed to keep some basic medical supplies, and he's found some other useful contraband."

Elmer asks, "What's the nature of the injury?"

"It's his leg—there's a lot of blood."

Elmer turns around and trots off into the dark hallway.

"My name is . . ." I'm not sure what to say. I still can't call myself Angel. It's like I haven't earned the right to be her.

The soldier with the ax puts his hand up and says, "We only use code names around here. The less they know about us, the better. That was our medic, Elmer. I'm Sam." He points to the guy holding the lantern, who seems to be the youngest of the group. "That's Sylvester. And that's . . ."

A muscular man steps forward and says, "Jerry." He gives me a flirty smile and touches his brow with his fingertips, saluting me.

"Otherwise known as Prince Charming," Sam says drily.

A moment later, Elmer returns with a small case with a red cross on the side and nods in the direction of the hallway. "Let's go."

I worry about what I'm doing getting involved with these guys, but Thomas might bleed to death if he doesn't get help soon. I'll take help from whoever I can get it from, even a bunch of guys who've named themselves after cartoon characters.

"Lead the way," Sam says.

I turn to head back the way I came, occasionally looking over my shoulder to make sure they're staying with me. As we make our way down the halls, the men move in unison, like a flock of geese shifting direction in the sky.

When we push through the double doors back into the hallway where I left Thomas and Oscar, I see that it's completely dark. A sickening pool of dread rises and soaks through me.

Sylvester raises the lantern. I see both Thomas and Oscar on the floor. Thomas must have rolled over onto his glow stick. I immediately rush to Thomas's side while

Elmer goes to Oscar, whose bullet wound is obvious. I'd forgotten about Oscar in my panic about Thomas.

"No, him first!" I say, pointing to Thomas, my hand shaking.

Thomas has gone a gray-white color. His eyes are frantic underneath his eyelids.

Elmer looks at me and then at Oscar and says, "I have to treat the worst first. Unless he's an enemy combatant."

"No! Yes! He's that, then. An enemy. Just . . . please, please help Thomas first!"

He turns toward Thomas to assess his condition. Thomas moans a little when the light from the lantern shines in his face but barely seems to notice when Elmer peels back his boot. I'm relieved to hear him, even if he's suffering, because it means he's still alive and hasn't bled out onto the floor.

"I need help moving them. I'll take a closer look when we get them back to camp," Elmer says.

Camp?

I'm worried he means back out into the storm, but then I look again at their bare feet and realize that wherever their camp is, it must be inside.

The men lift Oscar and then Thomas in turn, putting them on a drop cloth they find nearby. They drag both up the hallway. The four men break into a jog at exactly the same moment. I follow behind them as we head deeper into the basement. I doubt I could have backtracked and found my way back out again.

We finally come to a large room that looks very much like the rec lounge, except there is no television and no sofa. The only furniture is a folding table and several plastic chairs. I also see some blankets in the corner of the room.

Sam says to me, "We assumed something must have happened. They cut the power, and we haven't received our rations in the last twenty-four hours." He points to a door in the far corner. It has a largish swing door at the bottom, like a cat flap. "Usually it's like clockwork. Our captors come at precise intervals with food and water."

I'm only half listening because all I'm thinking about is Thomas, but the word *captors* snaps me back to attention. I look at Sam. I'm curious and confused. I guess you could see the nursing staff here as captors. But still. These guys talk like they're prisoners of war.

I look over at Elmer. He's covered Oscar with blankets and raised his feet onto one of the chairs. He's now working on Thomas. I watch as he cuts away the lower leg of Thomas's ski pants and then ties a tourniquet just above his knee. I find myself tensing, trying to look and not look. Sam sees the worry on my face.

"Elmer is the best medic around. He can work miracles, even with the few medical supplies they give us."

Sam is looking at my clothing, like he can't make sense of what I'm wearing but the wheels are turning in his mind. For some reason I decide it's best not to mention the blizzard outside.

"When was the last time you had any contact with your, you know, captors?" I ask.

"They rarely speak to us directly," Sam says. "Obviously, because of the language difficulties."

I shift my weight back and forth. I need more information from them, so no matter what they say, I nod in agreement.

"Have you ever tried to escape?" I ask.

"Where would we go?" Sam asks. "It's desert in every direction for hundreds of miles. That's assuming they don't shoot us first."

Desert? I don't know what's happened to these guys, but I'm not going to be the one to tell them they're about as far from a desert as you can get.

CHAPTER 20

Elmer works on Thomas for an hour or so. Just getting his boot off without aggravating the wound takes half that time. I try to stay away but can't, even after Elmer shoos me back for the tenth time. I rest the back of my head against the wall, my face tilted toward the ceiling. That dripping sensation is back. I feel like another memory wants to come, but it won't. I think the stress of what's happened has delayed it somehow.

Sylvester offers me something he calls an MRE. I'm not sure what he's talking about. It looks like a granola bar. I take one and thank him but don't eat it.

After half an hour of watching me pace, Sam approaches me and says, "There's a place to wash up down the hall. I strongly suggest you use it."

I look down at myself. I've got dirt, blood, and that weird blue dye that they use in porta-johns all over my coveralls and probably on my face. Maybe the smell of me is getting to them.

He holds his lantern out to me, but I show him my glow stick.

"I'll be okay."

I walk into the outer hallway. A deep, eerie quiet instantly surrounds me. I feel like I've been ambushed by the emptiness. I wave the glow stick around. Everything is the silvery gray of unfinished concrete.

A few yards up the hall, I see a bunch of construction materials, including a stack of plaques that haven't been mounted yet. I give them a nudge with my foot, and they topple to the floor, clicking like dominoes. There are four of them. I pick each one up and read what they say: "Custodian," "Mechanical Closet," "Recreation Lounge," and "Guest Reception." The last has an arrow pointing to the left, but I don't know which direction the sign was supposed to be facing.

Farther on I find the bathroom. It's exactly like the one we had on our ward. There are no mirrors. There's also no hot water. Teeth chattering, I pull a stack of paper towels out and swab myself off. They come away in my hands, filthy. I go through the whole contents of the dispenser, dropping each paper towel to the floor after I'm done, until I've made a tall, soggy pile. I feel like I've just washed off all my war paint after a long, unsuccessful battle.

I cup my hands beneath the running water to take a drink, and suddenly I'm swimming. No, drowning. I have to grab hold of the sink; otherwise, the terrible, spiraling sadness washing over me will suck me down.

I know what this is.

I know what's coming.

This is the moment. The very moment I found out.

I see the social worker standing in the hallway. The dark outline of her slumping shoulders. Her braided hair backlit by the bluish fluorescent light. She is the stranger holding a briefcase who has come to tear my whole world down.

I push the memory back, out, away. I slam into the wall behind me and press my hands against my ears, but there's no defense against a voice inside your head.

"Sarah?"

My mother told me never to open the door for a stranger, but this woman keeps knocking and holding up badges to the peephole.

"I'm afraid I have some very sad news to tell you. Please open the door."

Somehow, in this instant, I know what she's going to tell me, and I decide I won't listen. So long as I don't listen, then it hasn't happened. I sit down on the couch, put my headphones on, and ignore her. I won't open the door, no matter how long she knocks. I'll barricade myself in here forever.

But it doesn't work.

People with sad news always find a way to get to you. They just go find the building super and two police officers to escort him, and then you can't keep them out anymore. They bust in and tell you what you don't want to hear. They fill out paperwork about your status and your future. And then that's it. No matter what you do, no matter how hard you try, you can't ever be the same again.

I feel like I'm falling. I feel that tickle in my stomach as I plunge down into a shaft of darkness, and as I fall, I pull the emptiness around me right into my heart. I want to be one with this nothingness. The empty black nothingness.

But suddenly there's an abrupt shift inside my mind, and in an instant, this bad memory is a flag snapping in a too-strong wind. It tears loose and is carried off.

Now I'm climbing, hand over hand. Higher and higher. My feet slipping on metal bars that are not meant to be used as steps. I'm climbing to get closer to something, or farther away—I don't even know. And wrapped up in this pain, as inseparable from me as a parasite is from its host, is the name Erskine Claymore.

I'm on the bathroom floor again, panting.

I make myself stand up, and then I spit into the sink and rinse my mouth, because I taste stomach acid at the back of my throat like I'm going to throw up.

The only thing I can think to do is move. To run. Just like Thomas said. If I move fast enough, I can leave these bad dreams behind and they'll fall away and evaporate.

I rush into the hallway, dashing one way, then another, like a frantic bird that's accidentally flown inside a building. I run with no sense of purpose or direction. I just want to get more lost. The hallways are full of turns, full of choices that I refuse to make, and it wouldn't matter if I did. Because they all lead me to the same place. To pain, to the dull emptiness of grief.

I run and run and run, until I notice that beneath my feet the bare concrete floor has given way to soft carpeting. I stop and try to pull air back into my burning lungs.

Up ahead I think I see a light. I lower my glow stick, and there it is. A small green circle. I head toward it and come to a fancy door made of striped wood with a smoky glass center. The room beyond is dark, but now I see that the tiny green light is from a magnetic card reader. I seem to have come to the edge of where power and outage meet.

I wonder what this place could be. I pull my passcard out, debating whether I should use it. What if it gives my location away? I don't care. I'm too curious.

I zip the card through the reader and pull the door open.

The room on the other side looks like a hotel lobby, complete with concierge desk. There's a water feature—the kind that trickles and drips and is supposed to make soothing noises like a mountain brook. In the center of the room is a coffee table made of tangerine-colored glass, two clear plastic armchairs, and a huge sofa with square, white leather cushions and chrome legs. Looks expensive and extremely uncomfortable.

I walk in, sit down, and put my hands on my knees.

Obviously it's a waiting room.

It's the kind of place where you sit alone, chewing on a piece of your hair and bouncing your leg nervously. Before you hear adults say that they did all they could but it was too late. Before you pick out a casket. Before you're told that you'll be moving to a new home the next day, so gather everything you have into a single bag—everything, including all the happiness you've ever known—because they're going to shepherd you into a bleak new future and you can't refuse to go.

Before all that, you wait in a room like this. Except it's a lot less nice.

I stand up and straighten my back. A calm anger strengthens me, sharpens me, as I look around.

It's all so strange. This is newly built. I don't understand why the government canceled this project just to start decorating this place like a posh resort. It makes no sense.

My eyes sweep back and forth, trying to see if there's anything worth taking. I see a crystal candy dish on an end table marked with an *E.C.* It's filled with candy-coated chocolate mints. Without thinking, I grab one and toss it into the air. Before the candy lands in my mouth, a memory lands first.

"Catch it!" my mother yells.

I don't.

"Again!" she says, tossing another seed to me.

I miss.

"Ay, Angel, you're terrible at this!" she says, laughing. "I'm almost out of pepitas!"

"I can do it!" I pout. "One more time."

We walk and she tosses another pepita. It bounces off the end of my nose. We are now emerging from the subway onto the street. It's our mysterious yearly trek to the Upper West Side. I have never asked her why we come here before, but today I do.

She takes me by the hand and says, "I like this place."

"We have parks, too," I say, defending our neighborhood, which is not this nice or this quiet. And there are too many men without jobs hanging around, and they usually start drinking by noon.

"I know, but this park brings me happy memories," she says as she swings my hand high above my head.

We find a bench and sit to eat the lunch my mother has brought: beef empanadas, plain white rice, and a Coke. We always sit on this bench, directly across from a big mansion overlooking Riverside Park. My feet do not touch the ground. I swing my legs like I'm kicking the air.

"I wish I was rich. I wish I had a house like that," I say.

"Do you?"

"Yes."

"You know, I used to work for the man who lives in that big house."

"Really? What was he like? Are rich people mean? That's what Yolanda Cruz told me. They're all mean and selfish."

"No, they're not all mean and selfish. The man I worked for was very nice. He was the best man I ever knew."

"What happened to him?" I ask.

My mother does not reply.

"Mamá?"

She looks up to the uppermost window, and I think I see someone looking down at us. But only for a moment.

"My friends say things about who my father is," I mumble.

She sighs and waves her hand. "They don't know anything, Angel. Just remember that you are special, and someone is always watching over you."

I press the heels of my hands to my eyes and groan. It's so frustrating! To be so close to remembering and still not be able to see my mother's face, just a cloud of white. I need to remember things that will help me figure out who's trying to kill me and why, and this memory has given me nothing useful.

I look around the room again. I pick up one of the pillows. It's burgundy velvet, corded on the edges with gold thread. I push the nap of the fabric back and forth. My fingers leave streaks. This pillow alone must have cost a small fortune. I tuck it under my arm. I'll bring it to Thomas. Maybe it'll help him rest easier.

I continue searching the room, looking for anything else that could help him, and as I round the side of the tall concierge desk I see something even better. A laptop. I fold it up, snatch the power cord coiled next to it, and hang it around my neck like a scarf.

I've lingered long enough. I need to get going. I turn

around and stop in my tracks. I haven't entered this waiting area through the main entrance. I've come the back way. I face a set of large glass doors with the letters *E.C.* on them. And now I know what the initials stand for.

Of course.

Erskine Claymore.

I've seen these doors before. From the other side. This is South Wing.

CHAPTER 21

I may be smeared with blood and mud, but I'm hoping that the soldiers still see me as a girl, because only a girl would take such a long time in the bathroom. I don't want to have to explain too much about where I've been or what I've been doing. I doubt these strange, barefoot guys would get it.

After a few wrong turns I find my way back. As I approach the rec lounge door, I hear an agonized scream. It's Thomas. I burst back into the lounge and see Sylvester with his knees on Thomas's chest. I'm about to pull him off when I realize that he's doing it to keep Thomas from writhing around while Elmer works on the leg wound. I rush up to them and wish I hadn't when I see the extent of Thomas's injury. His lower leg looks like the muscle has been filleted off the bone.

I turn my head and nearly drop the laptop. I watch as Elmer wraps the leg from the knee down. He returns to his medical kit and produces a syringe and pops Thomas in the thigh. I pray that whatever Elmer's delusions are, they still allow for proper dosing of meds.

When I kneel next to Thomas, he clutches at me and his eyes open. He's focusing on somewhere far away, a place he wishes he could go to get away from this pain. I keep staring at him, wishing I could take the agony he's experiencing and pull it into myself. At the very least, I want to let him know I'm there with him, through every single second.

After a few minutes, I feel his grip relax, and he closes his eyes. His face becomes less ashen. I look gratefully toward Elmer.

"That morphine shot should last him a few hours," he says.

"Thanks. He seems more comfortable."

Elmer must have taken Thomas's hat off at some point. I slide the pillow I brought back with me under his head and notice something I hadn't before: the roots of his hair. Beneath the black dye, he's a redhead.

"I brought you a very expensive, fluffy velvet pillow," I say.

"And a computer," Thomas says. I put the laptop on the floor next to him. He reaches over and pets it. "Nice computer."

Elmer points to Oscar, who I now see has his shoulder bandaged. "I think the bullet passed through. Obviously, not his first gunshot wound. He must have seen a lot of action. Do you know which province he was stationed in?"

Province? I'm not sure what he's talking about.

Elmer motions toward Thomas. "His leg is pretty bad. He'll need surgery soon or it'll have to come off."

I pull him away so Thomas won't hear me. "*Come off? What do you mean, come off?*"

Elmer says unapologetically, "I'm a medic, not a doctor. I've done what I can."

"Help me sit up," Thomas says to our turned backs.

"No," Elmer and I say simultaneously.

"Seriously. I need to type."

Thomas rolls onto his stomach, trying to keep his injured leg still. He pushes the computer screen open and reaches into his pocket for his ugly glasses. The left lens is cracked, but he puts them on anyway. I realize I still have the power cord around my neck. I also realize it's useless because there is no working outlet. When Thomas presses the power button, the screen lights up, and I'm flooded with relief. If there's anything useful in this computer, I know Thomas will find it.

I crouch down next to Thomas as he works. Sam is staring at the computer, his eyes thin slits. He's confused by us. And suspicious. I don't have any hairs on the back of my neck, but if I did, they'd be standing up right now.

After a few minutes of typing Thomas says, "I've got good news, bad news, and everything in between."

"Let's hear it all," I say.

"First of all, this computer is swank. Like, even better than 8-Bit's computer. It's also chock-full of tasty information. They seem to have a completely separate, encased mainframe for just this area. I'm sure 8-Bit didn't know about it."

I glance at the soldiers and then back at Thomas, who notices something is wrong. I give a slight shake of my head: *Don't ask right now.*

"Go on," I say, lowering my voice.

Thomas lowers his as well. "I can get into their system easily enough. It'll take me maybe thirty minutes to bypass their security. Maybe an hour. I'm not really at my best at the moment."

I wince. "And the bad news?"

"This battery has about fifteen minutes of juice left, tops."

He closes the machine up.

"It's okay. I can take it back to where I found it."

"You don't need to take the whole thing. It's got a removable nuclear battery. Not exactly commercially available. This might be a prototype." He pops the battery out of the back of the computer and attaches the cord to it. "You found a place where the power hadn't been cut?"

"Yeah," I say, taking the battery from him. "I found this weird concierge waiting area thing. Thomas, this place is South—"

I snap my mouth shut and look up. Sam looms over me, radiating anger.

"This place is what?" he asks.

I see his grip on the ax handle tighten and realize much too late that we have a new problem.

"Whoa. What's up?" Thomas asks. His forehead crumples as he looks back and forth between me and Sam.

How stupid I've been. I go to the "latrine" and return with a laptop computer? They can't make sense of it. Part of what's keeping these men here is their belief that they can't leave. They're prisoners of their own minds. Maybe I've been living that way, too.

I take a deep breath and stand up to face Sam and his ax.

I may not have all the answers about my past yet, but I know that being timid, weak, indecisive—that's not who I used to be. And I need that girl back again. Right here and right now.

Sam is glaring at me. "Our captors could return at any moment. Unless you already know that. . . ."

Suddenly Thomas catches on to the danger we're in. "Hold on. Check that hostility just a second. Let me show you something."

He reaches into the inner pocket of his jacket. Sam raises the ax slightly.

Thomas pulls out the tablet we retrieved from the dead soldier in the construction pit. I'd forgotten all about it. He must have tucked it into his jacket like a father penguin sheltering its egg when Oscar got homicidal with the excavator. He hands the device to Sam.

Sam tips it back and forth in the light. "What is this?"

Jerry looks over Sam's shoulder, trying to see what he's holding. "How were you able to smuggle this in? They stripped us of everything."

"Yeah. Even our dang tighty-whities," Sylvester says.

"They don't know we're here," Thomas says. "Nobody does."

Sylvester lets out a whoop and elbows Sam. "I told you they'd send someone for us!"

But Sam is having none of it. He shakes his head and looks at me, unconvinced. "You think they'd send a girl to rescue us? Really?"

Sylvester's face dims as he looks at me anew.

"I guess it worked then," Thomas says as he nods in my direction.

"What worked?" Sylvester asks.

"Special ops is getting trickier and trickier these days, eh? Who would suspect her?"

Sylvester's face lights up at this answer. "Yeah. Absolutely. No one would."

I point at the tablet. "We stole this. We're still trying to figure out how it works, but see these red dots? This shows us where the, uh, enemy combatants are."

Sam clears his throat and looks down at the screen. I watch as he follows the red dots swarming all over. I can't read his expression at all. Finally he points at the tablet and says, "They've concentrated their forces here and here. That's bad for them, good for us. One well-timed ambush and they're wiped out."

I pick up the backpack and hold it out to him. "We also

managed to get our hands on some of—"

"Your captors' equipment," Thomas finishes, warning me with his eyes.

With a nod from Sam, Sylvester takes the pack from me, unzips it, and begins examining the contents. I look at the tablet in Sam's hands, and my heart sinks. I see that the red dots, about ten of them, are moving around near where I just was, at the entrance of South Wing.

"Can you bring up the security camera view for that area?" I ask Thomas, pointing at a spot on the screen.

He takes the tablet from Sam and calls up the feed. It's the waiting room I was just in. I take the passcard out of my pocket and think very seriously about snapping it in half. The soldiers were probably watching me the whole time. They must know exactly where I exited the room, but for some reason they just keep circling near the front doors.

I say to Thomas, "I will get you some power. But first, maybe you can use those last fifteen minutes to find out more about the, uh, situation here."

He nods and salutes me. "Sir, yes, sir."

"Sir." Sylvester smiles at me and then points a finger at Sam. "See? You didn't believe me, but I told you they'd come for us. I told you."

"Yes," Sam says, eyeing me. "It's a very convenient explanation for why they're here, isn't it?"

He walks away and leans against the wall, watching us as he considers what we've just revealed. I don't know what he's thinking, but I do know he's got his hand wrapped tightly around that ax handle.

CHAPTER 22

I hold the tablet in front of me and bite my lip. After a minute, the cluster of red dots in the reception area moves off. I'm relieved, but also wary. *Why would they back off like that?*

I want to talk with Thomas about it, but I don't want to interrupt him. Occasionally, I look over as he works. His face is set, betraying nothing but concentration. A few minutes later, he closes up the computer and motions for me to come over.

"What did you find out?"

"These guys are seriously—"

"Messed up. I know. Keep your voice down. They think they're POWs."

"Yeah. I found a whole slew of files, but could only get through a fraction of what's there. Basically they're Special Forces—some of the first patients to be treated for PTSD, using a new technique that completely and utterly back-fired. What they're experiencing is called a paradoxical treatment effect. The soldiers ended up trapped inside the traumatic memories the doctors were trying to remove."

"This must be why the staff was always so weird about South Wing. No one ever talked about it. They tried to act like the place didn't exist."

"I guess this is where the doctors have been ware-housing patients who didn't respond well to the memory modification treatment. The power outage must have set them free."

"Yeah, but they're only a little bit free. They won't go beyond this lounge, because it's what's familiar to them. I think our jackets and boots are confusing them. They think they're in the desert."

"It also explains why they're barefoot. I read somewhere that captors take POWs' shoes away so they can't escape. Maybe the hospital staff was trying to do what the soldiers expected. They've used these guys' delusions to keep them under control."

"That's horrible," I say. "And it makes me really, really mad."

Elmer gets up and checks Oscar's vitals, but I have the impression he's just trying to move closer so he can eaves-drop. I think Sam might have told him to listen to what we were saying—or to make sure it's difficult for us to have a private conversation.

I look over at Oscar. He's breathing loudly, making little

grunts each time he exhales. "You think this paradoxical effect is what Oscar's experiencing, too?"

"I guess it's kind of related."

I let my head fall into my hands for a moment and then look up at Thomas. "This is real, right? I'm just worrying . . . maybe I'm getting like him." I point to Oscar.

Thomas smirks and grabs my shoulders. "Remember what I told you? Does this suck?"

I nod. "It sucks a whole bunch."

"Exactly. Real."

He gives me a fist bump.

"What else did you find out?" I ask.

"Not much."

"Nothing about the pills?"

"Nothing specific. Like I said, this computer system wasn't hooked in to the other mainframe, but I did find a reference to someone borrowing medication from the locker on the third floor. We might start there. How much time have we lost?"

"I don't know." I look at his watch. It's after midnight. "I've got about fourteen hours."

He picks up the tablet and compares the two locations—the two medicine lockers and those menacing red dots. He sighs.

"It's bad. I know."

"If you like suicide missions, then I'd say these are perfect conditions for one."

"I can do it," I say.

"Angel, the only part of the main building that has electricity also has a lot of guys with guns. And that locker is just one giant red blob."

I ignore this as if it's old news. It is. "How long does the battery take to charge?"

"An hour or so."

"I've stayed alive this long; I can stay alive for another hour."

"That kind of bragging will get you killed."

"I'm telling you, I can do it."

"I know you can, but it's still a terrible idea."

"This whole thing was a terrible idea," I say, pushing away from him. "You should have done what 8-Bit told you to do. You should have never come back to this place with me."

"But look at all this self-destruction I've accomplished." He gestures at his bandaged leg. "No way I could have done this much damage on my own, Angel."

"Thanks. That makes me feel loads better."

"I have no regrets, okay? So you can stop looking at me like that."

"I can't help it." I almost choke on the words as I say them. "I feel awful."

"I feel awful, too. But I'd have felt awful no matter what. None of that's your fault, and at least this way, I got to spend some quality time with you, nearly dying. Not to mention Oscar. What a treat it's been getting to know him a little better."

"Thomas, you're not funny."

We stare at each other. He gives me a tired smile.

"Why are you helping me?"

"Because you deserve to be helped."

"No, really."

"Because maybe I've got a lot to make up for, and maybe I can't pay it back to the person I owe it to, so I'm paying you back instead. Who cares why? I'm clearly not the only one."

"What do you mean?"

"You remember right before the Fantastic Mr. O–No tried to crush us like a couple soda cans, I said I'd found something interesting?"

"Yeah?"

"The first thing these ninja soldier dudes did when they got here was shut off the one and only external security feed."

"But we just used the security cameras. We know they're working."

"Yes, the *internal* camera feed is working. But there was one feed that they blacked out."

"Meaning?"

"This system is supposed to be a closed circuit. Nobody from outside is supposed to be able to look in. Except somebody was. There was a feed routed through a computer here that was heavily encrypted—and I'll bet you anything that if I traced it back to its source, I'd find that it was your friend Larry's."

I sigh. "Please just tell me what you think this means. I'm too tired to put two and two together, but I promise to note your extreme cleverness."

"Okay, listen. What I think it means is, someone on the outside had a secret link into the security camera network here. Someone has been watching this place ever since you arrived."

"Who?"

"I'll tell you who. Someone with a net worth of seven-point-four billion dollars, that's who."

"You think Erskine Claymore has been watching the hospital?"

"Not the hospital. You."

CHAPTER 23

The idea that some reclusive billionaire has been watching me around the clock is less worrisome than what I see when I look up. This time there's no mistaking it. Sam has had enough of watching our private chat. He's staring right at me, his eyes cold and unblinking.

"We have a more immediate problem," I say.

Thomas turns and looks. "Secretive whispering does not sit well with our man Sam, does it?"

I know what I've got to do—what the nurses did: play by the rules of these guys' delusions. They think they're soldiers at war? Then that's what we'll let them think.

I lean over Thomas and mutter, "Sorry for this."

"Sorry for what?"

I grab a fistful of his hair, scowl at him for all I'm worth, and say, just loud enough that only he can hear me, "So. You're a redhead."

I let go, pushing his head back a little harder than I intended. He has that surprised and offended look on his face again, the same one he gave me after I punched him.

"Ow! What the heck? You got a thing against redheads or something?"

Through my clenched teeth I say, "I'm chewing you out for, you know, talking back."

"It's called insubordination."

"Whatever. Just go with it."

"Why?"

I point directly into his face. "You'll do what I tell you to do, you got that?"

He puts his hands up. "Okay! Okay! Sheesh."

I can't tell if he's playing along or really annoyed. I say softly, "I think it'll put them at ease if they think the reason we're whispering together is because I'm chewing you out. "

"Couldn't we just have pretended that we're boyfriend and girlfriend? Then it wouldn't look so suspicious—the two of us sitting together."

"You told them we were special ops. They don't send boyfriend-girlfriend teams to rescue POWs."

"Maybe we're the first of our kind."

"Thomas."

He shrugs. "Fine. Keep chewing."

I crouch down in front of him and shout, "I don't want to hear that talk from you again, you hear me?"

Thomas nods and then grumbles, "My idea was a lot

more pleasant. I'd rather be your fake boyfriend than have you shouting in my face."

I pace back and forth, trying to look as disgusted as possible. Sylvester hands Sam the backpack, and he begins rifling through it.

I whisper, "Is it working?"

Thomas glances behind me and his expression collapses into dread.

"What's the matter? What's Sam doing now?"

"Did you know there was a pistol in the backpack?"

"Really?"

"Afraid so."

"Great."

Thomas keeps watching Sam over my shoulder. "On the positive side, the gun does seem to have cheered him up a lot."

I turn toward Sam and give him a nod. He shakes his head like he knows what I'm dealing with. It's not easy to keep the troops in line sometimes. Ten tense minutes pass as I wonder what Sam might do with that gun, but he seems much more relaxed now that he's armed. I try not to look too concerned as he keeps putting the ammo clip into the pistol and popping it back out again, like he's playing with a jack-in-the-box. At least it's keeping him distracted.

I slide closer to Thomas, not sure what to do. He's gone very still. His eyes are closed, and I wonder if he's fallen asleep.

"Hey. I think you're supposed to stay awake."

"I am awake," he says, his eyes still shut. "I can see you perfectly right now."

"Another magic trick of yours?"

"Yeah."

He smiles up at the ceiling and then all of a sudden his face contorts. I can't tell if it's the pain or for some other reason, but he's quiet for too long. It makes me nervous.

I give him a gentle poke in the arm. "Come on. You have to stay alert."

"I'm completely alert. By the way, in case you've ever wondered, morphine is really nice."

"Glad to hear it. Now what are you thinking about?"

"What makes you think I'm thinking about anything at all?"

"The tortured look on your face a moment ago."

"That's just a thing I do sometimes. Girls can't resist it."

"Come on. Out with it."

"I was thinking." He opens his eyes and blinks slowly. "Maybe when all this is over, I can get my memory sucked out, too."

My mouth drops open.

"Angel, I'm serious."

"Why would you even say that?"

"You don't—you wouldn't—" He shakes his head. "When 8-Bit got this job, I read all the stuff about you guys. The patients here. The *tabula rasa* treatment to pull all those memories out."

"And?"

His brown eyes burn into me. "I envied you."

"*Envied?* How could you envy something like that?"

"Whatever it is you did—you don't have to remember it. You can start over right now like you're a brand-new person."

"But I'm not a brand-new person. Taking my memories didn't *give* me anything. It hasn't given me freedom or peace or whatever you're imagining. Believe me, you don't want to feel like I do. It's a terrible thing."

"Why?"

"Before I started getting my memories back, I felt like nothing."

"But that's what I want to feel. Nothing."

"I didn't say I *felt* nothing; I said I felt *like* nothing. Maybe that's what they don't understand with all this messing around in our heads. When you take memories, you take pieces of someone away. You may think you're better off, but you're not. You're less than you used to be. Obviously, I am."

"Listen, I know all about you," he says.

"You just met me."

"Maybe, but I'm a quick study, and I know something special when I see it."

He tries to sit himself up higher but can't manage it. I want to help him. I want to put my arms around him so he can save his strength. But that's not what commanding officers do.

"My mother used to travel all over the world buying

art. She'd be gone for weeks at a time. She's a rich woman, had always been rich, and she was restless, like she was looking for something and didn't even know what it was. The more she looked, the worse she got. I think traveling made her feel like she was doing something useful somehow, even though she was basically just going on long shopping trips while my sister and I hung out at home with the nanny."

"And?"

"Hush and listen. One time she brought this bowl back from Japan. She paid six thousand dollars for it. It was just this little rice bowl. Maybe the size of your cupped hands together. It had a few cracks in it, and I asked her why she was so excited about it, especially since it was damaged. She said it was the color that attracted her. There was something about it. It was the lightest, most fragile color green. A green-gold, my mother called it. The color of something about to grow."

"That's very nice, but what does any of that have to do with me?"

"Your eyes are green like that. Like the color of that bowl. The color of something about to grow."

It's a beautiful thing to say. I'm just not sure that I deserve to hear it.

"Thomas . . . I—"

I look down at my hands and notice they're shaking. He puts his hands on top of mine. They're pretty shaky, too, but together like this, somehow we steady each other.

"I wish you could see that bowl. You'd see what I mean. But you'll never be able to."

"Why? Because you think we're not going to make it out of here?"

"No. Because my sister took the bowl and smashed it to get back at my mother for something. My mother didn't speak to her for a month."

"Is this the sister you used to entertain with magic tricks?"

"Yeah. Lainey. Her name was Lainey."

His face goes white and his eyes become vacant. I know it's something to do with remembering her.

"Thomas, how did your sister die?"

He slumps down, his head missing the pillow. "I killed her."

CHAPTER 24

"You should know who I really am. You should know what I did," Thomas says.

"I know who you are. You're the guy who gave me my identity back. And I'd already be dead if it wasn't for you."

"You think you know me, but you don't. You need to hear this, Angel."

"All right. Tell me."

"My sister and I, we were close growing up. Lainey was smart and tough. I mean, here's this rich girl with everything. You'd think she'd be all spoiled, but she wasn't. I always thought that if she hadn't been born into a rich family, she would've been okay. Money didn't suit her. She wore grubby clothes, and her shoes had holes in them. It drove my parents crazy."

He looks at me. I wish I could say I understand, but I really don't.

"I used to think it was funny in a way. Here I'm the adopted kid, and Lainey's their biological child. I'm supposed to be the one with the issues, right? But no. She was a mess. I think she went into rehab for the first time when she was fifteen. But she was doing better. We all thought so. She'd been sober for a year when I took off."

He stops and swallows like he's choking down something bitter.

"A couple weeks after I left with 8-Bit, she smashed her car into a Jersey barrier on the side of some highway."

"How is that your fault?"

"Didn't you hear me? She went looking for me," he says. "Because I left with 8-Bit. Nobody knew where I'd gone or what happened. My parents filed a missing persons report. They thought something bad happened to me."

"That's why you said you just met your father?"

"8-Bit showed up out of the blue at my boarding school right after I'd just had this huge blowout with my adoptive dad for the billionth time. I'd always known I was adopted, but the story he told me . . . I thought I'd hit the jackpot. My real father's some infamous computer hacker? He's been living abroad for years, unable to return to the U.S. because of several outstanding warrants for his arrest, and the first thing he does when he gets back on American soil is come looking for me?"

"Kind of made you feel special, I'll bet."

"I thought, well, hey, that explains my talent with writing code. And rewriting other people's code. He offered to teach me the ropes, and I jumped at the chance. I took off without saying a word to anyone. They didn't know what happened to me. My adoptive dad can be a real idiot sometimes, but my mom . . . I mean, she's a superficial, rich lady who spends too much money on stupid stuff, but she loves me. Or she did. Until I killed my sister."

"You didn't kill your sister."

"I might as well have."

"How did you find out what happened?"

"I called them. I started feeling guilty about them worrying about me. Plus, you know, life with 8-Bit was a lot more complicated than I'd imagined."

I tug on his dyed hair.

"Yeah. Exactly. Being on the run is a huge drag. And 8-Bit wasn't really a *dad*, you know? I realized one night when we were playing video games and eating microwavable burritos for the tenth day in a row that my adoptive dad, he yelled at me about grades and stuff like that because that's just what dads do. That's what they're supposed to do. Not try to beat your high score in some first-person shooter game."

"What did your parents say to you when you called home?"

"I'll never forget my mom's voice. I told her I couldn't talk for long, but that I was okay. Then I asked about Lainey and there was this cold silence on the other end of the phone. She told me that Lainey got it in her head to go out looking for me. Then my dad got on the phone and screamed at me, told me not to bother coming home ever again. He said, 'You win, Thomas. You win. How does it feel?' Then he hung up."

"What does that mean, 'You win'? Win what?"

"I guess he meant that I'd won our power struggle. Me and him, we were always butting heads because I kept getting tossed out of all the fancy private schools he put me in, mostly for hacking into the school computers and messing with them. He told me that the reason I hacked things was because I was a cheater at heart. He said I did it because I never wanted to lose, because I wasn't man enough to lose. He said it takes courage to learn to lose gracefully and that deep down, I had none."

"That's horrible."

"It is horrible. And he was right. And that's why my sister is dead."

"I understand why you'd think that. I feel responsible for what's happened to you, for you getting hurt like this."

"It's different. I wanted to come, remember? I rudely insisted on it, as I recall."

"You forgive too easily. Everyone but yourself." I squeeze his hand. "I'm so sorry about your sister."

His eyes are wet. He shakes his head. "Don't feel bad for me. I don't deserve it. You should save your pity for yourself. Look what they do to angels in this place. I even feel bad for stupid Oscar."

"No, you don't."

"Yeah, you're right. I don't. I hate Oscar and I hope he

spends the rest of his life behind bars getting rabid badgers stuffed up his butt."

I look at the soldiers sitting around in a circle. "I wonder if I'm going to end up like one of these guys."

"You won't. Because we're going to get you that last pill. And we're going to find out why an entire squadron of elite soldiers is trying to take you out, you hear me?"

"I hear you."

"Good."

There's a sudden grunt from across the room. Oscar is rolling his head back and forth like he might be waking up.

"Oh no," I say.

"A more apt nickname there has never been," Thomas responds, wincing slightly as he shifts his position.

Elmer takes Oscar's pulse and then raises his eyelids. Oscar grabs him by the wrist and twists. Sam, Sylvester, and Jerry are on him within seconds, but it takes all three of them to subdue him. I rush over to help.

I try soothing him. "It's all right. You passed out. They're trying to help you."

Oscar opens his eyes but doesn't seem to see any of us. He begins thrashing around so violently I think he's having a seizure.

After a few seconds Elmer shoots him up with a syringe full of something, and Oscar's rigid body relaxes, but only slightly. Elmer looks at me, concerned. "I put enough sedative in him to knock out a rhino, but I don't know how long it'll be before he wakes up."

Oscar is twitching and rocking back and forth.

"Several of the cuts on his head have reopened," Elmer says. "We may need to put more stitches in. . . ."

"No." The last thing we need is a freaked-out Oscar waking up to some stranger knitting his head together.

"Angel," Thomas says. I walk over quickly and lean in close.

He whispers, "You should take a couple of these guys with you. For backup."

"I can't do that!"

"They're already at war, so what difference does it make?"

"They can't get killed by their imaginations, whereas, you know, those guys with the guns are shooting real bullets."

"You and I both know they have no future. Why not give them a chance to fight their way out?"

"It's taking advantage of them."

"Yes, it is. But it may be what you have to do if you want to get that pill in time."

CHAPTER 25

Thomas and I argue so loudly that Sam overhears us.

"We'll do it," Sam says.

Thomas shoots me a look. I'm about to speak, but he cuts me off.

"If you're gonna go on this mission, you should know something first. You were . . . you were transferred to a new location."

Sylvester is openly confused. "What? But how?"

"You were drugged and brought here," Thomas says. "They've been moving you around to different locations, to keep you disoriented and to keep people off the trail. They know you're valuable assets they can trade to get some of their own, uh, fighters back."

Sylvester immediately starts nodding, but Sam is still skeptical. "How did you find us, then?"

"To be honest, we were on the run ourselves and just happened to get lucky when we stumbled in here."

Sam paces. After a few more thoughtful moments, he seems to accept what we've told them, and Thomas begins showing them the layout of the upper floors on the tablet.

"There are three walkways that connect this wing to the main hospital building: on the main level, the third floor, and the sixth floor. It's possible the basements are linked together, too. But it's also possible they never finished the tunnel linking them. Half this place is half built."

Thomas shows them the most direct route to the medicine locker, though he doesn't say that's our "mission objective." He tells them we are looking for a communications center where we can charge the computer battery and that we've got only a few hours to do it.

He puts his finger on the map and looks at each of us in turn.

"I'm fairly sure—emphasis on 'I could be totally wrong'—that you'll find a working outlet in this area here, and it's far enough from where the enemy's camped out that you should have a better chance of not getting shot."

Thomas hands me the battery and cord. "Plug it in, stay alive, and get back down here."

I try to take the battery from his hand, but he doesn't let go.

"Those second two things are more important than the first," he says as he stares into my eyes.

"Got it." I yank the battery out of his grip, and after a quick glance at Thomas's leg, I say to Elmer, "If I don't make it back—"

"Shut up," Thomas says, looking right at me.

I ignore him and keep speaking to Elmer. "There's a garage on the lower level, on the other side of the main building. A small tractor is parked inside. If you can put Thomas in a wheelchair to move him—"

"Shut up," Thomas says again.

I spin around and glare at him. "Are you sure you want those to be the last words you speak to me?"

"Yes. I'm sure. Shut up. *Sir*."

He smiles lazily, and I try to return it. Or I think I do. I suspect my expression looks like I'm baring my teeth, and trying not to throw up. Which is pretty much what I feel like doing when I think about Thomas dying here.

I strap the computer on my arm so I'm wearing it just like the soldier who Oscar pushed into the pit had. Sam is taking supplies out of the backpack, distributing some to Jerry and Sylvester and stuffing the rest into his waistband and pockets.

"Here. Take a few of these," he says to me.

I look at what he's given me. They are shiny circles the color of pencil lead, maybe two inches across. Sylvester laughs like I've just produced his childhood teddy bear.

"Mines," Jerry says. He takes one from my hand and throws it carelessly against the door.

I duck, but other than a loud snap as it hits the door, nothing happens. Sam is smiling.

"Magnetic," he says. "You twist them, throw them at something metal, and they stick. Ten seconds later, boom.

You turn them a little, you get a smaller explosion. Dial them all the way to max and they can punch a man-size hole in the side of an armored vehicle. Very effective."

He puts the backpack down and kneels. "You also have a few other items in here: lots of bullets, a walkie-talkie, a knife . . . oh, and these." He shows me something that looks like a dark gray piece of chewing gum. "C4 explosive strips. They won't be of any use without blast caps, but you do have these." It's a packet with two circles of what looks like clay. One circle is black and one is white. "Commingle these two by kneading them together, put them on any surface, and they bore an inch-wide hole through it, no matter how thick the material is."

"How's she going to crawl through an inch-wide hole?" Thomas asks.

"She's not. But if she puts it on, say, a lock . . ."

All these gadgets and things cheer Jerry up immensely. They seem to confirm what Sylvester has been saying: that Thomas and I are some kind of unorthodox special ops team.

"We're ready, sir," Sam says to me as he picks up his ax handle.

Thomas looks at me, his face full of pride. "Looks like you've gotten a battlefield promotion."

CHAPTER 26

For people trapped in a nightmare fantasy, these three soldiers are all I could hope for as a security detail.

Sam, Jerry, and Sylvester lead the way through the passage that Thomas had indicated. Sam had told the guys to commit the layout to memory, and they had, almost instantly. Unfortunately, I had not, and after the first three turns I am completely lost.

That's when we hit our first problem.

The stairwell we were intending to use is blocked off by fallen debris. A strong draft of air and wisps of snow blow down from above. Sylvester puts his hand up and catches a snowflake in his palm, a look of wonder on his face.

"We must be up in the mountains," he says. "I heard they had snow here, even in the desert."

Rather than see this roadblock as an indication that we should turn back, Sam merely waves us toward another hallway. After about twenty feet, we come to a possible way up: a ragged hole in the upper floor. A huge beam has fallen, creating a steep ramp.

Sam jumps onto the beam and tests it, bouncing up and down to make sure it's secure. One by one we go up, crouching low and pulling against the I beam with our hands. It reminds me of crawling up a playground slide. Halfway up I remember that I've actually done this before, many times. But now I'm terrified, even though I'm only eight feet off the floor. Maybe when they pulled out the memory of climbing half-built skyscrapers, they pulled out my courage, too. How could I have ever gone into the sky so high?

We reenter the stairwell above where it's been blocked off, and climb up another level. A vertical sliver of light shines at the end of the hallway. Maybe it's the edge of a doorway. If Thomas got it right, we should be approaching the first walkway linking the third floor of this wing and the main building, and there should be no door here at all. I look down at the screen and give Sam the thumbs-up. No soldiers up ahead. Sam runs up the hallway, keeping low. He stops just outside the door and tries the knob, but it's locked. After quickly kneading the pieces of black and white putty together, he slaps it against the lock.

"Don't look directly at it," he says, and it's a good thing he does, because I would have watched.

The fire or chemical reaction or whatever burns an intensely bright white for about half a minute and then snuffs itself out like someone pinched the end of a sparkler.

I see the light in the hallway brighten as Sam pulls the door open, a little at first and then finally all the way.

We've found the walkway. What there is of it, anyway.

"Unfinished," Sam says.

We are staring at nothing but I beams. The walkway looks like two railroad tracks with a few diagonal braces connecting them, all of it dripping with icicles and coated with a thick hump of ice. It's a huge, backbreaking drop to the top of the first-floor walkway below.

I look across the space between the two buildings. Something's not right. I count the floors, trying to figure out where we'd be coming out if we did manage to get across this icy bridge, but it's hard to tell. The two buildings are on the side of a hill, and the main building is higher up.

I put one boot onto the beam, and as I shift my weight forward to try to walk, I move slightly too far to the side and slip. Sam catches me by the arm.

"I'll go first," he says.

He steps out onto the I beam, confidently, arms extended to the sides for balance. He does not look down. He moves in small, rapid steps, his feet turned almost perpendicular to the beam. One by one they cross to the other side. I look at the men's naked feet. For getting across this ice-slicked steel girder, they may actually have the advantage. I take my boots and socks off, and hang the boots around my neck.

I put the ball of my foot onto the beam and immediately pull it back like I've been stung. The ice is so cold it burns.

Fear now blooms in my chest like a drop of ink in water. It colors everything. I turn my legs and keep my toes pointed outward like a ballerina, like they did when they crossed. I force myself to put my weight on my feet, to make myself fully commit to what I'm doing. This was how I used to do it, I think. People aren't brave unless they need to be. Commit first, and the courage will follow.

I walk. As quickly and surely as Sam, Sylvester, and Jerry did. They say nothing to me as I'm crossing. No encouraging words. Nothing. They just let me get on with it without distraction.

Sam uses another burn charge to cut through the lock of the door on the other side of the bridge before pulling it open, staying clear in case someone's in the hallway beyond. We wait, and then Sam finally has a look. He motions for us to follow. The hallway is dark, but Sam doesn't want to risk using the lantern.

"Jerry, up front to find us a path. We'll use the walls to guide us," he says.

I put my hand against the wall, feeling my way. When we get ten or so yards down the corridor, the texture changes. I'm touching glass.

Sam finally asks, "What is this place?"

"I'm not sure," I say. "But almost every floor has observation windows."

Jerry walks ahead, and after a few seconds we hear a thump and then the sound of Jerry getting back on his feet.

"Blocked," he calls back to us.

We feel around. Concrete on one side, glass on the other. We're stuck.

"Let's just cut through the glass," Sylvester says. "Or break it."

"How?" I ask.

"We can use some of the burn charges to crack it," Jerry says.

I hear Sam say, "Let's do it."

A moment later I'm already closing my eyes and getting ready to not look at the chemical fire. I hear Jerry slap the charges onto the window.

"I'm going to cup my hands over them to block the light," Jerry says. "Just in case this area is still under surveillance."

We wait. The burn charges shouldn't take long. I lean against the wall, and my head touches something—a small plaque. I trace the writing. A number two. We're not on the third floor after all. We're on the second.

And then, too late, I remember why these walls are made of glass.

"Get that off the glass," I say. "Get it off now!"

"I can't. Once the reaction starts, I can't stop it," Sam says.

"It's an aquarium. It runs the length of this entire hallway!"

This massive tropical fish tank is supposed to be soothing to watch. Steve once told me it held thirty thousand gallons of water and cost the hospital two million bucks, as he grumbled about his latest lousy pay raise.

Jerry takes his hands away from the burn charges. As they flare and grow more intense, I can see inside the tank. The plants are still, and the water is cloudy. Most of the fish are dead, but a few still lurk at the bottom, looking desperate for oxygen.

I hold my breath and wait.

The first of the charges melts through the thick glass and burns itself out. Almost immediately we hear the sound of water shooting onto the floor, like someone just turned on a hose full blast. It smells of fish and briny, rotting greens. I step back and shove my feet back into my boots. My socks are still stuffed into the toes.

The other charge flames out, producing another spigot of water. Then the hallway is again dark. Within seconds, we hear a scratching sound over the noise of the spilling water. It sounds like someone is running a diamond across the surface of the glass.

I turn the tablet on and use the light from the screen like a lantern. We see a crack form. It connects the two holes, then travels horizontally, fast as lightning, across the length of the tank. Dozens more small cracks start to branch out from it.

The glass sounds like ice breaking up. Water begins to spurt from the center crack, just a little at first, and then . . . quiet.

A second later, the whole tank wall explodes outward.

CHAPTER 27

I'm pushed backward, pinwheeling through the water. It seems to go on forever, and I think my lungs are about to burst. Someone slams into me, and then my head hits the exit sign on the ceiling. I grab it and pull myself up, against the tide of the water gushing toward the exit door we've just come through. From below the water, someone grabs my ankle and pulls.

A moment later, the pressure on the door is too much, and it blows off its hinges. The person holding on to my ankle loses his grip. I watch helplessly as whoever it is gets sprayed out the door and over the edge.

The water gushes out quickly and the hallway clears. After a moment, I let myself drop to the floor. The hallway is littered with pebbles and fake ceramic coral. I slip on a good-sized striped fish, bright as a tennis ball. Sam's up the hall, still clinging to a piece of metal that hangs down from the ceiling. The metal is sharp and his hands have deep gashes that are bleeding heavily. He coughs, trying to clear his lungs. I look around for Jerry. I don't see him. I pluck a piece of plant off my neck and stagger toward the door. Jerry's holding on to one of the support struts of the unfinished walkway with his legs like he's riding a horse bareback. Sylvester's on the ground below, facedown, not moving.

"Jerry, can you climb back up here?"

He sputters a moment, then nods. The water has shifted some of the debris from the hallway. We climb through the broken tank to the other side. Neither Sam nor Jerry registers any emotion when I tell them that Sylvester has fallen, that I think he's dead.

Sam says, "We need to keep going. They'll come and investigate what just happened."

Jerry nods.

"Wait."

I take my boots off and use my socks to wrap Sam's bloody hands. Not much of a bandage, but it's something. I'm certain the tablet must be ruined, but when I touch the screen it lights up like a smile.

That's when we hear them—a group of soldiers approaching. They're sloshing through the remaining puddles on the floor, right behind us.

We hurry up the hallway, and I turn right abruptly. Sam and Jerry follow the light of the tablet as I go around the corner. I know just where we are: in the hallway that leads to the gymnasium.

"Where are we going?" Sam asks.

"Shortcut," I tell him. "Through the locker room."

Stupidly, I hesitate as I see "Men" on the door, but then I push forward into the changing room. Several rows of lockers have toppled over, tipping against one another. I hear a humming sound, low and steady. The sound of electrical current. Sam nods and says, "That sounds promising."

The only light we have is from the tablet strapped to my arm. I point it toward the far end of the locker room, trying to figure out if there's enough space for us to pass through to the other side with the lockers blocking the way. I don't think there is. Certainly not if we're standing up.

Sam turns to Jerry. "Help me shift this." Jerry reaches for the edge of a bank of lockers to set them straight again.

"Stop," I say.

On the far side of the room a cable is hanging down, sparking and wriggling like some vicious tree snake. The end of the wire is making contact with one of the lockers. And all the lockers are touching each other, creating a giant circuit. All the metal in the room is electrified, and we are soaking wet.

We hardly have time to take it in before I hear the soldiers coming up the hallway. We are inches from the metal. My skin prickles.

We were looking for power. I guess we found it.

There's nowhere to go. The voices are getting closer, and we have no choice. If they open the locker room door, we're caught. We'll have to squeeze ourselves through the tunnels created by the toppled lockers and pray we don't make contact with any of the metal.

I don't want to go in. It reminds me of being put into the MRI machine. Like I'm being entombed.

Sam points to the floor. "Down! Now!"

I still can't. He sees I'm too afraid. That I'm going to give us all away unless I get moving. He pushes me down.

"Pull your arms in. Stay straight." He practically throws me into the space between the lockers, like he's pushing a puck along the floor. When I come to a stop, I use my elbows to inch forward. I hear Sam dive onto the floor behind us.

No sooner do we get ourselves crammed into this small void than the overhead light comes on. My body is rigid with terror. I worry that the soldiers hunting us will hear the water still dripping off my clothes, or hear me panting, or my heart pounding. That I'll accidentally touch one of the lockers and fry myself.

Their steps are slow and cautious. A digitized voice says, "Careful. That's a live wire."

Another robotic voice answers back, "Let's head upstairs before one of us gets electrocuted."

After they leave, Sam, Jerry, and I continue crawling to the other side of the room. I'm not even sure how I'm pushing myself along with my arms against my sides. When we finally reach the other end of the locker room, the door to the gym is propped open and I can see inside. The gym floor is scattered with soccer balls, basketballs, volleyballs.

Dozens upon dozens of them. They must have spilled off their storage racks when the explosions shook the building. It looks like a hundred children were playing and then simply vanished.

And then I see it: an outlet beneath a desk. I crawl under and plug the wet battery pack in, terrified it won't work, but a red circle of light comes on.

Power.

Sam and Jerry slide in on either side of me, and we all push ourselves under the desk, our backs to the wall. I wait a solid ten, fifteen minutes before I turn to Sam and say, "I think they're gone."

Sam sits with his hands clasped, resting lightly on his knees. "Some of their men don't speak English, apparently."

"What do you mean?"

"That device he's using. We used them when we needed to talk to the locals and there was no one available to translate. Each man has his own earpiece. Commands are translated into whatever language he speaks."

Jerry spits. *"Mercenaries."*

In this moment of quiet, I think of Sylvester. Neither of them has mentioned him. Maybe it's part of their training, but part of me thinks otherwise.

"I'm so sorry about your friend," I say to them.

"Friend?" Jerry says.

"Sylvester. The man who was pushed out the door when the fish tank exploded."

"Yes. Right," Sam says. "He was a . . . good soldier." His eyes are vacant, like he's not sure who I'm talking about.

Jerry is staring straight ahead, confusion clouding his face. This was a close friend and fellow soldier, but they're already forgetting about him and neither is sure why.

Is this a side effect? Would anyone want to forget like this, so quickly, so effortlessly? The procedures have taken away these men's ability to remember, which is to take away their ability to grieve, which is to take away their ability to love.

I feel a cold, wet, slimy sensation in the pit of my stomach.

Is this what's going to happen to me if I can't get the last pill I need? Will I end up like Oscar, unable to distinguish dreams from reality?

The three of us wait for what seems like hours. I'm about to pull the battery cord out of the wall when the light on the charger starts blinking green. I look down at the computer on my wrist and realize something: Those two soldiers we saw earlier should have registered on the screen, but they didn't. They must have turned off the tracking device.

They know we're here.

CHAPTER 28

"They know we're here, and they know we've got one of their devices," I say to Sam and Jerry.

Sam clenches his jaw and digests this piece of bad news without comment.

I tie the power cord around my waist like a belt. "I think we can cut through the pool area and exit through the women's lockers to the central hallway. From there we can . . ." I'm about to say "get to the nurses' station," but realize they don't know that part of the plan.

"We can take the stairs down to the basement and find a way back."

Now that we can't rely on the tablet, we're flying blind. But the extra risk is just punishment for the detour I'm taking us on.

"This way," I say.

I follow the smell of chlorine. A column of snow is

falling through the broken glass above the pool. The wind has died down and the snow has changed. It's no longer light and wispy; now, each flake is the size of a dime.

We run quickly to the other side of the room, through to the women's locker room. It's dark and chilly and smells of bleach. We push the swinging door open between the locker room and outer hallway. I touch Sam lightly on the shoulder and point. A row of panicked eyes stare back at us. Six nurses are propped against the wall, gagged, their hands and feet bound.

"Hostages," Jerry says.

I scan the group quickly, and right away I recognize Nurse Jenner. I can't tell if she's relieved or worried. Certainly, all of them seem bewildered by the sight of us.

I kneel and remove the gag from Nurse Jenner's mouth as Sam cuts the plastic tie binding her wrists with a knife he's pulled from the backpack.

"How are you still alive?" she asks.

"I don't honestly know."

"Do you know what happened to the other patients on the floor? Oscar? William?"

William? Ah. The kid in the coma.

"William is dead. Oscar is alive, but he's not—there's something wrong with him."

"Of course there is. You think we're playing around here? These procedures are precise. Oscar needs to have his final injection of sealant. Soon. Sooner than now. Do you know what that boy is capable of?" She looks at me as if I'm being stupid on purpose, which I now realize is how she's always looked at me.

"I know where he is right now," I say. "I could give him the injection."

I begin to unravel the thick tape that keeps her ankles bound together, but she pulls her feet away and finishes it herself. "We've got to get to the medicine locker at the nurses' station on the third floor."

Sam looks at me. One of those soldiers in the locker room said something about heading upstairs.

I start to undo the tape on another nurse's ankles, but Jenner stops me. "You're better off leaving them where they are. The soldiers send someone by every fifteen minutes to check on us. If they see us all gone, they'll just hunt us down and shoot us."

"Where's Dr. Ladner?" I ask.

"Ladner." She says his name like it disgusts her. "This is his fault."

"That's not what I asked. I want to know where he is."

She looks at me, startled. I've never actually said a defiant word to the woman until now.

"He barricaded himself in his office on the sixth floor before they rounded us all up. They seem to be focusing their efforts on getting at him. And someone else."

I try to remain calm and not react to this statement. She must have missed the exciting announcement in the lobby about who they were looking for when they first burst in. I doubt she'd help if she knew these guys were after me.

Sam and Jerry run up ahead of us. Nurse Jenner is remarkably nimble as she climbs up the stairs to the third floor, leaping over fallen concrete blocks as she goes. She's about to open the door to the hallway when Sam steps forward. "Jerry and I will go first to make sure it's clear."

Jenner is about to follow. "Wait," I say. "They'll let us know when it's okay."

She doesn't like having to listen to me, but she does.

"Is there some way to put out a distress call?" I ask her.

"Of course there is," she snaps. "You can't have a hospital full of people like *you* and not have an evacuation plan."

"So how do we do it?"

"There's a panic button on the wall behind the security desk in the main lobby. If you hit it, there's a Special Forces unit that's supposed to come. Not that it'll do us any good in this storm."

I hear two knocks on the fire door. Sam's signal. "Quickly," Sam says, crouching low next to the main desk.

Though the outer windows are riddled with bullet holes and some of the monitors have fallen onto the floor, the nurses' station is still full of equipment that's gone onto battery backup. Something is beeping urgently. We duck down and make our way along, staying hidden behind the desk. Jenner crawls to the medicine cabinet, punches in a code, and quickly prepares a syringe. "Give Oscar this." She reaches into the cabinet again and pulls out another syringe. "And if he gives you any trouble, pop him with this. Just touch it to his skin, press the button on the top, and the syringe will automatically inject the sedative."

She hands both syringes to me and then suddenly stands up in plain view. Her head swivels back and forth, her eyes flicking nervously around the room and toward the ceiling.

"I also need something. It's a clear gel capsule."

She freezes, then spins around. "Who told you about those pills?"

What can I say to her that will make sense? That will make her help me without asking why?

I stand up straight and look her in the eye. "Dr. Buckley."

"You're lying. Buckley isn't even on site, and even if he were, he doesn't interact with patients as a rule."

She looks at the clothes I'm wearing. At my boots. Like she's trying to piece things together. "Someone helped you get out. Who was it?"

"I don't know."

I see her jaw working as she thinks. "It was Ladner, wasn't it? Yes, it had to be. I knew there was something funny about that power outage. This place has backup systems for its backup systems. And just when that consultant was here to make sure your procedure went as planned."

Jenner moves closer to me. Her blue surgical scrubs are filthy and torn. She looks like she wants to put her hands around my neck and break it. I have no doubt she could.

I sigh loudly, rub my eyes, and sit down in the desk chair even as she towers over me. I'm getting tired of people wanting to kill me. I really am.

She grabs the chair and spins it so that I'm facing her. "It makes sense now. All the delays. You were supposed to be done months ago, but every time you were scheduled for surgery, something would inexplicably come up. Twice, Dr. Buckley just didn't show up to conduct your procedure."

She puts her forefinger against the side of my head and presses on one of the remaining halo inserts.

"They were doing something different to you. And they didn't want anyone to find out."

"What was it? What did they do to me?"

"I don't know. I wasn't allowed near your surgeries. They told me I didn't have high enough security clearance. Nonsense. I've assisted with dozens of memory modifications. I know where all the bodies are buried around here. And then you come along, and suddenly I can't be trusted?"

She's inches from me, her eyes blazing and locked on to me like I'm a target.

"No one could observe. You were some big breakthrough. I heard them say it once, and I didn't understand at the time. I didn't get why Dr. Buckley and Ladner gave you special treatment. Why would that be?"

I have no idea. I really don't, but what's the point of telling her that?

"I don't think there's anything special about you at all. I think you're just a girl with a violent past, a bad attitude, and no future. Just like the rest of them."

The door swings open behind Nurse Jenner. I see the

outline of a soldier, and then I hear a scuffle followed by grunts and a crack. When I look again, a dark form lies crumpled on the floor. Sam and Jerry enter, stepping over the mercenary's body. Sam crouches down and picks through the soldier's utility belts and pockets. He takes the mercenary's gun and slings the guy's backpack over his shoulder, the model of cool professionalism.

Jenner looks at Sam and Jerry and shakes her head. "And now, as if things weren't bad enough, you've gone and opened Pandora's box."

"No, they're okay," I say. "A bit messed up in terms of geography at the moment, but they're still the same good men they were before."

"You don't know what you're talking about. They put those men here so they could gather every last bit of information about them before they died. Maybe learn from their mistakes. Those men are nothing but failed medical experiments."

She stares at me, her face steely and hateful, her coral lipstick smeared up into the lines around her mouth. She no longer has to care for me or pretend to be civil, and we both know it.

She pours a bottle of capsules onto the floor and then throws the bottle down. "If you want to know what you really are, by all means, take these pills. But be prepared."

"I'm not afraid of finding out who I am. Not anymore."

"You should be. The fourth floor was where they put the worst cases, and the soldiers upstairs who are after you, whoever they are—let me just tell you, they wouldn't be after you if you didn't deserve it."

Jenner grabs the microphone on the nurses' desk and blows into it. "Testing. Can you hear me?" I hear her voice amplified over the PA system. "This is Pamela Jenner. I have level 2A clearance. I'm at the third-floor nurses' station. She's here. The girl you're looking for is here. Sarah Ramos."

My whole body sags. Not because she's hurt my feelings or betrayed my trust—let's face it, I hate the woman and she hates me—but because I know what's going to happen.

"They're not going to reward you for turning me in, if that's what you're thinking."

"I'd rather take my chances with them than with you. Or them," she says, nodding toward Sam and Jerry.

"Nurse Jenner, Pam, whatever your name is, I don't know how much they're paying you to do this job, but it's not nearly enough, considering what's about to happen to you."

Almost instantly, soldiers pour into the room. They fire at the desk and hit the bank of monitors behind us. Sam looks at the approaching mercenaries; his eyes narrow like he's got crosshairs built into his pupils.

Nurse Jenner lunges at me and grabs me by my wrist, but trying to hold on to me is her big mistake. As I peel Jenner's fingers off my arm one by one, Jerry moves toward her with such grace I can't resist watching. He raises the handgun he removed from the downed soldier's body and squeezes off two quick rounds. Jenner hits the desk, her cheek knocking the phone out of its cradle as she collapses to the floor. He turns and pulls the trigger three more times, leaving three more soldiers dead.

I drop and try to find one of the clear capsules among the scattered, glittering bits of broken glass.

Another wave of soldiers arrives. Jerry fires at them so that Sam and I can retreat, but I don't want to leave without that pill. I keep sweeping my hands back and forth, hoping I'll get lucky and find it, but Sam pulls me by the arm back toward the stairwell.

I struggle to break free of his grip. A pill lies inches from Jenner's face, right in front of her nose. I scramble for it on my hands and knees. Sam grabs my ankle just as I'm about to reach the pill.

"Noooooo!"

He drags me along the ground, firing at the same time. I watch as Jerry is hit in the neck by a bullet. He goes down onto one knee, still firing, his hand over the pulsing wound. The last thing he does before he slips to the floor is shoot the surveillance camera in the corner of the room.

Sam and I spill into the stairwell, and I leap to my feet. We hear soldiers bearing down on us, their boots beating like drums. The sound is coming from above and below. We're trapped. Sam pulls another gun from the pack he's carrying and hands it to me along with the simple command, "Point and shoot."

Then he takes something from the bag, just as calm as can be. I know what he's planning to do. "You want to go up or down?" he asks.

"Down."

He twists one of the disks in his hand and tosses it up. The disk zooms toward the metal fire door and sticks.

The mine explodes just as we make it to the landing. I'm so startled by the noise I drop the gun as I try to cover my ears. We spill out of the stairwell into the main lobby near the elevator bank.

It's probably the worst place we could have ended up.

CHAPTER 29

We are going to die. Right here. Right now. This is where all those angry red dots are concentrated like a bull's-eye.

Sam keeps his gun drawn, and pushes me behind him, putting himself between me and whatever may be coming from the direction of the lobby. We press ourselves into the elevator alcove, against the closed doors. I expect soldiers to come around the corner and start shooting at any moment, but nothing happens.

"We should try to get to the basement. See if the tunnel connecting the buildings is really there," he says.

Of course it might not be. But we don't have any alternative.

Sam presses the elevator button, and I watch as the car sinks down, down, down toward the main floor. The mercenaries must see us on the security cameras by now.

I suddenly remember what Jenner said about the panic button—about how it would take hours for help to arrive. I wonder if we'll last that long.

I look toward the desk. The panic button is mounted on the wall, plain as day—yellow, big as the palm of my hand, with a plastic cover over it. The open space between these elevators and that button might as well be miles long, but I've got to try anyway.

"I'm going to try to get to the panic button to call for help. Wait here."

"No, I'll come with you to cover you if you need it."

The wind groans through the windows. I take a step toward the desk. I expect to hear gunfire, but there's nothing. No one is around. Sam and I quickly cross the ten yards to the guard's desk. I'm about to reach for the button when two soldiers walk into the lobby.

Damn.

Then Hodges.

Damn, damn, damn.

Sam and I drop to the floor. We hear a ding as the elevator car finally arrives. The soldiers rush toward it, guns drawn. The doors open; they see that no one is inside and lower their weapons.

Hodges is so close I can hear the jangle of her bracelets. I can see the tips of her ivory shoes under the desk. Now she's wearing a long coat with fur trim.

The elevator doors close again, and she makes a noise in her throat, slapping her hand on the desk. The sound makes me jump, and I thump my head on the underside of the counter just as a soldier says to her, "Not there."

"Well, obviously." Her voice is thick and so down-homey, she might as well be speaking with a mouthful of grits. "Go and find her. This is getting ridiculous. Seven million dollars for mercenaries. *Seven million.* I could have found her with a coonhound by now."

Sam gets into a crouch, ready to spring up and hit the panic button if we get the chance, which is looking less and less likely. As I look around, searching out our options, I notice something unexpected.

Steve!

His chest is rising and falling in a stuttered rhythm. A bubble of bloody snot expands out of his nostril. I don't know how he's still alive, but he is.

Hodges sends the two soldiers off. She's by herself now.

Sam points toward the elevator car. The doors have reopened, and it's just sitting there, waiting for us if we can get to it. I get up onto the balls of my feet, ready to slap the panic button and then make a dash for the elevators.

Hodges paces and curses. I hear beeping, like she's dialing the same phone number over and over, but she keeps getting cut off. She becomes more familiar to me just as everything begins to blur. It's like someone has taken two pictures and put them in the same place in front of my eyes, and I don't know what to focus on, the past or the present.

I feel myself fall back onto my heels and then onto the floor. I can't stop it now. It's the police station again. It's the same day, the same memory. I know because Hodges is still in her purple ball gown.

She spins her bracelets again.

"Nervous?" *I say.*

"No. I'm not nervous." *But she immediately stops and folds her hands in her lap.*

"I've never met you before today," *I say.* "How exactly am I ruining your life?"

"How indeed. Let me first ask you, what do you think you've been doing all this time at Mr. Claymore's worksites?"

"Um, climbing?"

"I don't mean the crane. You've been snooping around, asking for the building plans from the Department of City Planning. Tell me why."

"Those plans are a matter of public record. I'm an interested citizen."

She glares at me. "No, what you've been trying to do is embarrass Mr. Claymore. You think you're going to find something out that will cause trouble. Isn't that right?"

"Something like that."

She crosses and uncrosses her legs like she can't get comfortable in her chair. She says nothing for a long while; just looks up toward the ceiling like she's thinking.

"You went to the nursing home near St. Luke's to see Mr. Claymore's wife. The woman is eighty-two and demented. Why?"

"Oh, was that a nursing home? Do they always put razor wire around nursing homes?"

"What could you possibly be hoping to find out from her, Sarah?"

"Sarah. Did you know that's also Mrs. Claymore's first name? Interesting coincidence, huh?"

"It's a common enough name," Hodges says as she adjusts her earring. "Very common."

"Well, Sarah and I were just making small talk. And she's not demented. Heartbroken maybe, but hardly crazy. You'd probably be heartbroken, too, if three of your kids were dead and one was terminally ill. Well, I mean, maybe not you, but other people. You don't seem like the type to get all broken up."

"You're right. I'm not. And you know what else you should know about me? I can read people like books. Trashy, conniving little books. And I know that you're lying to me."

"Am I? I don't think I'm the one who's been lying all these years. Mrs. Claymore told me a lot of things. Really fascinating things about your boss."

Hodges looks like she's having a hard time maintaining her composure. She runs her tongue back and forth across her upper lip.

"Did you know that she was once married to Mr. Claymore's older brother? But then he died suddenly, tragically, and in her grief, she married her former brother-in-law. It's probably too much to get into here, but Mr. Claymore has a lot to answer for."

"Shut. Your. Mouth."

I lean back in my chair and try to act cool. My heart is pounding, but she doesn't need to know that. "I don't think you're all that worried about defending your boss's honor. I think what's really bothering you right now is that I know some dirt you don't."

"You know nothing. You are nothing. You will always be nothing."

"That sweet Southern accent of yours seems to come and go. What's up with that?"

She slaps me in the face. I won't lie: It hurts. A lot. But I smile anyway, even as my eyes start to tear. Then she slaps me again, this time with the back of her hand. Her bracelets tinkle as they slide down her arm.

I refuse to look at her.

"I'm going to make you very sorry, little girl."

Make me sorry? That's almost funny, and I might laugh about it, but I don't want her to slap me anymore. Instead I think about how tired I am. My hands are still sore from climbing.

"You can't take anything away from me, lady. It's already all gone."

"That's true, isn't it? It is all gone. And I, of all people, should know that."

"What's that supposed to mean?"

"You know who I work for? I'm Mr. Claymore's right-hand . . . woman. I take care of all the little things for him. Things like you, for example."

"That right?"

"I know perfectly well why you've been targeting his projects for the past year, and I'll start off by telling you that I'm not going to negotiate with you. I'm going to tell you what's going to happen here, and you're going to do it."

"Or else?"

"Oh goodness, I'm not going to tell you the 'or else' part. You're just going to experience that when the time comes."

I feel a shiver go through me as the woman watches me with an almost bland expression on her face. Somehow, she's still menacing. But I know my rights. I don't have to listen to any of this. I look over at the observation window. "Hey! Are you people there? This woman is threatening me."

I'm looking at her reflection, and she's looking at mine. She smiles. "There's no one in there who'll help you. Mr. Claymore has a lot of friends and a lot of people who are, okay, not exactly friends, but interested parties who want to stay on his good side. So it's just me and you right now, talking girl to girl."

I see something in her eyes that frightens me. There's an emptiness there. I am a thing to her. Nothing more. A thing that, for whatever reason, is in her way. It takes a lot to frighten the girl who climbs cranes. Who half hopes she'll fall off. The girl who is afraid of nothing because she has nothing to live for, except dealing some payback.

Maybe courage is the same thing as not caring about losing. And that makes courage a worthless possession. Like everything else I own.

"Here's what's going to happen. You are going to publicly admit that you've been harassing Mr. Claymore and extorting money from him. Then you're going to apologize and agree to spend two years on probation, doing community service for several of Mr. Claymore's personal charities."

I start laughing. I've spent the last year making trouble for Erskine Claymore, pointing out what coldhearted scum he is. After taking advantage of my mother, he just carries on like nothing while she works and scrapes to make a living? And this flouncy, red-haired woman thinks I'm just going to renounce all that? For what? I'm waiting for her to offer me money. That's what these rich people do, and when she does, I'm going to tell her to take her money and . . .

"Well? I'm waiting," she says.

"Are you trying to pay me off?"

"I didn't say I was going to give you anything in return."

I laugh harder now.

"What, precisely, is so funny? You don't agree to my terms?" She reaches over and gently brushes a strand of hair away from my forehead. I pull back in disgust.

"You don't know this, but I gave you a chance once, not so long ago. That was very much out of character for me."

"What are you talking about?"

"I was trying to be someone I'm not—that was wrong of me. I realize now that you have to know who you are, Sarah. You have to understand yourself. Do what you know has to be done."

"If you think I'm going to do anything to help you, you can just forget it."

She sits up straight and gives a girlish gasp.

"Forget it . . . hmmm . . . forget it. Now there's an idea."

Suddenly she's giddily happy, and it's scaring me more than anything that's happened tonight.

"So, are you ready to make a statement now?" she says. "We can get you a pen and paper. I assume you have a command of the English language. Unlike your mother."

The table jumps forward as I leap to my feet. I lean toward her, thinking I might head butt her, but I catch myself. What am I, crazy? I'm already in trouble. I can't attack this woman at the police station. I glance warily at the observation mirror and sit back down.

"That's right, Sarah. Sit, sit. If you keep raging like this, they'll lock you up for who knows how long."

I take a deep breath and close my eyes, trying to keep calm. I know she's baiting me.

"That's it. I'm sure you're good at keeping a level head. To a point, of course. Everyone has her limit." The woman lowers her voice to a whisper and adds in the sweetest Southern accent she can muster, "You know what? Just for fun, let's see if we can find out where yours is."

She reaches across the table to pat my cheek. I try to jerk my head away, but she grabs me by the chin and digs her nails deep into my skin.

"Let's see. When was it now? Just two short years ago, I think. Your mother was walking home from work, crossing the street. I'll bet she was tired, making up beds all day at the hotel. That's probably why she was walking so slowly. Because she was soooooo exhausted. All I had to do was tap my foot on the gas pedal a little harder than I should and whoops! Up she goes, over my hood and into the air. I stopped and got out and checked her pulse. If anyone saw me, I was prepared to pay him off and tell him to shuffle back to his dreary little apartment, but no one was there. I've never seen a New York City street so empty. A stroke of luck for me, really, but then again, fortune favors the bold.

"Anyway, there I was, standing over your mother's body, and I looked down onto the pavement and there were seeds everywhere.

Strangest thing. I thought, How odd! The woman is carrying birdseed. Why? What bird is she feeding?"

"Pepitas," *I say.*

"What?"

"They were pepitas."

She flicks her hand, and that's when I push the table forward like a sled. It hits her in the chest and she flies backward in her seat, her ball-gown skirt billowing out like a parachute. She shrieks as she hits the floor. I tip the table over onto her, pressing the edge of it into her throat. Then I put all my weight down on it. The next thing I know, I'm pinned against the opposite wall, crying and screaming and thrashing and biting like a wild animal until a Taser drops me to the floor.

"She's crazy!" Hodges shouts. She's clutching her neck with one hand, where the tabletop has left a bruise. Her other hand is dangling down oddly. I think I may have broken her collarbone. "She attacked me! Out of the blue! I offered to help her, and she attacked with no warning!"

I'm back. Sitting under the desk, my two hands clutching my bald head.

This is the woman who killed my mother.

Now I'm going to kill her.

CHAPTER 30

I rise to my feet like I've been drawn up with strings. Sam is still underneath the desk, not sure what I'm doing. I'm in full view in the lobby. No gun, no grenade, no anything to defend myself, except the strength of my own anger.

Hodges is turned toward the windows, her back to me. She's talking on a radio. "Speak up! What are you saying? She's where?"

I hear the static-filled response, the frantic tone, as someone shouts, "She's there! She's there! Behind you!"

"Behind who?" she shouts. "Give me your location!"

"Main floor lobby!"

"Don't be stupid. *I'm* in the main . . . floor . . . lobby. . . ."

She turns and stares at me.

I take several steps toward her as rage courses through my veins. I am a fountain of fury. I could fill up the whole world with it right now.

She puts her hand to her neck protectively.

"I see by the look on your face that it's all starting to come back to you, *Angel*." She pushes a long curl away from her face and pouts. "I've come a very long way to kill you. I hope you appreciate it."

I feel a prickle of adrenaline in my fingertips. Just as I'm about to take a step toward her, out of the corner of my eye, I see movement.

Soldiers.

I fling myself over the guard's desk like I'm hopping a fence. Sam stands up and begins firing.

"Go! Go! Go!" he shouts at me.

I rush into the elevator but know they'll be on me before the doors can close. Suddenly Sam is there, blocking the door of the car, firing, telling me to close the doors.

"Get in!" I shout.

"Close the door!"

"Get in!"

He pushes a button and then steps back out into the lobby to cover me. He's firing, and now they're firing back. He's hit in the shoulder, then the upper chest. A moment later his face hits the marble tile. He rolls onto his back, twists one of the mines, and hugs it against his chest.

The doors close. A second later a blast rocks the elevator shaft, and for a moment I think I'm in free fall. The car seems to tip a little and makes a horrible scraping sound against the walls before shuddering to a stop. I think it might be wedged in place, but when I take a step, my weight is enough to make the elevator wobble and slide farther down the shaft.

I'm within arm's reach of the little door that says "For Emergency Use Only." I try to keep my feet planted and, without adjusting my center of gravity, pull the door open to get the elevator key. I look at it. I had to use a key like this all the time when I was a kid, because the ancient elevator in our apartment building stopped at least once a week. Getting on it was sort of like playing the slots. You could take the stairs or you could take the elevator, but if you did the latter, you risked getting stuck for an hour or more while somebody called the super to get you unstuck.

I try to push this memory out and away like I did before. I can't give in to it.

"Not now! Not now!"

But I can't resist it. And I have nowhere to run to get away from the past.

I see the brown, scuffed tiles in the apartment hallways. I remember the sound of the buzzer when you let someone into the building. I remember . . . I remember . . .

Being at school. And Mrs. Esteban. Again. Why would these memories be connected?

I see the bright red painted doors of my swanky Upper East Side school, full of skinny girls who get dropped off in fancy cars every morning, their hair pin-straight and shiny, telling stories about what they'd done that weekend—the backstage concert passes, the trips to the Hamptons, the front-row seats at Fashion Week.

I've been summoned down to Ms. Janklow's office. She's the fairly useless guidance counselor whose only qualification seems to be that she can nod sympathetically.

"It's Debby. Call me Debby," she says. "I'm so sorry to have to ask you to come down here, but I'm wondering if there's been some sort of mistake."

"With what?" I ask. I honestly don't know what she's talking about. My grades are fine. Better than fine. I've even managed to keep them up since . . . since my mother died. That was three months ago. I do it because my mother would have wanted me to.

"Well, your tuition payment has . . . well . . . we haven't received one this quarter."

I look at her, confused and, I admit, somewhat annoyed. "I'm not sure how the scholarship works. I don't know what to tell you."

"Scholarship?" Ms. Janklow says. She has very nice skin. It's creamy and peachy, or whatever that expression is.

"My scholarship. I don't know how it works. I assumed the school took care of all that."

"What scholarship?" she asks.

What scholarship? The one that allows me to go to this ritzy school that I hate, but I would never say that to my mother, because she broke her back just to pay for the stinking itchy wool uniform I have to wear.

"You don't have a scholarship that I'm aware of," she tells me.

"Then how . . . I don't understand. How could my mother afford to send me here?"

"I have no idea, Sarah," Ms. Janklow—Debby—says to me. "Your tuition has been paid by check just like everyone else's. Did

your . . . did your mother leave money in a trust fund? For your education?"

I want to burst out in mean, mocking laughter. A trust fund? Me? If I had a trust fund, would I be living in a foster home with a woman who only seems to know how to cook three dishes, all of which feature ketchup as a sauce?

This has been my life since my mother died: pulling myself out of bed every day, even though I don't want to get up, don't want to see the sun rise, because every day that passes puts more distance between me and my mother being alive.

"No, seriously," I say. "My mother didn't have any money. That can't be right."

Ms. Janklow tells me again that my mother has been paying my tuition for years, and they'd hate to lose me as a student, since I offer such a diverse perspective. Yeah, the poor, New York Latina perspective. The girls in my neighborhood would get a kick out of that, right before kicking me to the ground and calling me "white girl."

"Well, the problem is still the same," Ms. Janklow says. "The tuition is not being paid. Do you have any idea who might have been funding your education? Perhaps you should talk to him or her about it. You obviously have some patron who's been helping you. . . ."

An hour later I'm running up the stairs of my old apartment building. I need to talk to Mrs. Esteban. I know it may be a waste of my time; she's been failing for a while, but I remember her comment, long ago, about me having green eyes. I think I must have put it out of my head the instant she said it, because I thought she

*was just being mean and gossipy. But now . . . now that I know
someone has been paying my way through school . . .*

I take the steps to her apartment two, three at a time. Her
daughter answers the door. She seems confused about why I'd want
to talk to her mother, but ushers me into their neat, shabby living
room, where Mrs. Esteban is watching television and picking over
a pan of rice looking for rocks and bits of twigs.

"She'll spend the whole afternoon on it," her daughter says,
motioning to the bowl in her mother's lap.

Poor Mrs. Esteban. She had such powerful arms, and now
she's little more than a child who must be kept busy. I haven't seen
her in nearly two years, but she knows me. I can tell because she
makes a face like, What are you doing here? I guess she'll never
forget that kick in the ankle I gave her.

"Mrs. Esteban. Do you know who my mother worked for?
Long ago? I need to know."

"Your . . . mother . . . que bonita," she sighs. The side of
her mouth droops slightly from her recent stroke. I ask her the question again, and she is annoyed with my impatience. She knows the
answer. She starts waving her hand at me, her index finger and
thumb pinched together.

Her daughter says, "That means she wants to write something."

I take a pencil and piece of paper from my backpack and give
them to her. She makes her hand work very slowly. I'm hoping for
a name, even just one. I watch as she writes the letters E C and
then circles them clumsily.

She smiles at me, and I try not to show my disappointment.

E.C. *This is meaningless to me, but I thank her and stand to leave. Her daughter, drying her hands on a kitchen towel, looks over her mother's shoulder to see what she's written.* "I'm sorry. She tries. Don't you, Mamá?"

I'm almost to the door when I hear Mrs. Esteban's daughter add, "Huh. That looks like the symbol at the top of Claymore Tower, doesn't it?"

CHAPTER 31

I don't need to remember any more. I know now as I knew then. That's what sent me off on my mission. My late-night raids. My desire to bring him down and embarrass him—to do whatever I could to make him look bad. My mother always had a dark grace about her; she seemed to bear the weight of a hundred lives. She was beautiful. He must have taken advantage of her. Pretty maids are like prey. There can be no other explanation.

The man who builds all the tall buildings.

Erskine Claymore.

I've somehow managed to keep myself balanced in the elevator all this time. The air in the car is close and warm—so filled with my panic that it feels crowded. My fingers are slippery with sweat as I work the emergency key clockwise. The car slides a few more inches, the metal screeching like a subway car coming to a stop. Finally I can turn the key no farther.

I put my fingertips between the two doors and push as slowly and carefully as I can, a centimeter at a time. The car groans. I keep the pressure steady. I'm stuck three-quarters of the way between floors. The car starts to slip, little by little, so slowly I'm not sure at first that it's even moving. Then I can see it's moving faster, and I know I don't have much time. I throw all my weight forward as I kick my legs out, and am able to just squeeze through the opening and pull my arms out before the car gives a last screech and descends with a horrific crash.

I sit in the hallway and look around, trying to figure out where I am. I need to rest. I think I'll have time. Hopefully, they'll assume that I didn't make it out, that I fell to the bottom of the shaft.

Like a lot of my hopes, though, it doesn't work out that way.

The other elevator car is coming down. I watch the numbers above the doorway until I see the *LL* light up.

I stand up and take out the last mine.

Wait.

Wait.

I twist it. Pull my arm back.

Wait.

Wait.

I hear the bell ring. The doors are about to open.

Wait.

Wait.

I throw the mine and then run down the corridor, toward the tunnel that may be an escape or a trap—or maybe it doesn't exist at all. The first few doors I try turn out to be closets, but then I fling one open and face a black, musty void. I walk in and pull the door shut behind me. I have no idea how long the tunnel is, so I keep walking blindly. About twenty yards later, my hands touch cool, smooth metal. I find the knob, turn it, and pull. It doesn't budge.

Panic explodes in my chest like fireworks, but I remember the burn charges. I use one to melt through the lock and, a moment later, burst out of the tunnel like I'm emerging from a tomb.

It takes me a few minutes, but I find my way back to the swank waiting area where I'd found the laptop computer. The passcard gets me in, but I use it with a sense of fatality. What difference does it make if I give myself away now or ten minutes from now? They'll find me eventually.

I untie the battery from around my waist and drag it behind me like a child's pull toy, running down the hallway, trying to match the route I took earlier. I think I'm going the right way.

As I round the corner a shot rings out. The bullet just misses my head. I slip and fall, then scramble sideways like a crab, trying to find cover. The shot has come from near the rec lounge.

I peek around the corner and see Oscar. He's standing at the end of the hallway, blood streaming down his head. It looks like he's clawed the metal inserts out of his skull. He's got a gun in his hand.

I call out, trying to sound amused. "What's goin' on, dude? You almost shot me."

"It don't matter, *mija*. I shoot you, they shoot me. We all get shot eventually."

"Yeah, well, I'll get shot another time. I've got things to do right now."

His laugh is a funny, strained *heh heh heh*. I take another look at him. He's walking toward me, shaking the gun like a maraca. I see that street swagger I've seen from so many boys, so many times in my neighborhood, especially when they first get home from jail. So much energy wasted on trying not to look afraid.

"No matter what you do, they kill you, you know what I'm sayin'? You can't get away from it, so why try?"

"Are you supposed to be up and walking around? You were injured."

"Doctor Man, he told me to stay still, but I can't, you know? I can't. Rich Kid, he tried to stop me, but he can't. I need to get up and move around, you know?"

Doctor Man. Rich Kid. I assume he's talking about Elmer and Thomas. I watch as he does a little dance step.

"Where are they, Oscar? Doctor Man and Rich Kid?"

"Aren't you listening?" he shouts at me. He sounds far away, but then suddenly he's there, next to me. I feel the warm, hard gun muzzle touching my temple. "He tried to stop me, and I shot him." He lowers the gun and pushes the barrel into my chest. "Right. In. The. Heart."

I put my hand in my pocket and grab hold of the syringe

Jenner gave me. I face Oscar, like this is all a big joke between the two of us. I make myself relax and push the gun away from my head, smiling and shaking my head back and forth.

"We don't have time for messing around, Oscar. Come on. Let's get out of here."

He slaps my cheek lightly and pulls me close to him, pressing his forehead to mine. I feel the gun against the back of my head as he hugs me roughly.

"*Chica,* you all right."

I stare at him at close range. The whites of his eyes are dotted with small, reddish hemorrhages. I puff my chest out like a bird trying to look bigger.

"Thanks, Oscar. Come on. We need to get out of here."

I try to peel his arm away and take a step back, but he tightens his grip on me. Then he spins me around and puts me in a headlock. He flexes his bicep into my throat.

"What you doing here?" he says. His lips are touching my ear. "What you in for, huh?"

"I don't know, man," I say. "I don't wanna know."

"Yeah. I know what you mean. Except . . . suddenly it's coming back to me. I keep seeing all these people's faces staring at me, and they want to know why I did it to them, why I put them in the ground. And I don't know. I can't remember why. They're all around me, all the time. I can't get away from them."

I pull the syringe out of my pocket and put my thumb on the end of it, ready to push the button.

"Did you shoot Rich Kid, Oscar? Is he all right?"

He lets go of me but starts circling around, keeping his face inches from mine.

"Oh, ho! Now I see what's going on!" He slaps me hard on the back. "You like him, don't you? You got a thing for Rich Kid, eh?" He grabs my ear and tugs on it, pulling me over to one side. "You from the hood? 'Cause I look at you and I think you got some white girl in you."

"I'll tell you who I am: I'm Angel."

He pushes the gun into my cheek so far I feel it against my teeth. That's when I reach up behind him, stick him in the neck with the syringe, and hit the plunger. He reacts to the shock of the injection by bobbling the gun. I hear it clatter onto the floor as he loses his balance and steps backward. He immediately recovers and grabs me by the throat with both hands, slamming me into the wall.

"What did you do to me?"

I can't breathe. He's pinching off my windpipe, his fingernails digging into my skin. The sedative I just used on him—either it wasn't enough or it'll be too late for me when it takes effect. Because I'm done. He's staring right in my face, his teeth gritted, trying to hurt me as bad as he can.

A few seconds later, my vision becomes an endless tunnel, and I slide to the floor.

CHAPTER 32

Everything is black. The air is gone. I hear something, though—a voice. I don't know who it belongs to. Maybe it's just the echo of a voice that called out to me long ago. It's been reverberating in the air, looking for me all this time. It's telling me to hang on.

Oscar falls to his knees and his grip loosens. I'm able to pull free and push him away. I watch as his eyes go glassy and his mouth hangs open. A small bit of saliva gathers on his lower lip and he falls forward, one hand still pressed to the wall. I take out the other syringe now, the one Jenner told me that he needed, and seeing as I've just gotten another taste of his psycho-killer side, I'm inclined to believe her. I give him a shot in the arm even though I'm sorely tempted to put it right into his eyeball.

He falls over.

I tell myself to breathe. To calm down. I need to get to

Thomas. I give Oscar a kick, and his limp body rocks forward before rolling over.

I grab the power cord and kick Oscar's gun along in front of me as I run down the hallway to the rec lounge. I'm so tired I can hardly keep moving. When I finally arrive, I find Thomas sitting up, Elmer cradled in his lap. Thomas's hand, sticky with blood, is pressed to Elmer's chest. I drop the battery and cord and skid on my knees across the smooth floor. Elmer is still alive. Barely.

He tries to speak to me. There's a question in his eyes, and I answer it. "You did good, soldier. Everything's going to be all right."

Seconds later he's gone. I take him from Thomas's lap, lay him on the floor, and cover his face with my jacket.

Thomas shouts, "I'm going to kill that crazy—"

"You can kill him when he wakes up."

"He's asleep somewhere?"

"He is now. I found that medicine locker and got a syringe full of sedatives from one of the nurses."

I leave out the rest of the details.

"Did you get your pill?"

"Yes."

"You're lying."

"How can you tell?"

"I can read people. It's what makes me a good hacker. I can put things together, figure out what people might do, how they might hide their secrets and where. More than anything else, I hack into people's heads."

"That right?"

"Yes. And that's why I know you're lying to me. You think it will somehow make me feel better, like it did for him." He points to Elmer's body. "Something terrible happened to you."

I look at Thomas. I am empty. The world is no place I want to be right now.

"Tell me," he says. "Trust me."

"She killed her."

"Wait, who killed who?"

"The woman I told you about, the one we heard on the radio. She's the one who's running this whole operation. She killed my mother, ran her down like a dog in the street, and now she's coming after me."

"What?"

He puts his hand on my cheek, and I let my face fall into his palm, let my head rest against his hand. I feel his hand start to shake and I lift my head up, but I can't quite bring myself to look at him. My nose starts to run. I wipe it on my sleeve and swallow the hot lump in my throat, trying to make words come out.

"She works for Erskine Claymore."

"Claymore? But that's . . . it doesn't make any sense. Why would he wipe out a project that he funded? And what's it got to do with you?"

"I don't know! Maybe he's just angry because I made him look bad." I look up and scream. "She killed my mother, Thomas!"

"Oh, Angel. Oh . . . I just . . . I wish . . ."

I hug my knees to my chest. I feel Thomas's hand on my head, but then it falls away and I look up. He's in bad shape.

"I'm so sorry," he says. "What can I do? What can I say? I'll do anything."

"I know nothing can bring my mother back, but I hate that woman. And I hate her most of all for making me remember how much I loved my mother and how she died in the same exact moment."

I don't tell him about Claymore being my father. I think I don't say anything because I don't want to believe it. I don't want to think that there's any of him running through me. For some reason that helps me stand and pull myself together.

"You're in pain," I say.

"A bit. I guess that painkiller is wearing off." He points to the cord I've dropped on the floor. "Did you find any power?"

"I did."

I hand him the cord attached to the battery, and as he plugs it into the laptop, I tell him how many people died to bring that to him. Not to make him feel guilty. But he should know.

"You better have the best hacking day of your life."

Hours pass. I don't know how many. I nod off at one point and awaken to the clacking of fingers on a keyboard. I feel a hand stroke my cheek, and I drift back asleep. I dream that I'm still in my hospital bed, and the bed is sitting in a field of white. Everything is white. The sky, the ground, all of it. I'm frightened by it. Terrified. How can there be such nothingness all around me? Suddenly Jori appears at my bedside. Her blonde hair is long, and she's wearing a red bow in it. I tell her she is beautiful, and she says, "Yes, I am." She's holding a crayon in her hand. She sits on the ground and starts to draw. "It's paper," she says, looking around at the whiteness. "Blank paper. Come and draw with me." I tell her I'm not a very good artist, but she says I can write a story instead. Any story I want. I tell her I don't like this white world. It's so empty. She smiles. "Not empty. Blank. Full of possibility." She holds the crayon up again and tells me, "I can fix your broken wing if you'd like."

I tell her no. No one can fix my wings for me.

She puts her finger to my lips and sings, "Be true. Be true. Be true."

It's all crazy Jori talk.

When I wake, I don't open my eyes for a long, blissful moment. I could be anywhere. I can tell I've slept a long time. My limbs are heavy.

"You shouldn't have let me sleep. Those guys could be here any second."

"Don't worry. I've kept our mercenary friends busy for the last few hours, setting off alarms all over the building."

I sit up and lean into him. He winces, and I pull back. "I'm sorry. I didn't mean to hurt you." I cross my arms over my chest. "It feels colder in here."

"Does it?"

When I can focus my eyes again, I look at Thomas. He doesn't look well. I lean over and put my hand to his forehead; he pulls away.

"You're burning up."

"Yeah," he says, still staring intently at the screen. "I'm sure that's all kinds of bad."

He stops and looks up at me. I can't read his expression. He could say anything right now and nothing would surprise me.

"I love you."

I was wrong about that.

"I assume you're trying to make me laugh. Which isn't very funny."

"No, I have a reason for saying it. A selfish one."

"You have a selfish reason for saying that you love me?"

"I have a weird bucket list, and that one was right at the very top. I never said it to anyone before, and I wanted to say it to someone before I died."

"You're not going to die."

"Odds are not looking good."

"I'm not talking about this anymore."

"Okay."

"What happened while I was asleep? Did you find anything useful?"

"Have a look."

He turns the laptop toward me, and suddenly I realize that he's leaning on me to keep from tipping over. "Maybe you should lie down."

"Okay."

He lets me lay him on the floor. I hover over him and stuff the blood-streaked pillow under his head. He looks sleepy now, like he's having trouble staying with me.

"So how did it feel?" I ask.

"How did what feel?"

"Saying 'I love you.'"

"Oh. It was fine. I mean, awkward, but it wasn't as scary as I thought it would be. Here, I'll say it again." He looks me in the eye and says softly, "I love you."

I look away. "Okay, now you're just showing off."

He smiles at me, but I know he's faking. He's in pain and it's getting harder and harder for him to cover it up. I reposition the pillow just as a way to divert attention from my own embarrassment.

"Well, I'm glad you said it," I say.

"Yeah? How come?"

"Because I doubt I'm going to hear anybody tell me that ever. Whether we die here or not."

"You really are brain-damaged, aren't you?"

"Hey!"

He sucks in a breath between his teeth and licks his lips before saying softly, "Let me explain something to you, Angel. There are two kinds of girls in this world: the kind that guys find it easy to say 'I love you' to and the kind guys find it nearly impossible to tell. You're the second kind of girl."

"I think I already knew that."

"You don't understand. See, when a guy is afraid to tell

a girl he loves her, it's because what he feels scares the crap out of him. Some girls inspire fear; others don't."

"I'm scary. Well, that's nice to hear."

"Angel, you're not getting what I'm saying. . . ."

I feel stung. I don't want to have this conversation anymore. When I look down at my arm for the tablet, I realize that Thomas must have removed it while I was sleeping. It's lying on the floor, and the screen is black.

He sees me searching and shakes his head.

"It's useless to us now. But that's okay, because I just discovered something about portable mainframes. They are easier to hack than you might think. Hacking into a system designed to hack into other systems—that's like a double negative. Anyway, we'll still be able to see them on the security cameras now."

"That's good news."

"Yes. But as you are no doubt aware by now, good news usually comes with bad news."

"What's the bad news?"

"There's only one place you're going to get another pill."

I close my eyes. "Of course."

"Getting up to the sixth floor is not going to be easy," he says.

I let out an unhappy little chuckle. The idea of carrying on against these odds is completely laughable. Getting up three floors took four lives and almost cost me mine. Now I'm going to go twice as far? By myself?

"Thomas. Come on. It's over, and we both know it. I'm not going to get that pill in time. And even if I did, I'm probably not going to get out of here alive."

"I don't want to hear that from you! You are going to get what you need. I'm going to help you. I don't care if you want to give up. You can tell yourself you're doing this for me now. Whatever it takes. Listen. There are seventy-two security cameras in this building. I'm going to scroll through all of them. You'll see four angles per screen. Tell me when you see something interesting; I'm going to have a little rest." He closes his eyes and lets his head tip back against the wall.

I watch as the images go by. Some cameras show static; some only display black. After twenty or so, I see the main lobby appear in the upper corner. My eyes pass over it for a moment, but then I think I catch sight of something moving on the floor.

"Wait."

Thomas takes his hand away from the keyboard.

"It's Steve!"

"Who?"

I'm still trying to get over being pissed that he tried to hand me over to the soldiers, but when I see what he's doing, it makes it a little easier to let that go. He's pulling his huge body across the floor, inch by inch, leaving a trail of blood; he's moving toward the security guard's desk.

"I think I know where he's going. There! See. On the wall. That's the panic button."

Thomas does a weak, sleepy cheer. "I hope whoever comes brings balloons and lots of painkillers."

In another shot I see more movement. There are four soldiers, rifles in hand, making their way toward a stairwell. The next camera angle shows them walking downstairs. They're one floor above the main lobby. I watch as they continue to descend.

"No," I say. "No, no, no."

"What?"

"Those soldiers are going to the lobby," I say. "They're heading straight for him."

We watch Steve's progress across the floor. He's using his elbows to move his big frame across the marble, brushing aside glass pellets as he goes. It's excruciating to see, like watching some inhumane sport.

Steve's got seconds before the soldiers come through the door. Slowly, slowly, he inches along, his hands trembling each time he pulls himself forward.

He just needs a little more time.

"Where's that radio?" I ask.

"What radio?"

"The one we took off the soldier who fell into the excavation pit."

"I don't know. It's still in the pack, I think."

I find it and turn it on.

"Hello? Hello? Can anyone hear me?"

The soldiers on the screen stop and look around.

"Seems you got their attention."

Steve is still three feet away from the button, and it looks like his strength is giving out.

"Angel," a voice coos over the radio. "I thought we agreed we weren't going to do long, drawn-out good-byes. It's uncomfortable for everyone. I'm still hoping we can just shoot you and be on our way."

"I remember," I say to her.

"Do you? Tut, tut, tut. That's got to be *very* hard on you."

As I take my thumb off the radio button, Thomas says, "Tell her you know what they did to you."

"What?"

"Tell her you know what Buckley did."

I look at the monitor. Steve's reached the guard's desk. He's stretching toward the wall, flailing blindly for the button. He pulls himself up, falls, pulls himself up again. The four soldiers are running down the stairs toward the lobby.

"Come on, come on," I say to the computer screen, trying to egg Steve on.

"Keep talking," Thomas says. His skin has gone gray, and his eyes are glassy. "Tell her you have what she wants."

"What do I have that she wants?"

"The data. Tell her you have all the research on the Velocius project. By now they've probably figured out that it's gone."

I press the radio button. "I have what you want."

I hear a hiss and a beep. Then Hodges's voice.

"I'm sure you don't have what I want, not unless you've got some size-six-and-a-half Jimmy Choos with you. No, be assured that the only thing I want right now is you, dead, preferably killed in a violent manner."

Thomas shakes his head. He's in agony. "Go on. Tell her you have the data 8-Bit took. About the Velocius project. Say it."

I echo Thomas even though I don't understand. There's no response for a long time. I wonder if the radio has cut out. After a minute, I repeat what I said. Suddenly we hear a humming sound, and all the lights come on. The brightness stings my eyes. I've never been so unhappy to see light. I feel like a hole has formed in my chest and the rest of me is falling into it.

"Guess they figured out where we are," Thomas says.

I look at the computer screen. Steve has collapsed onto the floor, his arm still extended toward the desk, inches from the button. A soldier with a smoking rifle is standing over him.

"That's really, really freaking discouraging," Thomas says.

I turn my radio off and take the computer from his lap.

"I'm going after her."

"No, you're not. Not yet, anyway. Not until you get that last pill. Then you can kill her all you want. Please, Angel. Please don't leave me right now. I mean . . . let's see what else we can find out first."

Thomas slumps down and takes his glasses off. They fall from his hand onto the floor. "I need to rest my eyes for a minute. You look."

I continue pressing the "enter" key, trawling through

the camera angles for something helpful. After a few screens, I see a man tied to a desk chair.

"Thomas."

He doesn't respond. I slap his cheeks lightly and he looks up, momentarily alert. I point to the man on the screen.

"8-Bit," he says, leaning forward, his eyes unfocused.

"Can we hear what they're saying?"

"No. The surveillance cameras are just images, no sound. Including that external feed I found earlier."

On the screen we see that 8-Bit's head is hanging limply to the side, and at first I think he's dead, but then he moves and starts to speak.

"Where is he?" I ask.

He reads the location of the security camera. "Director's office, first floor."

Suddenly Hodges comes into view. My whole body tenses up. We watch as she slowly approaches 8-Bit, sauntering toward him with her fists on her hips. 8-Bit smiles at her.

She tucks her hair behind her ear and then backhands him across the face.

He looks up and smiles at her again. Like he finds her amusing, or finds what he's doing to her amusing, even if she doesn't.

She motions for one of the soldiers to give her something. He does. A gun.

She puts the gun against his head. 8-Bit looks directly at the surveillance camera. His gaze is steady.

"I can't watch this," I say.

Thomas and I both hold our breath, unable to look. Unable to not look. Then Hodges leans in and gives 8-Bit a long, lingering kiss.

CHAPTER 33

"She must be messing with his head, right? That's the only explanation," I say.

Thomas says nothing. I can't tell if it's the pain of his injury or the image of 8-Bit and Hodges together that's got him looking so wrecked.

Then I lie. "We'll get to him in time. We'll get him out of there. Don't worry."

"It's not that . . . I—play it back again."

"What?"

"I need to see it one more time. It's a digital file. Just slide the little time stamp bar back so I can watch it again."

"Why?"

"Keep your eye on his left hand while he's talking to her."

I would have dismissed it as a nervous tic, but now that I focus on it, I can see that 8-Bit keeps making a fist and then extending his forefinger like he's pointing straight ahead as Hodges stands over him, shouting into his face. There does seem to be a pattern to it. We play it back two more times.

"What is that? Sign language?" I ask.

"Kind of. It's binary code. Ones and zeroes." He holds his finger up. "One is for 'on.'" He closes his hand into a fist. "Zero is for 'off.' It's the most basic language of all computers."

"So what did he say?"

Thomas stares a minute, thinking, and then types something into the computer.

"Go."

"What? I'm not leaving you here!"

"No, that's what he was trying to tell me. He knows I'm here, and he wants me to leave him behind."

We hear a crackling sound overhead, like a staticky radio. The PA system comes alive. There's a bit of feedback at first, and then someone blows into the microphone and clears his throat.

"Sarah."

It's Larry. He sounds exhausted, but I know it's him. My heart leaps at the familiar sound of his voice.

"I guess I should call you Angel now. . . . I just heard the good news from our very irate consultant that you're still alive and somewhere in the building. And that you have all our research data. I'm so proud. Although I wish you were miles from here, free from all of this. Angel, I need you to listen carefully. . . ."

I listen. Oh boy, do I listen.

"I couldn't let Dr. Buckley do it. I couldn't let him destroy you just because *she* wanted you to go away. I haven't got much time, and you need to know some things about yourself. Things that may save you. I'm going to say a word in a few moments, Angel. It will unlock abilities that you didn't even know you had. But you must be careful. Using these abilities builds you up but also tears you down."

And makes people want to kill me, apparently.

"The process you've undergone is different from the *tabula rasa* treatment. You've had your memories sealed off, yes, but the pills I gave you will bring them back. We made some additional changes to your brain chemistry. And for that I want to apologize. I can only say this: I lost my way. We had so many failures, and sometimes when you've been working on something for a long time, you get frustrated and you do things you know are wrong. You think you can sort it all out later. That your discovery will more than justify what you've done.

"She sent you to us, and you became our first success. At first we didn't know why. *I* didn't know why, but Buckley did. I found out much later, and when I discovered what they were planning to do to you during your last surgery, I couldn't let it happen."

In the background I can hear people shouting and banging on the door.

"They're coming for me now, Angel, and I can't hold

them off any longer, but I'm going to level the playing field a bit. I want to give you the chance to survive that you deserve. Do you know what a psychological trigger is? I created it so we could ease you into your new skills when the time was right. Once I say this word, you're going to be able to access all of your abilities. It may not seem like much at first, but what our Velocius project gave you is a huge advantage in battle."

Battle.

I never asked to be in the middle of a battle. How could Larry have done this to me?

My anger dissolves even before it's fully formed as I hear gunfire over the loudspeaker. I stand up, helpless. A door bangs against a wall. Then a small explosion. Larry is shouting. I can't hear what he's saying, something about my mother's name.

The PA goes dead.

Larry.

Larry, who saved me. I would have liked to meet him, just once.

I hear Hodges's voice overhead now. "Angel, you need to come upstairs and let us kill you. No more of this cat-and-mouse stuff, darling. I'll also be needing that data file. I know you have it. I'm sure your little *friend* must have given it to you, and yes, of course, I know about him now. I'm sure you don't want anything to happen to him. But I will tell you this, Angel: you're going to have his blood on your hands if you don't do exactly as I tell you."

I look at Thomas. He can't even keep his head up anymore.

"I know that if you don't get the pill you need to flush the plasticizer from your system, you're going to gum up your brain. And I have them all. Or rather, I did, before I popped them all with my heel. All except one. So here's the deal. You bring me the data files and I will give you the pill you need and a five-minute head start. That's my first, last, and best offer."

The PA cuts out. I feel numb, and lost, and confused. What am I going to do? I try to think if I have any cards left to play. I don't.

And then I remember one thing. One small, pathetic hope, probably no more effective than casting a message in a bottle. But it's all I have.

That external security feed. Someone has been watching all this time. What if it isn't Claymore who's been observing me? What if it's someone else? Who, I can't even imagine, but I'm about to place all my trust in that person. It's cruel to try to rouse Thomas, but I've got to. I shake him, gently at first, and then so hard that I'm afraid I'm breaking his neck. "Thomas, I need two things from you! I need you to turn on the feed!" I shout directly into his face. "That external feed you were telling me about before."

Slap!

"Thomas!"

I'm about to slap him again when he grabs my wrist and holds it. "What's the second thing?"

"I'm sorry. I thought I was losing you."

His eyes open to slits. "I'm still here. For you."

"What is it? What is the Velocius thing?"

"We should kiss now," he says.

"Thomas, please."

"No, I mean it. Circumstances require it. Plus, it's the second thing on my bucket list: Kiss a bald girl. You can't say no."

"Thomas, stop messing around."

"Kiss me and I'll tell you what Velocius is. What you are."

"That's not fair."

"I know. I'm a huge jerk."

I kiss him quickly.

"That didn't count."

I growl. "Thomas, we don't have time for this!"

"Kiss me like we have all the time in the world," he says lazily.

I lean toward him and kiss him again, softly this time.

"That's a little better, but not much. Do it again."

"I don't have much practice with kissing."

"That's okay. I have some theories about what makes a good kiss, if you think you'd like to hear them."

"No. I don't." I put my hand against the side of his face and close my eyes. I kiss him just like he asked me to, like we have all the time in the world. Like this is the last good thing that's ever going to happen to me. Because in all likelihood, it is.

CHAPTER 34

Before I've even pulled back from him, he begins moving his fingers across the keyboard, without opening his eyes.

"I know you're only kissing me for my mad hacking skills, but that's okay. I'll take it."

He opens a file, and I see that he's showing me a doctoral dissertation from MIT written by Joseph Purcell Wilson.

"I really don't have time to read an entire book right now."

"Too bad. It's interesting stuff." Thomas's voice is barely a whisper now. "See, when people are under extreme stress, they literally think faster. It's why people say they feel time slow down when they're in a car crash or a similar situation. It's not that time slows down; it's that your brain speeds up. Amazing, eh?"

"Yeah. I guess."

"It's not just that. You can push your body further, survive longer in extreme conditions—you can be stronger, better, faster—all because your life is threatened. The only trouble is, it only works when your life is truly in danger. The brain kinda knows if you're trying to trick it."

"Okay. And?"

Thomas tries to sit up, but I make him lie back down. He's exhausted but somehow frantic at the same time. His hands tremble as he points to the computer.

"Buckley wanted to figure out a way to replicate what the body does in those rare moments of extreme stress. But instead of the process being dependent on a near-death experience, what if you could choose to turn it on and off whenever you wanted? The government paid him a lot of money to do further research. That's what's in all the files I have on this flash drive. Top-secret research. That's the reason Dr. Wilson had his little accident and became Dr. Buckley. They knew that if Buckley could pull it off, figure out how to give soldiers this ability, it would change the world as much as the atom bomb did.

Imagine whole armies of guys with the ability to think at hyperspeed, all the time. That's what this whole place was devoted to doing: helping soldiers become better soldiers and then helping them recover from being good soldiers who couldn't hack remembering all the brutality they dished out. Velocius and *Tabula Rasa* were distinct research projects that got sort of murkily combined at some point. Probably once Buckley discovered that only certain kinds of people should be used as test subjects for the *tabula rasa* process, or else it didn't work so well. See Elmer, Sam, Jerry, and Sylvester for proof of that."

"Young people," I say.

"Yes, that's what they thought at first. That's why they started trawling juvenile detention centers for test subjects. They said it would help them reclaim their lives, rebuild their futures. It was the only way they could get anyone to allow them to experiment. Most of these kids were wards of the state anyway, and they had nowhere else to go except jail, so why not give them a chance to fix their lives, right? Makes perfect sense. And just about every kid they offered this opportunity to jumped at the chance."

"Maybe that's why they were always telling us how lucky we were, and that we should be grateful for this second chance we were being given."

Thomas squeezes his eyes shut for a moment, trying to gather the last of his strength.

"I'll jump right to it, Angel. They realized that the process could work, but only on an undamaged mind. That's why it worked on you."

"On me?"

"Buckley gave *you* this Velocius ability. The same stuff that happens during an 'I'm gonna die' adrenaline rush. But you can access it whenever you want."

"But I can't!"

Thomas must have missed when Larry explained the trigger mechanism.

"But what about Claymore?" I ask. "What's he got to do with any of it?"

"I don't know. He's been putting money into this kind of research for years. Claims he's just trying to push the frontiers of medicine, but who knows what he's really after."

Thomas fumbles toward his jacket pocket. He takes out the flash drive. "Take it and go. When you get far enough away, destroy it. This is scary." He opens his eyes and glares at me. "You're scary."

"That's right. I'm scary."

"So scary," he says, putting his fingers to my face. He grabs the front of my shirt and pulls himself up toward me. I lean closer and he kisses my bottom lip.

"That's my theory, by the way," he says.

"Your theory?"

"My kissing theory. You kiss one lip and then the other." He kisses my upper lip. "Then both at the same time."

He gives me the kind of kiss Sleeping Beauty would envy. Slow, sweet, full of promises that everything will be all right because he will make sure I get my happy ending. As I look into his eyes, I no longer feel not good enough. I know this has nothing to do with me, and everything to do with him. When someone looks at you like that, it elevates you.

For a moment anyway. I blink, and all the good feelings vanish.

"Take this and go," he tells me again.

I push the flash drive away. "After all this, you think I'm just going to run off? I'm not leaving you here so that woman can kill you."

"You have to go."

"Thomas, please."

"She won't kill me, Angel."

"Of course she will!"

"I opened the file."

"What file?"

"The 'In Case Something Happens to Me' file that 8-Bit left me. Didn't even have to hack it. Her name was the password."

"Who's name?"

"Evangeline."

"I don't understand. Why would—"

"Angel, she's my mother."

CHAPTER 35

The room spins. Thomas looks away from me, arms crossed over his chest. He's shaking from fever, and his teeth are chattering.

Three times I try to speak before I can finally manage to ask, "Why didn't you tell me?"

"I told you I was adopted. 8-Bit came and got me eight months ago. I've never met her, but some of the things he told me before this job . . . they make sense now."

"No," I say as I back away from him. "There's some mistake. That can't be right."

"Look for yourself!" He tips his head forward. "See that? My roots are showing. Red hair."

I run my hands through his hair.

"She probably dyes her hair. Maybe she's got gray hair," I say.

"Yeah. Maybe she dyes her hair the exact same color it

used to be when she was younger. Isn't that what women do?"

"A lot of people have red hair."

"Angel."

I stare at him, trying to make sense of this horrible fact, still hoping that he's wrong.

"That woman took every single thing in my life away from me."

"I know. I'd give anything for this to not be true. Anything."

Thomas can barely keep his eyes open now, and he's fallen to the side, cradling the computer, unable to push himself up again. I take him in my arms, propping his head up with the crook of my elbow.

"They were married. 8-Bit says he didn't know about me until after I'd been adopted. By then he had problems of his own to deal with. Like fleeing the country."

Thomas again holds the flash drive out for me.

"No." I push it back at him.

"Take it."

"No. Keep it, hide it. She wants it. You need something to bargain with."

"I don't need it to keep me alive. Nothing will keep me alive now."

"What does that mean?"

"I told you, I read a lot. I know a lot about things. Shock, for example. And sepsis . . . Angel, I want you to promise me something. . . ."

"No."

"You're going to take this drive and promise me that you won't give them the data. You can get the pill another way."

His voice is fading now.

"How? It's impossible!"

"Not for you, Angel." He raises his hand slowly and points toward the ceiling. "You've got wings."

I don't want to leave him, even though he's unconscious and there's nothing I can do to help him. Still, I'm torn.

Suddenly the choice is taken from me.

I hear an explosion from above. The soldiers are coming. It sounds like they're blasting through the rubble in the stairwell. This gives me minutes to get out. If I'm lucky.

I think of Hodges. Then my mother. I'm blind with rage and sorrow and fear. I want to run, and I want to curl into a ball and cry. I can't do both. I must choose.

Thomas is right.

I know what to do. There's only one way to escape now; I have to go back out into the storm. And then I have to go up.

Thomas's jacket is lying on the floor nearby. I take it, plus his hat and gloves. Then I sling the soldier's backpack over my shoulder. Just as I'm about to leave, I go back for two more things. I take the headlamp, because I might need it. Then I whisper in Thomas's ear, "I love you, too."

Because if I've ever said it to anyone before, I don't remember.

CHAPTER 36

Retracing my steps, I try to go back out the way we came in. I reach the conference room near where I first saw Sam and his fire ax. As I round the corner, Oscar is standing there, holding on to the wall like he's trying to steady himself on a boat.

Oh no!

This is just what I don't need. I make a fist. He looks at me and makes a fist, too. But then he starts punching himself in the side of the head. I should let him keep doing it, but instead I rush toward him and grab his arm.

"Everything hurts. Everything in here," he says, punching himself again.

Whatever was in that shot I gave him has turned him inside out. He looks at me like a scared little boy. I'm about to walk away, I really am. But I stop. Now, I understand what Thomas was trying to tell me and how I'm going to do it.

"Oscar, you want to make it all better? You need to help me, okay? You need to help me now, and we need to go because they're coming for us."

"Who?"

"The bad guys."

"I'm the bad guy."

What am I going to say to him? He is. I must have given him a dose of truth serum with that syringe.

I pull him by the arm. "Oscar, you remember the crane, right? The big one, like the kind they use to build sky-scrapers back home?"

I hear men shouting, their robot voices getting closer. Beams of light bounce up and down as they search for us.

"Oscar. Come on. We gotta get out of here."

We burst out the door into the white world beyond. I have no idea what time of day it is. The air is still achingly cold even though the storm has died down.

I point to the crane. "Can you operate that?"

He rocks his head from side to side, as if he's thinking about it. "I can figure it out."

That'll have to be good enough.

I know I've done this before. Many times. Unfortunately, I don't remember how.

There are rungs that run up the interior of the crane structure. I put my hand on one and pull myself up, hop-ing it will all come back to me. I make it about six feet off the ground before realizing that I don't need to climb. Unlike back in New York, when I was always sneaking around construction sites at night, we can use the operator's cab.

Oscar looks over the controls. The crane is gas-powered, and after a few attempts at firing up the ice-cold engine, he gets it working. He plays with the controls a little, testing them. The cab rises and falls a few feet. I hear the groan of the swing arm moving overhead. Then the entire crane rotates, and I watch the hook at the end of the arm move back and forth like a pendulum. The wind is still blowing hard, and it sends the hook around and around in a circle. I start to feel afraid. I *should* feel afraid. This is crazy.

The cab shudders up a few feet, and Oscar feels satisfied that he knows what he's doing. There's something in his face that's different.

"This is a nightmare."

From the way he says it, I'm not sure if he's asking or telling me.

"Yeah, it is, Oscar."

We rise. The cab slams to a jarring halt at the top. Oscar takes my hat and wraps it around his hand. He punches the window out. Between the two of us and a few good kicks, we're able to clear the frame of glass. I crawl out onto the swing arm.

The wind is much stronger up here. I look out at the long climb ahead, at the hook swinging back and forth, and I want to stop this madness. I used to like it up here. I know that. But not anymore.

The crane's arm lurches sickeningly to the right, and

I fall onto one of the struts, right onto my pubic bone. It hurts like crazy, but I hold on tightly with my arms and legs. I guess I should expect sudden shifts like that. The wind seems to be aiming for me.

"Make sure the arm is over the top of the roof," I shout to Oscar.

He moves some levers, and I feel the crane turn. First we go the wrong way and shudder to a stop. Then he swings the arm into position directly over the main building. He begins lowering the hook.

The fastest way to get to the end of the swing arm is to get on my belly and pull myself along. I reach and pull, reach and pull, my whole body burning from the pain as I fight against the gusts of wind. Thomas's jacket and his hat are making this attempt at bravery possible. Oh, and his gloves. Without them, my hands would be raw and bloody.

I wonder if they've found Thomas yet and if they've, if *she* . . . Would Hodges really do it? She had mercenaries cut down unarmed people, but would she order her own son shot and killed?

His mother is Hodges.

I don't care.

It changes nothing about the way I feel for him. The only reason I'm here, that I'm alive, is because of him. So I keep pulling myself along until I get to the end of the crane arm.

Oscar is supposed to lower the hook as far as he can, all the way onto the rooftop if he's able, but nothing's happening. I turn and look toward the cab, and I see that it's descending. This was not what we agreed to. I want to kick myself for trusting him, but I can't waste any thought or energy on it, because I have to focus. Now comes the worst part. I've got to get myself onto the cable and down to the hook at the end, which means swinging my body out over the edge and grabbing the cable with my legs. For a moment, I'll be holding on with just my legs. This is the most dangerous time. Because worse than the fear of falling is the desire to fall.

Every time I ever climbed, I felt it. And every time I felt it, I fought it.

I close my eyes, trying not to look down. I can hear it: my own fear disguised as longing. It's calling to me. *No more pain, no more loneliness, no more fear.*

Let go.

Let go.

Let go.

I need to think of something, of a point in the future, a place I want to get to. I need something that will overpower gravity's seduction.

I can't have my mother back. I may never be able to get all of my memories back. But there is something I do want very much.

I want to see Thomas again.

I believe he's still alive.

I believe that with all that I am, and I won't be able to see him again if I don't get through this.

The hook is still impossibly high above the roof, and Oscar has abandoned me. Even if I got myself all the way to the bottom and hung down as far as I could, I'd still have a long drop. I can't judge the distance from here, but it's at least one, if not two, broken ankles far.

I open my eyes to take one last look around. It's not a bad place to die—beautiful and ferocious and indifferent. It's like the city in a strange way. The lawn, covered in white, sparkles in the stray bits of light showing through the breaks in the storm clouds. So clean and new. Like a blank piece of paper.

The snow!

There must be six feet of it. It will soften my landing—maybe just enough to let me get up again after I jump.

I swing over the edge and nearly lose my balance.

And then . . . the flutter of a memory. Delicate as a feather. It's there. The answer is there. I hear Larry's voice in my head, and now I understand what he was trying to tell me.

Sometimes the answers to all our questions are staring us right in the face.

That whiteness, the blank white space that I see every time I remember my mother. It's not a cruel trick. It's the answer.

Blanca. My mother's name was Blanca.

Suddenly my mind is flooded with peace. Because that's what clarity is: peace. A slow-moving peace. Peace on my own terms. I wrap my legs around the cable and take my hands off the crane arm. I feel sure of myself. I will not let go. I will not listen to the whispers. They have always lied to me.

I tighten and release the cable between my thighs, moving in a controlled descent until I reach the hook; then I use my arms to lower myself the rest of the way. I know that I have to get as far down as I can so that the drop will be as short as possible.

I hang there, at the end of the hook, swinging back and forth in the wind.

It's time to let go.

With one hand I unzip my jacket, and as I release the hook, I pull the jacket wide, trying to catch the wind. After a split second of joyful flight, I land with a hard thud. My kneecaps hit like two overripe plums against concrete. Whatever breath I had in my body is squeezed out, and for a long moment I have a hard time inflating my lungs again. Finally, I gasp and roll over. I test my arms and legs, moving them back and forth to see if they're working.

When I rise a moment later, I realize I've made a snow angel.

I look down over the edge of the roof, searching for where Oscar went. Below me, near the base of the crane, the lights of a cement mixer turn on. *What is he doing?* Oscar backs up, stops, and then circles the truck around. Then he guns it. The mixer is barreling through the snow like a plow. He's heading directly for the crane, and as he gets closer to the base, I realize that he's not stopping.

I don't fully appreciate how wobbly I am until I try to run. Then those knees that cushioned my landing—they don't work so well. But I still feel that peace. This must be what the Velocius project has given me. It's both a small thing and a huge advantage. There is speed, yes, but more than this, there is a sense of calm to my thoughts, and every sense is heightened.

Fear? There is no fear whatsoever. It's all just questions and answers. What needs to be done and how I can do it.

I watch as Oscar collides with the crane's base at full speed. He doesn't hit it straight on, and this may have been his plan. One of the struts buckles and destabilizes the whole thing. I know where he wants it to land.

I keep watching the truck. Whether he meant to do it or not, the cement mixer sails past the base of the crane and into the construction pit. There is no way he can survive that fall, and no way I have time to stand around thinking about it, because the crane is now coming down.

Directly onto the roof.

CHAPTER 37

Time seems to elongate as the crane comes toward me. I run to the edge of the roof and look down on the glass walkway connecting the main part of the building with South Wing, just like the ice-covered bridge that Sam, Jerry, Sylvester, and I came across, except this one is finished. Or at least it has a roof on it.

It's maybe twenty feet down. I remove my backpack and feel around inside. I have three mines left. All this happens in a matter of seconds. I look over my shoulder. The crane has bent at the base and is now collapsing. The arm will hit the center of the roof, but the real damage will come when the ten-ton counterweight lands shortly after that.

I twist the mine, hold it for what seems like three seconds longer than I can possibly stand, and throw it at the metal roof of the walkway below. The falling crane is getting closer and closer. Part of me is screaming to jump, *now now now.*

That's not the part that's in control.

I force myself to wait, jumping only a fraction of a second after the mine detonates and creates a hole in the roof wide enough for me to pass through. I keep my arms at my sides, sinking through the air like a deep-sea diver as the crane crashes, dividing the roof in two. The counterweight plunges down, and then the swing arm crushes one edge of the building. The sound is horrendous—an exploding plane crashing into my skull. I can tell it's over only when I see papers and file folders flying out of the hole in the side of the building.

I cannot move at first. I've landed hard and hurt myself badly, though I'm not sure where exactly. I'm pretty sure "everywhere" would cover it. As I try to push myself up, I realize that my left arm doesn't work. I think I've dislocated my shoulder.

But I'm alive. Only because of what they did to me. Because I can refuse to give in to panic. Because I can find peace, clarity, and strength at the moment I need it most— now and possibly every moment from now on, assuming I have a "from now on." And for the first time, I do assume it. More importantly, I want a future.

Because I have work to do.

As distractions go, a tower crane falling onto a roof is very effective. I limp toward the main building, wondering how deep the crane has penetrated. It's probably too much to hope that Hodges is ground paste beneath a steel beam or pile of concrete, but I hope it anyway. Of course, I know that the crane also may have destroyed the medicine locker. But last chances, first chances, only chances—they're all the same. A chance is a chance.

I open the door between the walkway and the main building. There is snow blowing in through the roof, but oddly, sections of the floor are completely unscathed. I need to go up to the sixth floor, and I don't dwell on the insanity of rushing headlong into an unstable, half-crushed building toward a woman who's determined to kill me.

My shoulder is definitely dislocated. My arm hangs limp as dead meat on a hook. I don't care what I've done to my legs or my knees. They must work. I make this clear to them and ignore the pain crawling up my shins like fire.

The layout of this floor is no different than the others. There's a large, open center area where the partially destroyed nurses' station is located. Patient rooms ring the rest of the floor. Stairwells positioned at opposite ends. I'm sure the one at the far side has been obliterated by the crane, but the nearer stairwell looks passable.

I go up the stairs, heavily, noisily. It feels like I climb for an hour, but I'm sure it can't be that long. At the top, the sixth floor is open to the sky. The crane is wedged into the building, its giant metal carcass motionless.

I hear a grinding sound. Then moaning.

I find a soldier pinned on his side under a long piece of metal—one of the support struts of the crane. The riveted metal bar sticks through the soldier's abdomen, protruding through his back.

The soldier has very dark skin, dark eyes, a heavy set of brows grown nearly together. His gaze is focused but lacks emotion. Maybe he's assuming I'm going to kill him and he's simply waiting.

He has one of those voice translators. Maybe he doesn't speak English. I pick the translator up and speak through it.

"Where is she?"

The language that comes out is unrecognizable to me. I hold the translator against his face and wait for his response. He says nothing, just reaches out feebly with his fingers. I now see that his rifle is near my foot. I kick it across the floor and the handle falls off. A few other parts come away as well.

I don't understand how you can pay a man to be *this* loyal. His injury is grisly and he's in agony, and still he's trying to kill me?

I hold the translator up and tell him, "Your rifle is toast."

Who knows if *toast* will translate? I don't really care.

At first he pushes the translator away. He keeps saying the same thing. He looks at me, pleading. I put the translator to his mouth again.

"Please. Shoot me."

He says it over and over again. I now know how to say "Please shoot me" in whatever language he speaks.

He points down toward his boot, and I see that he has an ankle holster with a small handgun in it. I take the gun out. I will not shoot this man, even if it would be a mercy to do so. Of course, he doesn't know that.

I put the translator to my face and say, "Tell me where she is, and I'll shoot you."

It's strange to say this to him. It's like we have this situation all backward. I'm supposed to be threatening him to tell me something *or else* I'll shoot him.

"Director's office."

"Who's with her?" I ask.

"The computer hacker, four soldiers, the boy."

Thomas. This could complicate things.

I take the soldier's radio. I may need it. He closes his eyes and waits for me to pull the trigger. Instead, I walk back toward the stairwell with the gun in my hand. When I reach the stairs, I bend down and slide the gun across the floor. It skitters to a stop against his body and he puts his hand on it. I won't shoot him, but he can shoot himself if he wants.

As I descend the stairs, he does.

Although I'm still in pain, still limping, my head still filled with holes and my memories little more than shadows that lurk just beyond my grasp, I'm feeling lighter. And I know why.

I am extremely pissed off.

I don't know why, but I feel anger like I've never felt it before. It's pure, crystalline, freeing. It feels like power. How can anger feel so good? Because it's anger without hate. I don't understand it, but it's true.

I press the button on the radio as I walk up the third-floor hallway. I start with a simple pleasantry.

"Hello."

Hodges responds almost immediately.

"Not a very nice trick, trying to crush us all to death."

"I wish I could take credit, but I can't."

I continue walking down the hallway into the darkness. I know where I am. I don't need a map or even light. I count my strides the way I used to count the tiles on the floor.

"I don't want any more of this nonsense. Just get yourself down here so we can finish our transaction. I should warn you that I'm in a much less generous mood now that you tried to drop a crane on my head. That five-minute start is now off the table. I've sealed off all the exits. Bring me the data. Now."

"What's in it for me?"

"For you, not a thing, but I would be willing to save your friend's life."

"Your *son's* life, you mean."

There is a long pause before she answers, "Whether he's my son or not is none of your business."

"I don't have the data," I say calmly, like I'm telling her that we're out of the soup of the day. "Can't help you."

"Your friend here says you do."

I'm about to deny it again, but then I put my hand into the front pocket of my coveralls and sigh. That boy and his stupid sleight of hand.

"Turns out he's right."

"Hurry up, then. If you don't come promptly, I may send a few men to escort you here."

"I see. Well, in that event, I'd like to apologize," I say.

"Oh? Why?"

"I *am* coming to get you, but if I need to deal with your soldiers first, I might be a little late."

I throw the radio out the next open window and make my way downstairs to get some supplies.

CHAPTER 38

I'm now reaping the benefit of the excruciating boredom of my previous existence. All those days of counting floor tiles and doorknob handles, of scoping out which doors are the supply closets and where they keep the linens. I have the home-field advantage now. These soldiers—they're on *my* turf.

The building has again gone dark, but it doesn't matter. I know my way around. I put Thomas's headlamp on. Not to give me light—the battery has pretty much given out—but for luck, I guess.

I head for the east side of the floor, to the surgical procedure rooms. I stop at the medical supply closet and, as I reach for the doorknob, remember that I need to fix my dislocated shoulder first. It's a very painful prospect, but I get it done. Once, I was climbing a fence and fell off. I remember the nurse at the free clinic resetting my arm.

Then she winked at me. I think she knew who I was.

I find some useful things—a stethoscope, surgical tubing, tape—and use it all to fashion a slingshot. I'm ready now.

Speed is my advantage here—actually, not so much raw speed as uninterrupted motion. I don't need to stop and start and move with careful deliberation. I feel myself speeding up or the world around me slowing down. Whichever it is, my thoughts, my actions, are nothing but sure, swift movement. Hearing footsteps coming up the stairs, I pile as many blankets and pillows as possible on top of a gurney and push it in front of the stairwell door. Obviously, it won't stop the soldiers, but that's not what I'm trying to do. I just want to obscure their view when they open the fire door.

I hop up onto the nurses' station counter, the slingshot in my lap, and let my feet dangle like I'm sitting at the top of a steeple. The soldiers have reached the landing, and they're about to find out that body armor can sometimes be a disadvantage.

I hear the doorknob turning, and begin kneading a burn charge in my hand. Then I put it into the slingshot and release it. I hit the first soldier square in the chest as he pushes the pile of blankets out of the way. I shoot a second charge, this time onto his upper thigh. He looks down and realizes what is sticking to him. He tries to bat at the intense white flame, tries to push it off of him, but he knows it won't work. He steps backward, blocking the guy behind him, and drops his rifle. If he's quick enough, he may get his body armor off before the burn charge hits his skin, but he'll be preoccupied while I get rid of his companion.

I swing my legs over the counter and drop to the floor as the second soldier bursts into the room. I only have two mines left, and I already have plans for at least one. I need him to follow me. Predictably, he sprays the nurses' station with bullets, but I'm already almost around the corner.

He doesn't see me at first, so I stand up and wave. "Hey there!"

He aims, and I run down the hall into one of the procedure rooms, holding the door open with my foot a moment to make sure he knows where I've gone.

Seconds later he kicks the door in. Here I am, standing in the middle of the empty room, out in the open. I put my hands up. He's got me.

"Put your hands behind your head," he says.

I do.

I guess he speaks English, because he doesn't use his translator when he barks at me.

After two steps he lurches clumsily to the left. He shakes his head. He looks dizzy. I tilt my head, like I'm concerned, wondering if he needs help. He keeps walking, but his body is growing heavier with each step.

He hasn't noticed, but I haven't drawn a single breath since we entered the room. I don't need to breathe. It's like I've put everything on pause except my heart. I let that beat. Once. Twice. Enough to keep my blood moving, but only just.

He sways. His eyelids flutter. Down he goes.

I stand over him and think about taking his rifle. I've done perfectly well without using a gun so far, but I decide to take it anyway. It's nice to have options.

Before I leave, I close the nozzles on the tall canisters of anesthetic gas. I don't take a breath until I'm well clear of the area.

If what that dying soldier on the sixth floor told me is true, then Hodges is down to two soldiers. 8-Bit's role in all this is still unclear. I don't know if he's helping Hodges or not, but he might be.

Back in the hallway, I hear the sound of men shouting. I stay low to the floor, well below the glass partitions that divide the hallway from the rec lounge. I know this lounge faces south. That's where I want to be. At the end of this hallway is another medical supply closet. My last burn charge takes care of the lock. Inside I find several oxygen canisters. I tip them over and push them into the hallway one by one with my foot. They roll noisily along the floor, bumping to a stop against the wall near the rec lounge.

I need to get to that set of outer windows. The door to the lounge is locked. It always is. The nurses would unlock it, let us in, and then lock it again when we left. But this will not be a problem, especially since the wall is made of glass and I have a rifle.

I can see the outer windows are cracked but still intact.

I fire at the wall. It shatters. I fire again, taking out the windows. The men are coming. I drop the rifle, get a running start, and dive through the broken glass wall into the lounge. I roll and stand up.

Just as the soldiers arrive, I throw one of my two remaining mines back into the hallway, toward the oxygen canisters. The soldiers raise their rifles to shoot me. I clear my throat and point. Then I watch their faces as they look down and realize that they can either kill me or save themselves.

Climbing out the window, I balance momentarily on the narrow ledge, then let go and drop. I have no idea what they ultimately decide. All I hear is a really big boom.

CHAPTER 39

I slip eight or ten feet before reaching for the trellis on the side of the building, screaming as I get a handhold. I never realized that these pretty, fluttering pieces of foil are razor sharp. As I cling to the trellis, they spin in the wind like a thousand coppery buzz saws. They easily cut through the fabric of my pants, and the palms of my hands are slashed where I'm trying to hold on.

I need to load the slingshot, which means letting go for a moment and leaning into the rotating razor blades to keep myself from falling. Trying to get the last mine out of my pocket, I lean too close to the wall and get a nick on the end of my nose and one on my cheek.

I can see the helicopter about fifty yards away. The helipad is free of snow. I guess it must be heated.

The shot I need to make is a difficult and long one. If I arc it up into the air, the mine may land near enough to the helicopter that the magnetic force will pull it the rest of the way. I'll have to shoot the mine immediately after I twist it; otherwise, it will detonate in midair. I have no illusions. This has little chance of working, but I don't want Hodges getting away before I have a chance to kill her.

As I'm setting up the shot, I realize that there's no way I'll be able to hang on and pull the slingshot back far enough to reach the helipad. I'll have to let go in order to get a shot off. And once I do, I won't be able to grab back on again. This shot will be a one-way trip.

I can't waste any more time thinking. Leaning back against the trellis, I feel the foil cut into my back and legs in a dozen places, but I ignore the pain. I twist the mine and quickly load it into the slingshot. Just as I'm about to release the trellis, I hear a distant shot, then feel something hit me in the side. I drop the slingshot, and the mine zooms toward the metal trellis and clings there.

My last thought as I watch the ground speeding toward me is that I need to flip if I can. The mine explodes. I feel bits of metal bite into me. I force my head down and feel myself somersaulting in the air. If I land flat on my back, I may survive this fall.

That's assuming I'm not already dead by the time I hit the ground.

I won't let myself lose consciousness. I keep my body limp as they drag me up the steps and back into the lobby. I'm fairly sure my right lung has collapsed. It just feels not there, not useful.

They say that your whole life flashes before your eyes

when you're dying, but that's not happening for me. Maybe it's because I don't have much to remember, or maybe it's because I won't let myself remember anything. Remembering won't do me any good right now. Thinking about the here and now will.

I've slowed my heart rate down, and though I know I could speed it back up again, bleed out, and leave this world behind, I won't.

I am way, way too angry to die.

The soldiers drag me across the debris field of the lobby, and I open my eyes just enough to figure out where they're taking me—the Director's office.

They lay me on the floor at Hodges's feet like a prize, right next to the desk chair where 8-Bit is tied up. I keep my eyes slightly open, with just a sliver of iris showing. I figure that makes me look a little more dead.

8-Bit's lower lip looks like a cooked sausage that's burst out of its casing. There is dried blood caked in his nostrils. He's tall like his son, mostly legs. His hair is gray at the temples, and his eyes are the same black-brown as Thomas's.

"Is she dead?" Hodges asks.

"Yes," a mechanical voice responds.

"Are you sure? She faked it before. Check her carefully."

The soldier puts his hand over my mouth and pinches my nose shut, closing off my air for almost a minute. I do not react. This seems to satisfy her.

"How did it happen?"

"She was climbing up the side of the building when we shot her. She fell about forty feet."

Hodges bursts out laughing. "The angel has fallen. I love it!" She abruptly stops celebrating. "Can you survive a forty-foot fall?"

"How would I know?" 8-Bit says. "Ask a member of the medical staff. Oh wait, you can't. *Because you shot them all.*"

Hodges won't come near me. She has one of the soldiers unzip the coat I'm wearing, Thomas's coat. He rolls me back and forth as he rifles through all my pockets. As I rock to one side, I see Thomas lying on the couch next to me. His skin and hair are damp with sweat, and he's taking rapid, shallow breaths, but he's still alive.

I feel the soldier's hand probe the inner coat pocket. He removes the flash drive. "Found it."

Hodges is still wearing her coat, but she's shivering. Her hair is looking a little greasy and disheveled. Obviously, she hadn't planned on staying this long. She sits down heavily on the chaise next to Dr. Buckley's desk. She's holding something in her lap. Something heavy and sparkly. It's a crystal candy dish just like the one I saw in the South Wing reception area, with an *E.C.* etched into it.

She plunks it down so hard on the desk, I think she must have cracked it.

"Aw, what's the matter, Ev?" 8-Bit says. "You seem disappointed. This is the girl you've been hunting, and now she's been killed in cold blood, at your direction. I'd think this would be such a proud moment for you."

"Shut up, David. She deserved what she got."

8-Bit looks down at me and sighs. "Somehow I doubt that."

Hodges walks over to the soldier holding the flash drive. "Give me that." She snatches it away from him before he has a chance to comply with her order.

"I hope you got your money's worth out of this whole operation," 8-Bit says.

"I did." Hodges closes her fingers around the flash drive. "And I'll be able to tell Mr. Claymore that despite the unfortunate events at the Center, we were able to recover Wilson's research data."

"I wouldn't be so sure about that."

"What's that supposed to mean?"

"Thomas is a smart kid. I'm sure he encrypted those files. And he's in no condition to tell us what the password is right now."

Hodges walks toward the couch and looks down at Thomas. She crosses her arms, then turns around suddenly. "So you'll hack it for me."

"No, I won't."

She walks slowly up to 8-Bit and gets right into his face. "Yes. You. Will."

"Sorry. Unlike your mercenaries here, I'm not going to accommodate your every ruthless whim. Guess you hired the wrong guy."

"Believe me, had I known I was hiring you, I would've saved myself the trouble and shot you instead."

8–Bit gives a tired, bitter laugh. Hodges begins spinning her bracelets and pacing.

"You know, David, I have to admit I'm impressed. You were always brilliant. But you were also sloppy—lazy even. Without an ounce of cunning. Yet here you've managed to engineer quite the opportunity to settle a grudge. I didn't think you had it in you."

"Well, you were my wife. And when I got caught, you let me rot in a foreign jail cell. Then, after telling me that I had a son, you didn't let me see him. Not to mention that whole *giving him up for adoption after having me declared legally dead* thing. I guess all I really needed was the proper motivation."

Hodges flicks her hand toward Thomas. Her bracelets jingle as they collect on her wrist. "Was that the point of bringing him along? You thought I'd take one look at him and melt?"

"I just thought you should see him."

Hodges slaps 8–Bit across the face. "It was a mean thing to do."

"I guess we're even then."

"We're far from even. I still haven't decided what *even* is going to mean for you."

Thomas moans and twitches. I see his fingers curl and uncurl, like he's trying to grab for something. It's all I can do to not reach up and touch his hand so he knows I'm still alive.

8–Bit says, "Look, do whatever you want with me, but let Thomas go. You did it once before."

Hodges paces faster now. A few times she steals glances at Thomas. She stops suddenly and stands over me, then pushes my head back and forth with her high heel. I keep my neck loose to make my "death" more convincing. This is the chance I've been hoping for. I let my hand fall to the floor and keep my forefinger extended.

One.

On.

I'm alive.

I hope 8-Bit sees. I hope he understands. I just need more time to think.

A mercenary comes in and Hodges is momentarily distracted by something he's saying, something about a helicopter being deiced and not yet ready to go. She dismisses him, walks back across the room, and then sits down on Buckley's desk.

8-Bit clears his throat. "What's going on?"

"Nothing that concerns you."

I feel him press his foot to my hand, and I push back slightly, hoping he'll feel that I'm resisting. That I haven't given up yet.

"You made a mistake, you know," 8-Bit says. "A big one."

"No, I didn't."

"Sorry, but this raid sort of proves that you did. I'm sure Erskine Claymore prefers to have his employees deal with messy problems discreetly. Not with guns and rockets and high body counts. So, come on. I can help you identify your error. I'm good at finding bugs and glitches. I'll even waive my usual consultation fee."

"No, thanks."

He gestures toward me with his head. "All this just to kill one girl? It shouldn't have been necessary. Not unless . . ."

Hodges glares at him. I can tell she doesn't want to give him the satisfaction of asking what he means.

"Not unless you needed to cover something up. Yes, that's it. You couldn't just bust in here and kill the girl. That would've raised a lot of questions. No, you had to wipe out everything and everyone to make it look like maybe some foreign country had done it. But what would you be hiding? And from whom?"

Hodges looks at 8-Bit, her face like stone. After a moment, she chisels out a smile.

"You don't want to tell me, Ev? That's fine. I understand. I'll tell you instead. I've read all the research files on Velocius. I've read all your email exchanges, all the texts you've sent. Everything. I might as well have hacked into your soul these last few months."

"Then you'd already know why she had to die."

"Because she's Erskine Claymore's daughter? Yeah, I figured that one out already. So what?"

"She's not Erskine Claymore's daughter. She's—"

Hodges clenches her jaw. She and 8-Bit stare at each other and then his expression begins to change. He nods in recognition.

"*Virgil*. She's Virgil's daughter, isn't she? Virgil, who's now your *fiancé*. Congratulations, by the way. I saw the announcement in the *Times* a while back. Hope you'll keep me in mind if you need someone to walk you down the aisle."

I feel 8-Bit flick his boot against my fingers again. Hodges is seething now. She walks past and kicks my hand out of her way.

"I was surprised to learn about the engagement, of course," 8-Bit says. "Not upset, mind you, just surprised. I mean, how did you get close to Virgil Claymore in the first place? He's got ALS—Lou Gehrig's disease, or whatever. He's been homebound for years. I didn't think he could even communicate."

Hodges walks up to one of the soldiers and adjusts her hair in the reflection of the soldier's goggles. Then she turns around and smirks.

"The translator," 8-Bit says. "I read about that in one of your project files."

"Claymore Industries adapted the military technology in this," Hodges says, pointing to the mouthpiece covering the lower half of the soldier's face. "They developed a device that could translate Virgil's brain wave patterns into spoken words. Claymore could have made millions off it if he'd wanted to, but he decided to keep it in the family."

"An ever-shrinking family. There aren't many members of the Claymore clan left, are there?"

Hodges tenses and turns her head away to look toward the office door. She seems eager get going, but things aren't moving fast enough. Or maybe something's wrong.

"Let's see if I remember my Claymore family history. It's a sad story about very rich and powerful people. There were four children originally, right? The oldest son died in a boating accident. The older daughter was strangled by her boyfriend, and the younger one pulled into the family garage with the engine running and fell asleep at the wheel. . . . That left Virgil, the sole surviving Claymore heir. Feel free to jump in and correct me if I get the facts wrong, Ev. I'm sure you know the Claymores intimately at this point."

Hodges doesn't look at 8-Bit directly as he speaks. She licks her dry lips and flicks a piece of hair away from her face.

"Let me guess," 8-Bit says, "Charming Southern girl that you are, you manage to get yourself hired by Claymore Senior, and then you what? Sit for hours patiently talking to Virgil? That doesn't sound like your cup of tea. There had to be something in it for you."

Hodges shrugs and smiles. "Claymore Senior was obsessed with his legacy, and his only son couldn't stand him. I saw an opportunity to be . . . *helpful.*"

"Yes, I imagine you did. If you could broker peace between father and son, Claymore Senior would be forever indebted to you."

"Yes."

"Did it work?"

"Not really. Virgil knew how his father had made his money over the years. He thought the entire Claymore family was toxic. If he hadn't been trapped by his condition, he would've walked away from all the money long ago. Stupid, really."

"I can't imagine how long it must have taken for Virgil to decide *you* were a reliable confidante."

"Two years."

"Ouch, Ev. That had to be excruciating for you. I guess it paid off, though. Virgil finally told you all his secrets. He told you he had a daughter."

Hodges leans against the desk and plays with the crystal bowl, swirling the pill inside it around like a marble. "When Virgil found out his hired help had gotten herself pregnant, he sent her away. He thought his family was cursed, or something. He wanted the maid and the child far away from the Claymores, especially his father. So Virgil set up a small trust fund thinking it was only temporary. His condition was deteriorating. The doctors told him he had a year to live at most—more likely a matter of months. He made a will leaving everything he had to the maid and her brat but then . . ."

"Then he didn't die."

"That's right. He didn't die. Because Claymore Senior did everything he could to keep his son alive. He spent millions on medical research and invested in every conceivable experimental procedure, no matter how far out it was on the fringes of science . . ."

"Or how ethically questionable it was," 8-Bit says.

"Virgil was at his father's mercy, helpless, with no way to reach out to what's-her-name—*Blanca*. Not until I came along. I was the friend he could trust to find his lost love and the daughter he'd never known."

She flicks her hand toward me.

"So you pretended to be the kind emissary, interested only in reuniting them all?"

"Something like that."

"Was that before or after you realized what a potentially lucrative position you were in? Trusted employee of a very rich man whose only heir is probably going to die young. Just imagine the possibilities."

"I did imagine them."

"But a lost love and newly discovered granddaughter would ruin everything for you, wouldn't it?"

Hodges tips her head. She picks up the crystal bowl again and looks at the ceiling light through it. After a moment she says, "I was thoughtfully saving everyone a lot of trouble. Every king wants an heir, but that doesn't mean he wants it to be the maid's daughter."

The maid.

My mother.

And now—now I can see my mother's beautiful face.

The blank white emptiness is gone. I see her laughing brown eyes. I remember the way she looked at me. So proud. So proud that I was her Angel.

The anger boils up inside me. I can hardly hold it back, but somehow I do. I do it for my mother.

"Why didn't you just kill the girl?" 8-Bit asks. "That would have been the simplest solution. I mean, I don't know for sure, of course, but I assume Blanca Ramos's *accidental* death was no accident. Why give the girl a pardon instead of executing her, too?"

Hodges walks to the door and looks toward the lobby, checking her watch.

"Oh, don't tell me, Ev," 8-bit says and laughs. "It couldn't be *that*."

She whips around. "Couldn't be what?"

"Were you . . . ? Did you actually feel the tiniest bit of *remorse*? You kill the love of your *fiancé*'s life, but can't bring yourself to kill his kid? I don't know, Ev. Sounds to me like your conscience was giving you trouble."

She walks toward 8-Bit and leans over his chair, her voice low. Almost sultry. "I didn't kill the girl because it wasn't *necessary*."

"Why?"

"Because she didn't know Virgil was her father."

Hodges pushes back, hops onto the desk, and crosses her legs. "When I met with Blanca, she confessed to me that she'd never told the girl who her father was. She thought it was easier that way. Better her daughter know nothing than know the painful truth." Hodges rolls her eyes. "She *really* shouldn't have told me that."

"Once Blanca was gone, and with no other family, the girl disappeared into the foster care system?"

"Yes." Hodges blows me a kiss. "Goodbye, *Sarah*! Off you go, into the arms of an overburdened city bureaucracy! Have a statistically unlikely nice life!"

8-Bit nods toward me. "But she went after Claymore back in New York. How did she figure out the connection?"

"I don't know." Hodges's upper lip curls in disgust. "Here I am looking at wedding venues and suddenly I find out someone's sabotaging all of Mr. Claymore's projects. A teenage girl, the rumors said. The media turned her into a sensation. And I knew! I just *knew*. I'd made a mis—"

She looks over at 8-Bit, probably hating that she has to admit he was right. She *had* made a mistake. She killed my mother, but she let me live.

"I tried to find this girl everyone was talking about. The girl with the wings on her back. I offered up reward money—a lot of it—for information about who was vandalizing Mr. Claymore's building sites. And if I'd been able to get my hands on her before the police did, all this could have been avoided. But she got caught. And then she told the cops who she thought her father was. They didn't know what to do with the information, so they called me to see if there was any merit to her claim."

"That's when Virgil found out she was alive?"

"He overheard me talking on the phone to the police about her. I had to think fast. I told him that I'd tried to spare him the pain of the truth. I told him that I'd discovered Blanca was dead and the girl was a mess—a common criminal. I told him that maybe she deserved a fresh chance, free of the Claymore money, the Claymore 'curse.' Just like he'd wanted all along. So Virgil agreed to send her here, to the Center. It was the perfect solution for everyone."

"Well, mostly for you," 8-Bit says. "But now I understand how it all fits together. Wilson was *this* close to a breakthrough with the Velocius project at the same moment that the government was *this* close to pulling the plug."

Hodges runs her fingertips along 8-Bit's swollen cheek. He jerks his head away.

"Couldn't have asked for a more perfect solution," she says. "Once Wilson's research was deemed a failure, the military would walk away, and without bothersome ethical restraints and government oversight, he could move forward. Which he did."

"And when Wilson finally succeeded," 8-Bit says, "all the proprietary research that the military had largely paid for would land in the lap of Claymore Industries. They'd be free to develop the technology for the private sector."

"Claymore Industries already had paying customers lined up for Velocius. Who wouldn't want to be able to think ten times faster? What CEO wouldn't want a crack at that?"

8-Bit looks down at me and then over at Thomas, who is now moaning like he's struggling to speak.

"Seriously gotta hand it to you, Ev. Letting Wilson use the girl was a brilliant move."

"Thank you," Hodges says. "I know that's got to be hard for you to admit."

"Although . . ."

"Although *what*?"

"You give the girl to Wilson to have her mind wiped, which he does, but then he also uses her for the Velocius project. Not part of the deal, I'm sure. Worse still, she turns out to be the project's first success. That's got to grate on your nerves, huh?"

Hodges gives a huff of irritation.

"Wilson kept putting me off, saying he wanted to study her further. But I told him that either she died or his career did. Simple as that. She was supposed to have a little accident during surgery. If he'd done what I *told* him to do, this whole rather expensive raid wouldn't have been necessary."

"Wilson reneged on your agreement then?"

"No. He knew what I was about to call down on this place if he didn't get rid of the girl."

"If he was going along with your demands, how did the girl escape?"

"Wilson's assistant ruined"—she pounds on the desk with each word now—"the . . . whole . . . thing!"

Larry!

My body wants to explode toward her like a bomb, but it's not time. Not yet.

8-Bit sighs dramatically, but Hodges refuses to look at him. She squeezes her eyes shut like she's trying to push all these ugly thoughts out of her mind.

"It was a good plan. It really was. If my hands weren't tied to this chair right now, I might even clap for you. Getting rid of the girl, keeping all the data on a multibillion-dollar research project, and marrying into the Claymore billions? Great idea. Too bad it didn't work."

"Who says it didn't work?"

Hodges walks past me. I can hear the rustle of her skirt, the tinkle of her bracelets. She digs through her purse and pulls out a hairbrush.

"Got a date?" 8-Bit asks.

"I do, actually. I need to freshen up a bit before my flight. And, David, let there be no mistake. This will be goodbye for us."

"I guess we'll never get our issues settled then, will we?"

She sits down on his lap and plays with the collar of his shirt for a moment. "Oh, we will. We will, David." She kisses him on the cheek and then, without looking up, says, "Shoot him, please. Right about here." She touches his chest, just below his heart, and then leaps off his lap.

The soldier raises his rifle to comply. Just as he fires, Thomas uses his last ounce of strength to throw himself off the couch. In the process, he knocks the candy dish into the air. I watch the arc of the pill as it flies out of the dish.

I roll and turn just in time to catch the pill in my mouth. Hodges is too distracted to notice. She glances at Thomas, who is now lying on the floor next to me, then turns her back on us both as she kneels in front of 8-Bit.

"I'm sure you understand why I had to do this. I need to make a fresh start. I need to let go and erase the past. And that means I need to erase you, David."

A storm gathers on Hodges's face at the sudden sound of helicopters approaching, a sound she's clearly not expecting.

8-Bit has slumped forward, gasping. He looks up. "Problem, Ev?"

"Give me some binoculars," she says to the soldier who's just shot 8-Bit. She leaves briefly and then hurries back into the room. "No problem, darling. That helicopter has *E.C.* on it."

She turns away from 8-Bit as if she's already forgotten he's there and stands in the center of the room for a moment, spinning the bracelets on her wrist round and round. As the sound of the helicopter grows louder, a robotic voice prompts her. "What do you want us to do with the boy?"

She doesn't answer.

"Ma'am?"

She exhales in annoyance and closes her eyes. She waves her hand blindly toward the floor. "Give me a minute. . . ."

She kneels beside Thomas, almost as if her legs have given out, and runs her fingers roughly through his hair. I know she must see the red at the roots. Her voice betrays a twinge of feeling, of softness, even as she says in exasperation, "We'll have to take him with us. I need the password for the data files. After that, who knows? Maybe I'll take him under my wing."

And there is my limit. Right there.

I spring up and crouch over Thomas, my hands on his chest. I say calmly, almost in a whisper, "Do *not* touch him."

Hodges falls back clumsily, and one of her high heels snaps off. She looks astonished, in shock, like she's seen the dead rise.

8-Bit manages one last smile before his head droops and his chin comes to rest on his chest.

Hodges screams, her voice high and shrill. "What are you waiting for? Shoot her! Kill her! That's what we've been trying to do for the past two days!"

But they don't shoot me. One of the soldiers puts his

hand to his ear, as if he's listening to something inside his helmet.

She runs up to each of the soldiers in turn, trying to pull the rifles out of their hands. "What are you doing? I've paid a lot of money for you to do exactly what I tell you to do!"

The lead soldier pushes her back so hard she trips and falls. He turns his weapon on her. She is furious and bewildered. The soldier adjusts something on his translator and begins to speak.

The robotic voice addresses Hodges. The words come slowly, haltingly. "The good thing about mercenaries is that they can be bought. Unfortunately, the bad thing about mercenaries is also that they can be bought."

The helicopter is landing outside. The sound pumps through the windowless lobby. I feel the air pulsing against my eardrums. Hodges looks toward the office door, her face teetering between fury and terror.

She stands and smoothes her hair and rumpled clothing. "Who are you? Why are you talking to me like this?"

"Don't you recognize my voice?"

"Of course not! You all sound exactly alike!"

"It's Virgil."

"Virgil? That can't be. . . ."

"This man with the gun has just shifted to my employ. I've been watching the girl's progress for months. The security feed went dead, but came back on again a few hours ago. I saw everything."

She's shaking her head so fast her red hair flies out to the sides like flames. "We turned that feed off."

"He turned it back on," I say. "Your son did. He saved me."

The robot voice addresses me. "Sarah, there's so much to this story that I don't understand. I'd like you to tell it to me."

"Angel. I go by Angel."

I stare out the door, past the wreckage of the lobby, and look at the helicopter. I watch the blades spinning. I can see it move, and wonder how it will ever lift off with its rotor going round that slowly.

I don't see Hodges anywhere. I try to ask a question. *Where is she? Is she gone?* I want to make sure she can't get to me or to Thomas. But I can't get the words out. My mouth and brain are out of sync.

"My men here will escort her from the building."

Suddenly there are more men in the room. They must have been on the helicopter. Just like that, Hodges is in handcuffs, and they are taking her away.

Is everything going to be okay? Is that what's happening? Is this real?

I unclench my fists and put one hand to my lower back. All this time I've managed to slow the bleeding, but I can't hold it back anymore. I can't hold back anything. My legs give out and I'm kneeling.

"Do you need help?" Virgil asks.

"No."

Why did I say that? It's a habit. I do need help. I should admit that. I should shout it. *Help me. Someone please help me.* This time when I try to speak, nothing comes out.

In the slow-motion rush of activity around me, I now hear what I know are words, but they are just sounds disconnected from any meaning. I want to ask what's wrong with the soldier's translation machine. I can't understand what he's asking me. Something about New York City.

I think he said the word *home*.

Time seems to rush, stop, and then hurry again. Paramedics appear. I turn my head and see them working on Thomas. He's completely unresponsive. I use the last of my strength, the whole of my broken soul, and crawl toward him. I want to tell him to hold on.

I put my hand out to touch his hair, but I collapse before I reach him. I try to say his name, but I can't. It's too late to speak. I've run out of time. Oblivion has come for me at last, but I won't let it take me without a fight.

CHAPTER 40

I can't shake the habit of looking down and counting the tiles. These sidewalks near the park are full of them. Thousands of little granite hexagons.

A cab whizzes by, blaring its horn. I turn and watch it go. Slow and plodding as I am, I'm quickly overtaken by people hurrying home at the end of the workday.

The city carries on as fast as ever. I just can't keep up anymore.

I hate walking with a cane, but still can't manage without one. Every week I get a little stronger, and my physical therapist says that if I keep up with my therapy, I'll be all better before I know it. But that's not how I feel. Every tap of my cane reminds me my life is frustratingly slow. And the being "all better" part? I'm not sure if that's ever going to be possible.

Things are coming back to me, yes, but not as much or

as fast as I'd hoped. And while I'm grateful for what I do remember, I wish I could have more than my memories. And more than my mother's grave. I go there about once a week and shell *pepitas*. Some I eat; the rest I leave for the birds.

As for Thomas . . . I have nothing. Nothing but memories of him, and that's not enough. Not enough by a long shot. I knew him three days. That's all. But I think I've fallen in love with him since then.

Is it crazy to fall in love with a memory? Probably. I wish I could ask Thomas about it, because I'm sure he'd have an opinion.

Sure, it's a bit crazy, Angel. Not that I don't understand. I am pretty amazing.

I have conversations with him in my head so we can finish talking about all the things we didn't have time to discuss back at the hospital. Back when everyone was trying to kill me. And we always laugh. I think if we'd had the chance, we would have laughed together a lot.

"Remember that time you told me you loved me because you thought you were dying?"

Yeah. That was horrifically embarrassing, wasn't it?

"I told you the same thing."

It doesn't count when the person you say it to is unconscious, Angel.

"Yeah, I know. You were way braver than me."

I reach the end of the block and pivot with my cane to face the steps of the cathedral. There are a lot more to climb than these, I know. The elevator isn't working yet. That keeps most of the tourists away. It's a long walk to the top of the steeple, more than five hundred steps. My physical therapist would probably think I'm working too hard. Or maybe not hard enough. They're tough to please, those physical therapists.

I hang the crook of my cane over my forearm and grab the railing. The pain in my spine will get worse with every step, and by the time I get to the top, I won't be able to think of anything else. This is probably not the best way of dealing with my grief over losing Thomas, but I've never been able to figure out what you're supposed to do. The only solution I've ever had is to go up. Somehow up is closer to wherever they've gone—those people you've loved and lost.

I have to stop a few times and rest, but finally I push the door open to the observation deck and look at my watch. Thirty-one minutes is a new best time, but it's cost me. I'm exhausted. The twinges of pain in my back have now fused together to become one continuous, unyielding ache.

I find a bench and sit down. It's always colder up here than I'm expecting, but I'll stay until closing time. I have nowhere else to go. Well, nowhere else I want to go. Being home again hasn't been easy. I can't go back to living my old life, and inventing a new one means letting go of some things and holding on to others. That hasn't worked too well so far. I still can't seem to figure out the right combination to get me back to feeling normal, so I guess I've kind of stopped trying.

I watch a mom and two kids who both look thoroughly unimpressed with the view as they hustle toward the door. There's also a guy leaning against the railing with his hands clasped. I'm hoping he'll leave in a minute, too, so I can have the place all to myself.

I rest my hands on my cane and push it against the ground, trying to give off whatever sad, impatient vibes might encourage him to leave. I hear sirens wailing down below. They're getting more persistent, ever louder as they head north up Amsterdam Avenue.

Somebody's in big trouble. I'm glad it's not me this time.

Almost instantly the guy by the railing spins around and begins to walk across the deck. I turn my head toward the setting sun, watching him come closer out of the corner of my eye. At first I think he's heading toward the stairs. It takes me a second to recognize him, and at first I don't believe it.

So many times I thought I'd seen him. In a crowd or on the subway platform. I'd limp closer, only to be proven wrong. I don't want to be disappointed again, so I wait until he's standing right in front of me. Then I close my eyes.

"Are you real?"

"I am."

"You can't be real."

"Why not?"

"Because this doesn't suck."

"This is the one exception to the rule."

I try to leap toward him but end up falling instead. He catches me. "Does this help you believe?"

He takes out his clunky eyeglasses and puts them on. I kiss him with such clumsy enthusiasm that I knock those awful glasses right off his face.

"I had no way to find you," I say. "They wouldn't tell me anything. Even if you were alive or dead."

"I know. Except I knew you'd be alive. I knew you would make it. And I knew I'd find you again."

"But how did you know to look for me here?"

"I told you, part of what makes me such an excellent hacker is that I'm good at figuring out the way people think, what they do, what habits they have. I spent the last few weeks thinking, trying to come up with a place that you might go. Then I saw the article in the *Times* about this place opening up. St. Philip's new observation deck. Upper West Side. I thought, ah, that's it. That's where my angel will go. I'm so glad I got it right. I knew I'd only get one shot at finding you."

"Why?"

"I'm kinda . . . under house arrest." He lifts the leg of his jeans and shows me his ankle transmitter.

"For what?"

"There were at least a dozen international warrants out for 8-Bit, but since they couldn't have him, they settled for me instead. I'm locked up at home with my parents. No computer. No phone. Basically, no contact with the outside world. I can't even go to school."

"For how long?"

"Until they figure out what to do with me and my lawyers cut a deal. Leniency in exchange for information."

"House arrest. I'll bet your mom is glad about that. Glad you're alive, I mean."

"She is. I . . . I know I've got a lot to make up for. I'm doing my best. My dad's still very angry."

"But Thomas . . . no computer? How can you stand it?"

"It's been easy. Compared to what else I've had to live without."

He kisses me, then stops. It's way too short a kiss for me.

"What's the matter?"

He lifts my hat up a little in the front. "I don't know if this is going to work out between us. I usually only go for bald chicks."

"I understand. How's this?"

I tuck my hair into my hat and pull it all the way down to my eyebrows. He kisses me again. A little longer this time, but still not long enough.

The sirens are getting louder, closer, and there are more of them. We walk to the edge of the observation deck, arm in arm, so I don't have to use my cane. Down below, three police cars have pulled up onto the sidewalk. Pedestrians scatter like pigeons as the officers leap out and charge up the church steps.

"Are they here looking for a handsome, red-headed fugitive?"

"Yeah. And if they catch us up here, I'm going to be in even bigger trouble. I'm sort of breaking the law two times right now. I'm not supposed to have any contact with you."

"Why?"

"I don't know. I guess they think they need to protect you from me."

"It's probably the other way around. My 'handlers' can't seem to decide if they should be bossing me around or placating me. I don't respond very well to either. I'm sure that's got to be confusing for them."

Thomas pulls me toward him by my jacket lapels. "Before they get here, tell me how your life is. I just need to know you're okay."

My head falls against his chest, and he presses his cheek to the top of my head.

"I'm all right. Virgil is a kind man. My mother was right about him. He hasn't told his father about me yet. We were waiting for things to blow over. Hodges . . . your mother—"

"Please don't call her that."

"Okay. But she was practically a surrogate daughter to Virgil's father—my grandfather. He did everything he could to cover things up, but he couldn't save her from being arrested. Couldn't even get her out on bail."

"I saw they busted Wilson, too."

"Wilson. I think I hate him almost as much as I hate Hodges."

"You should. That Velocius thing is no gift. Angel,

you know what it does to you? They told you that, didn't they?"

I step back so I can look into his brown-black eyes.

"They told me. I guess they wanted to keep me from using my new tricks. Nothing like a radically shortened life span to put a damper on your superpowers. They told me every time I speed my mind up, I wear myself out. They said it's like running a car at two hundred miles an hour. You can't keep it up forever."

We hear men shouting in the stairwell. Thomas looks over at the door and says, "Seems like old times."

"Tell me how to reach you."

"I have no computer and no phone. I guess you'll have to do things the old-fashioned way. Write me a letter."

"Okay. I will. What's your address?"

He pulls a folded-up piece of paper from his pocket and hands it to me. "It's on here."

I take it from him and whisper, "Thank you. Thank you for . . . for still being alive."

The men are almost to the top of the stairs now.

"Quick. Go hide behind that column while I turn myself in. Maybe they'll give me credit for semi-good behavior."

"Aw, but you're a good guy."

"That's me. Hacker with a heart of gold. Now go!"

He kisses me again. My bottom lip, then the top, then both together. He pushes me toward a column crowned with exceptionally gruesome gargoyles, all of them with their tongues sticking out. If only warding off evil was that easy.

"Stay here until they're gone, okay?"

"Do you want me to bust you out? I could, you know."

"I have no doubt about that, but I don't want you shortening your life by even one day for my sake."

The door swings open, and Thomas spins around and puts his hands behind his head, ready to cooperate. I wait in the shadows as the police take him into custody. The sun is low. Why it feels warmer now, in this cold wind, I don't know, but it does.

After a few minutes, I look out over the railing of the observation deck, down at the street below, and watch as they lead Thomas away. The police cars are long gone before I finally unfold the piece of paper that he gave me.

It's blank.

I flip it over. It's the same on the other side.

For a moment, I think it's a mistake. Or some kind of joke. I don't know why he would give this to me. It's not until I'm about to head down the stairs that I think to put my hand into the inside pocket of my jacket. There I find a second piece of paper. On it is written Thomas's full name, address, and three words I know he's never said to anyone else but me.

ACKNOWLEDGMENTS

I always read ACKNOWLEDGMENTS pages, don't you?

At one time, weirdly—perhaps ironically—reading the acknowledgments at the ends of books convinced me that I'd never be a published author. Most authors had so many people to thank, reading their lists of thankees was like watching film credits roll at the end of a movie. I used to think, "Really? I don't even *know* that many people."

Now I'm happy to say that I do. And I hope you'll stay and read all the way to the end so you'll know who made this book possible.

My "Without Whom" Agent

Molly Jaffa, for your unflagging support and patience and vision and for not letting me give up on this book. You couldn't be more perfect if you were dunked in chocolate.

Executive Producers
Andrea Cascardi and Bonnie Cutler, for giving *Tabula Rasa* a warm, safe home for its many bullets and explosions.

Director
Alison S. Weiss, my own winged editorial Valkyrie, a shockingly nice person and excellent editor who made this book better in every possible way.

Art Direction
Georgia Morrissey, for my fabulous, eye-catching cover.

Set Design
Alison Chamberlain, for designing all the pretty, gritty pages of this book.

Associate Producers
Ryan Sullivan and Laaren Brown for catching my mistakes so I don't look like (too much of) a fool.

Script Supervisor
Denise Logsdon, who has possibly read every word I've written the last fifteen years. Dude, you are the best. Truly. I'm not even going to be more specific than that. You're just the best.

Key (to My Keeping a) Grip

For critical feedback, tea and sympathy, and general awesomeness: Sierra Godfrey, Angelina Hansen, Vivi Barnes, Julie Bourbeau, Renee Collins, Tara Kelly, and the fabulous YA Valentines—Sara Raasch, Sara B. Larson, A. Lynden Rolland, Jen McConnel, Philip Siegel, Lynne Matson, Jaye Robin Brown, Paula Stokes, Lindsay Cummings, Bethany Crandall, Bethany Hagen, Kristi Helvig, and Anne Blankman.

Boom Operator

Amy Crandall Lippert, who always asked, "How's the book going?" and then listened to the (often whiny) answer.

Casting Directors

Mom, for your help, support, and assistance in innumerable ways, including clutch babysitting in the eleventh hour of manuscript revision. And my writer dad, for saying, "Wow. Look what you did with your brain!" upon hearing I was going to become a published author.

Technical and Military Advisor/Stunt Coordinator

Andrew Lippert, for making my childhood an excellent adventure. I'm exceptionally lucky to have had you as a big brother.

Special Effects

I'd like to acknowledge the work of Dr. David Eagleman, whose research on neuroscience—the concept of "brain time" in particular—got me thinking one day, "What if . . . ?"

Personal Assistants to Ms. Lippert-Martin

People ask me often how I'm able to write when I have four kids, and the reason is I have awesome kids. I thank you, my glorious progeny, Caroline, Lucy, Emma, and Augustus. Never has a writer been constantly interrupted by lovelier children.

Best Boy

I'm not sure what a "best boy" actually is, so I'm using this term literally. Thank you, Philip, for always laughing at my jokes and never once laughing at my dreams. There's a reason I named a cathedral after you.

FIN